# Gangsta Twist 3

# Gangsta Twist 3

*Clifford "Spud" Johnson*

www.urbanbooks.net

Urban Books, LLC
300 Farmingdale Road, NY-Route 109
Farmingdale, NY 11735

Gangsta Twist 3

ISBN 13: 978-1-64556-123-1
ISBN 10: 1-64556-123-2

First Mass Market Printing December 2020
First Trade Paperback Printing June 2015
Printed in the United States of America

10 9 8 7 6 5 4 3 2 1

*This is a work of fiction. Any references or similarities to actual events, real people, living or dead, or to real locales are intended to give the novel a sense of reality. Any similarity in other names, characters, places, and incidents is entirely coincidental.*

Distributed by Kensington Publishing Corp.
Submit Orders to:
Customer Service
400 Hahn Road
Westminster, MD 21157-4627
Phone: 1-800-733-3000
Fax: 1-800-659-2436

# Chapter One

Akim Novikov and his longtime comrade Alexander Sokolov both stood and watched as Akim's private jet slowly taxied toward the runway to make its departure from Moscow's Domodedovo International Airport to the United States—Los Angeles, California, to be exact. The twenty-one-hour flight would make one stop before arriving at LAX and their new business associates would be back safely to their home. Akim smiled, turned toward his comrade and spoke in Russian: "Well, my friend, it looks as if we now begin this new business arrangement with Taz and the Network. I'm confident this should prove to be very profitable for us and all parties involved."

"You should be confident; you've put a tremendous amount of time and effort into this decision to deal with Taz. It's been over six years now and we've missed out on a lot of money in America because of you and your patience with this man. My question for you is, why did it take you this long to make contact with Taz? You have told me numerous times how you trusted Won totally. If that was the case I figured you would have made contact with Taz and put everything in motion years ago."

As they turned and began to walk toward the airport exit Akim's smile seemed to brighten when he spoke. "That was my dear deceased friend Won's request. He wanted me to sit back and be patient and watch Taz from a distance to make sure he was in fact ready to do the type of business that Won and I had planned on doing. Won was never one to jump into anything without being absolutely positive things would come out in his favor. Even in death he prepared for everything to work in Taz's favor. He wanted to make sure Taz was in fact ready to take on such a tremendous responsibility being the leader of the Network. After six years of watching Taz lead the Network to soaring profits I felt it was time for us to help him soar even higher. Just as Won predicted Taz is a leader in every sense of the word. The power given to him by Won made him a man with enormous resources. Those resources accompanied with the intelligence and ruthlessness Taz has displayed over these last six years has shown me that he is more than ready to embark in our very profitable business ventures. Taz is not a man to be taken lightly. I respect that and I am anxious to see how this evolves."

Once they were inside of their chauffeured limousine Alexander asked, "What about the rest of the council? You know they aren't going to accept what Taz will tell them about the drugs."

"This is true, comrade. Taz loathes drugs; the council knows this. The Network's primary profits come largely from the distribution of drugs. The fact that drugs have made the Network very rich is secondary to Taz. He possesses the power to take the Network well beyond their current position. Taz will make sure that this transition within the business dealings of the Network will go smoothly."

"And if there's any problems?"

Akim smiled. "Then we will assist our American comrade."

"This should prove to be very interesting."

"That indeed, comrade, that indeed," Akim said as he relaxed in his seat and lit a cigarette.

Taz, Wild Bill, Red, and Bob made themselves comfortable as the G5 smoothly lifted off the ground and was airborne headed home. It had been a long, tiring week spent in Moscow. Taz smiled as he thought about the fun they had while in Russia. Partying with Akim and Alexander had been something he hadn't expected. Those Russian mafia guys sure know how to kick it. Shit, he still had a slight hangover from all of that vodka he drank while partying with them.

What surprised him most was how they handled their business. No word games or beating around the bush with Akim; he got straight to the point and laid down the rules and what he expected from Taz and the Network. Taz respected that. Now it was time to bring this to the attention of the council to see if they would agree with the decision he made while in Russia. He really didn't care but he had to do it the politically correct way. So far, he chose to never throw his weight around the council and for that they seemed to have more respect for him. Again, this was something he really didn't care about; as long as his crew was with it and by his side he would do whatever he wanted to. Won left him in power and he was determined to make the best of this, not only for Won but for everyone that was important to him: his crew, Red, Wild Bill, Bob, and Tari; his family, his wife Sacha, his mother Mama-Mama, and his children, Tazneema and his twin sons, Keenan and Ronald. Every move he made was for the well-being of his loved ones and Won's memory. He was winning so far and it felt real good. Real good!

In six years Taz used the influence Won left him to hook the Network up and take their criminal enterprise to an international level. Won had a game plan and he secured contacts for Taz with some very serious criminal organizations. Sicilian mobsters, South American drug cartels, Cuban drug lords, Asian gangsters, and finally the Russian mafia. Originally Taz wanted to remove the drugs from the Network, but he saw that would be basically impossible because the distribution of narcotics was where the majority of the Network's money came from. So he bided his time and waited patiently. He even made some stronger moves to help the drug trade elevate for the Network through Won's connection with the Orumutto family in California. The money earned from their X pills was enormous.

So far every move Taz made had been the right move and that gave him the confidence to make this next move with the Russians: weapons arms dealing. The money they would make in arms dealing with the Russians would surpass all of the drugs they dealt ten times over. He knew he could be greedy and make these moves with the Russians and keep the drug trade the Network ran intact and everything would be good.

But that's not what he wanted; he still loathed drugs and wanted no part of it any longer. At the next quarterly council meeting he was going to present his plan of removing the Network from the drug game altogether. Not only did he dislike drugs or selling them, he felt that it was too risky of a business to continue with. It was only a matter of time before things got wicked. Yes, they were not the average street-level drug dealers; that didn't matter to him. He wanted peace of mind and as long as the Network was involved with drugs he would never have that. Sooner or later the DEA or the FBI would catch wind of certain people and when that happened the snitching would begin. That meant murder would come in play because he knew without a doubt he would order the death of anyone he even thought was running their mouth. Though every move that had been made thus far under his leadership had been calculated to a tee it didn't mean every move had been made right. To him they had been extremely lucky and luck runs out sooner or later. It was time for the Network to switch shit up. Time for the drugs to stop. If the council didn't agree with what Taz was going to propose then there were going to be some serious issues, issues that would most likely make Taz use his position of power, and that meant a division within.

*Oh well,* Taz thought as the jet reached its cruising altitude. He reclined in his seat and wondered what his wife and sons were doing at home. He yawned and closed his eyes and began to doze as the rest of the crew was doing.

By the time Taz woke up Wild Bill was arguing with Red about who had the most money between Diddy and Jay-Z. For the life of him Taz couldn't understand how two men in their early forties could have such a childish argument. But these were his lifelong friends and nothing they did could ever destroy their friendship. He sighed and said, "Will you two fools shut the fuck up, acting stupid and shit."

Red, the biggest man of the crew at a little over six foot two, smiled at Taz and said, "You know this little man gets to tripping when he's wrong, G. Everyone knows that Diddy has way more money than Jay."

"Little man? Nigga, I can still out bench your big yellow ass any day, anytime, so kill that little man shit, fool!" They all started laughing because Wild Bill was extra sensitive when it came to his height. Any reference toward how small he was set him off instantly. Red knew this and used this tactic frequently to piss his friend off. Wild Bill, the smallest member of the crew at five foot seven, was extremely strong; his muscular physique was something he was very proud of, that and his long, permed hair that he refused to cut even after Taz and Red decided to cut their long braids for a more conservative businessman type look. Wild Bill laughed at them both and told them that he was like Samson: his strength came from his hair. Another one of his funny moments.

The next member of the crew was Bob. Bob was another comedian of sorts. Over the last few years since becoming a father he had calmed down considerably with some of his wild antics. His wife, Gwen, had a lot to do with this transformation. They were a perfect match for each other. She was the only person other than any crew member who could keep Bob in check when he got to tripping.

Bob was five foot eleven, with dark skin and a four-inch knot right in the middle of his forehead that made him the brunt of a lot of jokes over the years. Only from the crew, though; several men and women had been punished for trying to clown Bob about his knot, and he did not play that at all. Though his wild days seemed to have been behind him, Bob still was just as dangerous as the rest of the crew.

Taz, also at five foot eleven, was the head of the crew in a way but chose to lead by example. He tried to make all of the right decisions when it came to his friends. They were crew, but they were friends forever in his eyes and he loved them all like brothers. They had been reduced to a four-man crew when originally they were a six-man crew before losing two of their close friends in a beef with some Hoover Crips in their hometown of Oklahoma City. That beef nearly destroyed Taz and his relationship with his daughter Tazneema.

Taz and the crew went all out to get revenge for the murders of their friends, Bo-Pete and Keno. In memory of their friends each crew member put tatooed portraits of Bo-Pete and Keno on each side of their chest. So no matter what, as long as they were still breathing their friends would always be with them. Taz took it a step further when he found out that his wife, Sacha, was having twins; he chose to name both of his sons after his fallen friends. Ronald Michael Good was Li'l Bo-Pete and Keenan Mitchell Good was Li'l Keno. Sacha chose the middle names. The crew was composed of four men, but the total number of crew members was five because of Tari, Taz's ex-lover. Tari was a drop-dead gorgeous white woman who had held Taz down for many years after they were first introduced by Won, Taz's mentor/father figure. Their lives took a major turn because of Won and because of those turns they were now on a private jet returning to America from Russia.

"All right clowns, chill, we need to talk some business for a minute here. I thought we would wait until we got back home but since you fools have so much energy we might as well handle this now," Taz said seriously. Each member of the crew sat up in their seats and gave Taz their undivided attention. "So, you all heard what has been proposed by Akim and Alex. You know I am on board with it because I want to move the Network in a different direction away from the drug game. We don't get our hands dirty directly but if anything ever went left we could all be caught up in some heavy federal conspiracy shit, and I am just not trying to go out like that over some damn dope money. You know how I feel on that shit. Your thoughts?"

Bob reclined in his seat and spoke first. "If you're with it, Taz, then I trust your call. I mean you've made every move the right move since you've become the man over the Network. You've taken us just as far as Won figured you would. You know I feel the same as you do when it comes to the dope game. I say let's roll with these Russians and get this money with the gun thing."

Taz laughed and said, "Guns thing, huh? It's bigger than that, my nigga, but I feel what you're saying. We'll be participating in some heavy arms dealing. Not just some guns, this will be some major army type shit. Missiles, rocket launchers, automatic assault rifles as well as pistols, silencers, and such. This move will bring us way more money than the percentages we collect from the council of the Network. It will also solidify the Network as major players internationally."

"I agree with Bob, dog. I feel we should continue to trust your judgment because every move you have made has been on point," said Red.

"I agree too, but I do have some concerns," said Wild Bill.

"Talk to me, G."

"The drugs have been the main get down for the Network since the beginning. That's how Won has always ate and made the moves he was able to make. He kept all of the right connections and did his thang major with the dope game. The entire council except for you have a direct hand with the ho game. True, you collect a large percentage from the drugs as the rest but it's mostly how they eat. By making this move you would be taking from them what they have been dependent on for decades. Two things can come from this: one, they could roll with it and be willing to make this change; or, two, they will not want to make that move in fear of change. Fear of the unknown makes people hesitant, dog. Especially when you're talking about some heavy figures like what they bring in quarterly. I personally feel that if they choose not to roll with you on this it will cause problems within the Network. That will then cause someone to die because if I even feel like someone in that council is thinking about bringing you any harm I will take their head off myself. Real spill," said Wild Bill.

Taz gave him a nod and placed his right palm over his chest where the tattoo of Keno's face was and said, "Love, my nigga. I feel every word you have spoken. Now let me break it down to you as I see it and feel it. The percentage that we collect, not just me, dog, whatever I get I split with you guys evenly. That will never change. Yes, I am the head of the Network, but we are the crew and that comes before anybody and anything." Each member gave a nod and placed an open right palm over their chest. "Now, I know that change will be something that won't be easily accepted within the council and that is why I will propose an extra incentive for this move. I will give them one year, one year to get full profits from their drug moves. I will concede my percentage during that year. That means they will make over sixty or seventy million dollars during this last year of drug activity. But when that year is over the Network will sever all ties with all drug business. I think this tactic will make that fear of the unknown a tad bit better to deal with."

"Maybe. But have you given thought about how it will affect the others involved with the drug business? I mean you got the Orumutto fool with the X pills. You got Jorge Santa Cruz from the South American drug cartel in Buenaventura. It's bigger than the council only, my nigga. This shit could cause a major war with you pulling the Network out. You would be taking money from more than just the council members," Wild Bill said logically.

Taz sat and thought about those words for a few minutes then said, "You've made a good point with that, Bill. I can make the decision over the council whether they're with it or not because though it's a vote I have the authority to overrule all and make it happen. I didn't give much thought to what you pointed out though. That's why I love this crew; we will never let each other miss a thing. Five minds are better than one. This is what I intend to do: I'm going to have Sacha set up the next Network quarterly meeting out in Miami. Have her pick a real fly resort so we can kick it and have some fun while handling the business out there. In the meantime I think we will be doing some more international traveling. Colombia to get at Jorge is a must because you know he don't play no phones or e-mails at all."

"Miami because of the Cuban?" asked Bob.

"Exactly."

"Are you trying to bring them in on the business with the Russians?" asked Red.

"No. I will offer them some serious action on the weapons though. You know they will definitely want some action on them with all of the beefs they go through yearly. I think if I do this right I can avoid war with them."

"I feel you, but I feel that one of them ain't going to be with it," said Wild Bill.

Taz shrugged his shoulders and said, "Then that's the one who will get rolled on."

Wild Bill smiled and said, "Real spill."

"Okay, this is how we'll work this: we'll keep this close to our vests until we've spoken with Jorge Santa Cruz, Danny Orumutto, and Señor Juarez in Miami. Then we'll proceed from there with the council."

"I wanna go home. I miss the City, G. Can we add that trip into this mix?" asked Red.

Laughing, Wild Bill said, "Nigga, you need to dead that weak shit and go on and wife Paquita and bring her ass out west with the rest of us. You know you just wanna go back home because of her!"

Red gave Wild Bill the finger because he knew he was right on target with that jab.

"I was thinking the same thing actually. I need to see Mama-Mama and Tazneema. You already know the white girl is gonna want to know the business. So this is what we'll do: before we bounce to make the meeting needed we'll go back home and chill for a week, check on the businesses and our rental properties out there, and relax a little bit before we roll out. Agreed?"

"Agreed!" the rest of the crew answered in unison.

"One more thing, Taz?" asked Wild Bill.

"What up?"

"Didn't you give the Russians a yea on the guns, I mean, arms dealing thing?"

Taz gave Wild Bill a faintly mocking smile that Sacha said he had become known for and answered honestly. "I told them that I would deal with them whether or not the Network's council was with it. So, yeah, dog, I gave them the green light."

"I thought so. That's why you not really tripping on a war with any of these clowns. What we packing with the Network combined with the Russian mob we got enough power to handle shit."

Taz gave his friend that smile again and said, "Exactly."

# Chapter Two

Sacha Good was all smiles as she watched her twin sons as they slept soundly in their beds. She was amazed at how much her sons looked like her twin brothers who had been murdered almost twenty years ago. When she watched her sons she was so full of mixed emotions at times that she didn't know whether she wanted to smile or cry. She missed her brothers so much it hurt. She loved her sons so much that she knew that there was nothing in the world that she wouldn't do for them. She did what she had to do to avenge her brother's death and she felt no remorse for it at all. Killing Keno gave her the most satisfying feeling she had ever felt in her life. She could close her eyes and remember, as if it were yesterday and not six years ago, ringing his doorbell waiting for him to come to the door while she had her hand inside of her purse. She remembered the strange calm that came over her when she saw Keno open the door with a surprised look on his face.

*"What's up, Sacha? Everything straight with Taz?" Keno asked with a puzzled expression on his face.*

*"Everything is fine, Keno. I came over because I wanted to talk to you about all this violence. You're the closest to Taz and if anyone can talk him out of something you're the man who can do it. I understand you guys need to get revenge for Bo-Pete, but this has to stop before I lose the*

*man I love more than anything in this world. I want my baby
to have a father around, Keno. I need your help."*

*Relieved, Keno sighed and said, "Come on in and let's
talk, Sacha." He turned and started walking, followed
closely by Sacha.*

*Sacha stopped, turned, closed the door, and said, "I
hope I'm not interrupting anything, Keno. I know you and
Katrina been doing it real tough lately."*

*"Yeah, we good. You ain't in the way though. I was just
about to go out and do some shopping. Ring shopping,"
Keno said with a smile.*

*"Ring shopping? Wow!"*

*"I know huh? Never thought I'd be the one to wife a
female. Come on; let's go in the den so we can chop it up."*

*Sacha smiled as she pulled out a small .380-caliber pistol
and shot Keno three times: two in the back of the head and
once in the back of his neck. She then stood over his dead
body for a moment to make sure he was dead then said,
"That was for my brothers, you bastard. I hope you burn
in hell." She calmly put her gun back inside of her purse,
pulled out a scarf and wiped the doorknob, then opened the
door and left with the door wide open.*

That had taken place six years ago and to this very day
she was so afraid of what Taz would do to her if he ever
found out she was the person who murdered his best friend,
not the Hoover Crips in Oklahoma City who he had been
beefing with at that time. She was more than afraid; she was
terrified. So terrified that she made sure that no matter what
Taz was never able to spend time alone with her parents.
When they were married she made sure she kept them apart
or Taz was never alone with either of them. Taz knew nothing about her brothers let alone that they had been murdered.
She didn't want him to find this out and start to put two and

two together. He was no dummy and it wouldn't take him long to realize what she'd done.

Living with this constant fear in the back of her mind was maddening at times, but there was nothing she could do about it but continue to live and try to enjoy the life she had with her husband and her children. Taz had given her a good life, no worries at all. She had everything she ever wanted materially and had become an intricate part of Taz's businesses both legal and illegal. She smiled at that thought; she called herself the unknown member of the Network. That always got a good laugh from Taz. But he agreed because he knew she would always give him solid advice and that made her feel even better knowing that her husband trusted her like that.

They started Good Investments Inc. in Oklahoma City and moved west so Taz could take control as the head of the Network. She gave up her partnership at Whitney & Johnson, a prestigious law firm in Oklahoma City, to follow her husband to the West Coast where they now lived in a beautiful estate located in the most prime section of lower Bel Air through East Gate. It was situated on just under one acre of expensive park-like grounds with a large, flat grassy yard. Taz loved the yard because there was plenty of room for his beloved Dobermans, Precious and Heaven, to roam around and be comfortable. The interiors were classically proportioned with elegant formal rooms on a grand yet intimate scale, which Sacha totally loved. Hardwood floors and paneling gave it an even more expensive feel. The master featured dual baths and walk-in dressing rooms that gave them the space they needed because Sacha was well known for her shopping binges. Clothes were a top priority, so gigantic closet space was a must. There were seven more bedrooms, a gym for Taz and his crew to get their workout on, and an entire wing of the estate solely for the twins. Play rooms and their video games along with all of their many, many toys completed their dream home. The property was set back from the street behind gates with a spacious motor court and three-car garage that housed Taz's Ferrari and Bentley as well as her brand new seven series BMW. Everything about their home, even the location, was perfect. It was within minutes of UCLA Medical Center, one of the best hospitals on the West Coast, and within walking distance to the famous Bel Air Hotel and Country Club. Everything a couple from the country would just love.

Coming from Oklahoma City to living that lavishly absolutely fascinated Sacha for the first few years. Now she was used to it and had become a well-known socialite within the Bel Air community. She even talked Taz into attending certain social events from time to time. Her motives behind this were to solidify them as a legitimate power couple living amid so many other ultra-rich people. Taz was proud of her every move because so far everything had worked out perfectly for them.

Good Investments Inc. was doing quite well in Oklahoma City so the legitimate money continued to flow, but the main money came from the illegal moves from the Network. Taz made anywhere from $70 million to $100 million a year tax free and it was Sacha's duty to make sure that money was properly handled as well as laundered. This task she had taken seriously by completing several online courses for accounting and being taught the ropes by Won's financial advisors. Taz had introduced her to them when they first arrived in Los Angeles.

Tazneema, Taz's daughter, along with Tari ran the day-to-day operations of Good Investments Inc. This which basically consisted of making sure all of their properties and businesses were running smoothly and looking for new ways to invest the millions that they were making. Over twenty-five fast food chains: Subway, IHOP, Popeye's Chicken, and several McDonald's and Burger Kings, added to over 350 rental homes around the Oklahoma City area. The Good family along with the crew were doing quite well financially. Quite well indeed.

Sacha gave her sons a kiss while they slept peacefully and left their room quietly. By the time she made it to the bedroom she decided that she wanted to do something instead of being stuck in the house bored all night. She missed Taz. The thought of him made her smile; he was on his way home and that meant she would be able to get her hands on her handsome husband. *Mmm, yummy,* she thought as she slipped out of her jeans and top.

In only a pair of boy shorts and a bra she stepped to the dresser, grabbed her cell and called her best friend Gwen. When Gwen answered the phone Sacha said, "What's up, mommy? What are you doing?"

"Nothing much, mommy. Playing mommy for real; just put these two of Bob's kids to bed," Gwen said laughing. "Now I'm bored, wishing Bob's ass was here so I could put this pussy on that knot and get freaky."

"That's so crazy because that's exactly what I had on my mind too."

"What? Since when have you wanted to get freaky with my husband's knot, mommy?"

"Shut up! You know what I meant. This weeklong trip to Russia has me missing some Taz."

"I know that's right. But all of that will be over in the morning right?"

"Mm-hmm. They're supposed to be home around ten or eleven a.m. mommy. So, what you got up for tonight?"

"Nothing. Done playing mommy for the night so I was going to take me a long, hot bath and watch some TV so I can be well rested when Bob gets back. As soon as his black ass walks in that door we are fucking right there in the foyer!"

"Nasty ass."

"At least I ain't fake with it, 'cause you know damn well you feel exactly as I do!" They both started laughing. They had been best friends for so long that they knew each other inside out. After Sacha met Taz she introduced Gwen to Bob and their love connection shocked everyone. They were a match made out of true opposites: Gwen, the highly intelligent psychiatrist, and Bob, the wild man of the crew.

They seemed to be opposites, but in reality they were the perfect yin to each other's yang. It was love at first fuck for them because they were two of the most insatiable human beings Sacha ever met. Bob complemented Gwen and did so much for her in so many different ways; whereas Gwen did equally as much for Bob.

They were married right after Sacha and Taz and soon after were blessed with two beautiful kids: a boy, Bob Jr., and a girl, Gwendolyn, who Gwen affectionately called Bob's kids. It had been a good six years for them as well and Sacha thanked God every single night for Gwen's happiness. She'd been through way too much pain with the loss of her first husband and son, William and Remel, in a tragic accident over ten years ago. Now, that tragedy was stored in the back of their minds as they continued to live and try to make the best out of their lives together.

Gwen was just as dedicated to her man as Sacha was to Taz. She also became more involved with the business side of things. Though Bob's role with everything wasn't as intense as Taz's, Gwen made sure she did her part to help out when called upon. Like Sacha she left her thriving private practice as a psychiatrist to be by her man's side on the West Coast.

As soon as they made it to California Bob made his first purchase, which was some beach front property in Malibu for his bride. Their home was so lovely that Sacha tried her best to find a reason to get out there at least twice a week. The Malibu residence was located 115 feet from the beach. The property was known as one of Malibu's original beach front residences. The hacienda-style home had been meticulously restored with three bedrooms including an ocean-side master suite, top-of-the-line finishes, controlled private entry, and walls of glass doors. Gwen's personal touch to it made the home warm and inviting. Though much smaller than Sacha and Taz's estate it was worth more than $17 million. With Bob being a millionaire himself he felt it was nothing to make sure he kept his family in the very best home.

Gwen was in heaven and loved the life she had stumbled into with Bob. She was his bride, best friend, and his ride or die. She would do whatever it took to make sure they made all of the right moves together. Where Bob liked to get emotional at times, Gwen was the calmer, more calculated of the couple. She would bring the thinking to the equation, which made them a hell of a part of the entire crew. The crew was all one big happy family; everyone played their part. Together they were all winning, big time.

Both Sacha and Gwen stood five foot five and could pass for sisters. Sacha was the thicker of the two with a bronze skin tone that gave the impression that she was from the islands somewhere. Long, silky hair passed her shoulder with some firm C-cup breasts to bring heavy emphasis to her small hips. Taz loved her shapely ass and constantly reminded her that it was her ass that drew his attention to her at a club in Oklahoma City six years ago. Gwen, with her boob job C-cups, was just as easy on the eyes as Sacha. Though two kids had put some weight on her thin frame she packed a nice ass herself. With hazel eyes and a light brown complexion, she was everything Bob had ever dreamt of having for a wife.

Before either of the best friends had children they used to refer to one another as "bitch" and "ho" affectionately, Sacha being the bitch and Gwen being the ho. After they each gave birth they decided that that type of terminology was too graphic for mothers to be calling each other so they chose to stop calling each other bitch and ho and now called one another mommy. Taz thought it was funny, but it stuck with the women and that's how they referred to one another.

"All right, mommy, how long will it take for you to make it this way?" asked Gwen.

"What are you talking about?"

"If you don't quit that . . . You know damn well no one knows you better than I do. You're bored and you want to do something. Since you have the live-in maids and whatnot you can move around and I can't, so that means you want to come out here and kick it for a little while. Which is cool with me because I'm equally bored. I'll break out some XO and fry up some hot wings and we can go kick it on the deck out back, sip and eat while watching the gorgeous Pacific. I swear no matter how long we stay out here I'll never get tired of this ocean view, mommy, that's real."

"I know that's right, mommy. I'm on my way! Get to frying up them wangs!" Sacha hung up the phone laughing as she went into her walk-in closet to get dressed in something comfortable for the drive out to Malibu to kick it with her best friend for a few hours.

# Chapter Three

After being home for less than a week Taz and the crew were ready to get back on the move. First, they were going home to spend a week in Oklahoma City; then they would embark on their trip to Colombia to meet with the ruthless leader of the Buenaventura Cartel, Jorge Santa Cruz.

They would then fly back home to California so Taz could set up a meeting with Danny Orumutto, the top man of the Orumutto crime family. It was rumored that he was a cold man, a man so cold that he had his father and two uncles murdered so he could take over the family's X pill drug ring in Southern California. Taz met him a few times and was shocked at how young Danny was and how his demeanor definitely didn't fit his age. He knew instantly that Danny Orumutto was as dangerous as everyone assumed him to be. If there would be any beef Taz was almost 90 percent certain it would be with Danny Orumutto.

The last meeting would be set up right before the council meeting in Miami with the Cubans. The Suarez operation was run by Señor Suarez, a good-natured older Cuban who was known for being fair, especially when he had something to gain, so Taz wasn't worried about him at all in this mix. Time would tell though because all three men he would be meeting with had the potential of going haywire after he told them of his plans for the Network.

He thought about his friends within the Sicilian mafia and smiled. They had already agreed to do business with him so there was no reason for him to meet with them. When everything was ready they would be some of his first customers for heavy firearms.

Taz went over everything in his head several times before he presented it to Sacha. He really hated when she outthought him, which was often, he thought with a smile. When he told her his plans she agreed and that shocked him, but pleased him as well.

"Okay, let me get this straight, we're going home for a week and then you and the crew will head to Colombia?" asked Sacha as she fastened the seat belts on the twins in the back seat of Taz's Bentley.

"That's the plan, li'l mama. It's been a good minute since I seen Mama-Mama and Neema. You know they want to see the twins so I decided to make a family trip out of it. Plus, Red needs to get his Paquita fix taken care of," Taz said laughing as he pulled the big luxury vehicle out of the driveway of their estate.

Sacha rolled her eyes at him and said, "Whatever."

Twenty minutes later Taz pulled the Bentley up to the security gates of the Winners Circle. Once the security guard saw who was at the front gates the big wrought iron gates electronically began to open so Taz could enter the $20 million estate that Taz chose to call the Winners Circle in remembrance of its former owner, Won.

This totally secluded estate had belonged to Won. It had been his home for as long as Taz could remember. It was also the place where Won had been murdered. That was the reason why Taz didn't reside there. When he told Sacha that Won had been killed there she refused to live there. So they decided that Red and Wild Bill would hold

down residence at the Winners Circle. It also served as the
headquarters for the crew. Sacha had an office where she
could work her magic with the figures and Taz used Won's
old office as his own. All meetings and business were
handled at the Winners Circle.

The $20 million estate had by far the best view in the
city. It basically sat back on its own island off the famed
Sunset Strip. The number one view lot in the city sitting on
over three acres, totally private with no neighbors next to
or below and that fit Taz's taste perfectly. Security was a
must for him, his family, and the crew. The Winners Circle
had its own private street, gated with parking that could
accommodate twenty-five within the gate. The estate was
over 10,000 square feet and had two guest apartments.
Wild Bill and Red had plenty of room and never seemed to
clash with one another even though they got on each other's nerves as much as they could. When there was tension
they would go swim in the Olympic-sized swimming pool
or play some volleyball on the built-in volleyball court.

The Winners Circle was one of Won's most prized
possessions so there was no way Taz would ever get rid
of it. When Gwen asked him why he chose to call it the
Winners Circle knowing that Won died there Taz smiled
and told her:

*"Even though my man Won died here he still won. I can't
really explain it, Gwen, just know that this estate is the
Winners Circle because we all gon' win."*

*"Hell, we already winning! So I'm with that shit!"* They
all started laughing.

When Taz made it to the front Gwen and Bob were
standing in the doorway. Bob's daughter, Gwendolyn, was
standing next to her father smiling at them and Gwen
was holding Bob Jr., a spry little two-year-old. Taz got

out of the car and helped grab one of the twins as Sacha grabbed the other. When they were inside of the Winners Circle Taz asked Bob, "Where is Wild Bill and Red?"

"They went out looking for locations for the club."

Sacha told the boys to go and play with Gwendolyn and they all ran toward the play area located in the back room. Once they were out of sight she slapped her forehead and said, "Are you really going to let them go through with that, Taz? Seriously, a damn strip club?"

Taz started laughing and said, "Come on, li'l mama, they're bored and if this is something that they feel can make some money with, might as well have some fun with it, why not?"

"Why not? Why not is because you and Bob's ass here think you'll be going to that damn strip club to get your jollies off watching them young, stank broads and I can speak for my mommy here, that shit ain't happening, Taz!" Gwen said with much attitude.

Bob laughed, turned, and started walking toward the office. Laughing, Taz said, "And I can speak for my boy Bob; if we want to go watch the li'l minxes at a strip club that's nothing. We both know what we got at home and ain't tripping off no broads like that. Right, Bob?"

Bob looked back over his shoulder and shook his head from side to side. "Come on, man, leave her the fuck alone; she's going to drive me crazy with that weak shit. Let's get to the business. What time are we leaving?"

Taz was still getting used to this all-business atti-tude Bob had going on; not that he didn't like the new Bob, just that the old Bob was more fun to be around. "I was waiting until a decent time to get at Akim in Russia. I'm going to see if he'll let us use his jet for the trip to Colombia and back here."

"Why don't you charter a private jet for us? It will be much faster than waiting for Akim to send his plane all the way to Oklahoma City from Russia," said Sacha.

"True. But it would be cheaper if he let us use his jet."

"Since when have you started pinching pennies, Mr. Taz?"

Before he could answer his wife their son Keenan came into the office and said, "Daddy, I want to help you with business. I don't wanna play no more."

Taz smiled brightly at his son and said, "You want to come work with Daddy, Li'l Keno? You sure can. I need a little help, too. Come here and help me figure out how to send an e-mail to my friend." Taz smiled as he watched as his son ran to him and jumped on his lap. He turned and faced the PC on his desk and let Li'l Keno watch as the PC powered up. When he was ready he typed an e-mail to Akim and then told Li'l Keno to push the ENTER button to send the e-mail.

"This one right here, Daddy?" Li'l Keno asked as he pointed toward the correct key.

"Yep, that's right, buddy. Now send that e-mail and then we can go to the kitchen and raid the fridge. I'm hungry. By the time we come back we should have the reply from this business e-mail." Taz set his son down and then turned toward Sacha. "You may want to check on the kids and then I need you to get things ready for the council meeting in Miami."

Sacha was sitting on one of the comfortable leather chairs inside of the office tapping on her notebook. She looked up at him and said, "I'm on top of that now. I am down to two resorts. The St. Regis Bal Harbour Resort or the Palms Hotel & Spa."

Taz grabbed his son's small hand and said, "Whichever one you choose is fine with me. Get it together so we can have everything forwarded to the council members. I want that taken care of before we bounce up out of here tonight."

"It will be ready. Have you talked to Neema?"

"I'll give her a call in a little while. What's up?"

"Nothing, just wondered that's all. She's been doing quite well at Good Investments Inc. I'm sure she's waiting for some praise from her father."

Taz stared at his wife for a moment and then gave her a nod. "I feel you." He then turned and took his son to go raid the kitchen for something to munch on.

After Taz left the office Gwen stared at Bob then at Sacha and asked, "Is everything okay with Taz and Neema?"

Sacha shrugged and said, "After that Cliff stuff they seem to try to avoid each other to me. I've spoken to Taz about it but he swears everything is good between them. That's a crock of crap but it is what it is. That's another reason why I came up with the idea to let Neema run things at Good Investments Inc. That way she could be hands-on with the family business and feel more a part of everything."

"That was a real smart move right there, Sacha," said Bob. "But for real, I would have thought they would have moved on from that ill shit that happened with that fool Cliff."

"Me too. It's more from Neema's side but Taz is so damn stubborn sometimes so he's just as much at fault as she is. Hopefully this trip can help because I intend on making sure we have some family time. So you two don't get lost when we get back home. I've already spoken to Mama-Mama and she wants to cook a gigantic meal for all of us."

Laughing, Bob said, "Since when Mama-Mama don't want to cook a gigantic meal? I can't wait!"

"I know that's right, that woman can burn. Mmmmm, my tummy is growling now just thinking about some of Mama-Mama's food," said Gwen.

"I know that's right. Damn, I miss Oklahoma City," said Sacha. "Yeah, there's no place like home. No matter how much money we got we're not gon' get all the way used to living way out here in the West."

"Shit, speak for yourself. I'm never leaving my beach front home!" said Gwen and they all started laughing.


Tazneema was sitting in her office talking to her besty, Lyla Winston. They'd been best friends since they met as freshman in college. Ever since then they were insepara-ble. After they graduated Lyla moved to Oklahoma City with Neema and opened a small clothing boutique in the Bricktown area. For the last three years to everyone's sur-prise, except for Tazneema's, Lyla's boutique had done quite well. Catering to women's tastes in clothing and perfumes Lyla was building her small business into a force to be reckoned with. Tazneema had been equally successful in making sure that the day-to-day running of Good Investments Inc. continued to run smoothly.

She not only ran the company along with Tari, she was also heavily involved with acquiring new homes and businesses such as food chains that they added to the many they already owned. She was extra excited about her latest idea and was sharing it with Lyla as Tari entered her office.

"Hold on a minute, Lyla," Neema said as she put the phone down. "What's up, Tee?"

"Good afternoon. Anything special going on I need to know about?"

"Nope. Just sitting here telling Lyla about the chicken and waffle restaurant."

"That's what I need to talk to you about. Could you give me a few?"

"Sure," Neema said as she picked the phone back up and told Lyla she would call her back. After she was off the phone she stared at Tari and said, "What's up?"

"You know I'm behind you totally on this restaurant deal. It's going to be kind of costly to try to find a spot in Bricktown where you want it. I was thinking maybe we should try more for somewhere along the north side, like N.W. Expressway first and then maybe bide our time for a move toward Bricktown."

Shaking her head no and looking exactly like her stubborn father, Tazneema Good said, "Nope. The best way to introduce this restaurant to the city is in Bricktown. Look how commercial Bricktown has become over the last decade. There's no hotter place in the city for the restaurant to be. It's a win all the way around, Tari. It may be costly but I feel it will be well worth it and extremely profitable. We won't lose money on this only gain it."

Tari smiled at Taz's daughter and couldn't have been more proud of her. Tazneema had grown into a beautiful and confident young lady. Looking like a female version of her father she kept her long hair pulled back in a modest looking ponytail and refused to wear any makeup except for some lip gloss. This was a concern of Tari's, but she knew that Neema was still somewhat distraught over what happened between her and her first love Cliff. She had moved on with her life determined to do well for herself and she accomplished that so far in a major way. Just as she was determined to succeed in the business world she was equally determined to stay away from men and any form of relationship issues. That bothered Tari greatly. She felt Neema was denying herself the pleasures of a man all because of one bad call. Whenever she tried to bring the subject up Neema would give her that coldblooded stare that her father was well known for and she would know to change the subject. She was definitely Taz Good's child.

Tari sighed and said, "Okay, fine with me. Now all you have to do is run it by your boss. Get his approval and then we can start scouring Bricktown for a nice building to get things started."

"Aw, come on, Tee, you know Taz might trip out on this. Why can't we go on and make the moves ourselves and surprise him?"

Laughing, Tari said, "Surprise him? That's funny. Have you forgotten that his loving wife oversees all financial matters for Good Investments Inc.? There is no way we could pull this off without Taz knowing about it."

"Yes, there is. I haven't had to touch any of it. Shoot, I haven't even bought a new car 'cause I've been driving all of Taz's."

"True. I still wonder why you haven't sold those damn cars. You don't drive them all. You stuck in that six-year-old Mercedes when you should be pushing something brand new."

"You know that's not my style, Tee. That's my daddy's way not mine."

"Whatever. Even if you tried to spend your own money he would know it. That money Won left you is still in the offshore accounts and Taz would be notified. I'm sorry, baby girl; Taz is going to have to be in on this from the start. He trusts you, Neema; he's proud of you for what you've been doing here. I don't think he'll give you any problems with this restaurant."

"Are you sure?"

Laughing, Tari said, "I'm about as sure of it as I can be. You know your father; he switches up whenever he feels like it."

"I know. Shoot, this is all his fault anyway. If he wouldn't have ever moved to California I wouldn't have never went to that Roscoe's Chicken & Waffle place and this idea wouldn't have came to my mind. Now it's become somewhat of an obsession for me. I want Good Investments Inc. to be the first to bring a chicken and waffle restaurant to the city. And, dammit, Tee, I'm doing it."

"Go for it, Neema, you have my full support. Now call your daddy."

Tazneema smiled at Tari and said, "Nope. I'm scared!" She started laughing louder and said, "He's flying out here tonight. He doesn't know I know. Mama-Mama called me this morning and told me Sacha called her and told her that they were all coming home to spend a week out here. I'll talk to him when he gets here."

Tari smiled and shook her head from side to side and said, "That way you can have some big time backup."

"Yep. Some major backup. With you, Sacha, and Mama-Mama on my side that restaurant is good as ours."

"You're a grown woman and I am so proud of you, Neema, but you're still that little spoiled brat we all love so much."

Neema smiled happily and said, "That I am, Tee, that I am!"

# Chapter Four

The Network was formed by three men who felt that it was time for the black man to control more within the streets of the ghettos across the U.S. The Italians had their mafia, the Colombians and the Cubans had their cartels, but there was no one representing the black man in the urban community where most of these illegal enterprises were making their absurdly large amounts of money. The three founding members of the Network knew that there was no way that they would be able to remove the Italians, Colombians, or Cubans because they were already firmly positioned across the U.S. They were not afraid to make a stake and claim certain areas across the country because they knew without a doubt as long as they stuck together and continued to earn money for those in power sooner or later their position of power would increase. So their plan for over thirty years was to continue to make money, save money, recruit new members, expand, and gradually gain the power that would be necessary to make them a respected criminal organization in their own right.

Floyd "Cash Flo" Harris along with this two cousins Franklin Flintroy and Marcus Flintroy started the Network and recruited the first three serious members within their organization: William "Won" Hunter, Patrick "Pitt" Thomas, and Charles "Mack" Brown, three men who they

felt were intelligent enough to understand their goals and
would bring the right type of hustling and money-earning
skills to help further the goals set for the Network. Three
men who were ruthless enough to be able to handle the
bloodshed that they knew would be sure to follow once
they began their quest for their position of power. Three
men who they knew without a doubt would be 100 percent
loyal to the Network.

These men were the original members of the Network's
council. The first twenty-plus years of the Network's existence was a turbulent one to say the least. Plenty of violence and more death than any of the men within the
council had anticipated. But they prevailed and the
Network became a highly respected criminal organization along with its Italian, Cuban, and Columbian peers.
They were strategically scattered across the country and
continued to grow and make the necessary moves to gain
even more power. They knew they had to continue to
grow; the power came with numbers so more members as
well as states were added.

Now here it was a little over thirty years into their existence and the original members of the Network's council were no longer among the living. Frank and Marcus
Flintroy had been the first casualties in a war against the
Italians while vying for a stronger position in New York.
That was a crucial war. It cost the Flintroy brothers their
lives but it also showed the Italians that the Network was
serious and there to stay. Before the Flintroys had been
slain they made sure that they killed several key members of the Italian mob's hierarchy. This helped the in-
famy of the new, upcoming criminal organization called
the Network.

Charles "Mack" Brown had been kidnapped and murdered by the Cubans because he made the terrible mistake of bedding the wife of one of the top Cuban leaders. That had been an embarrassing moment for the Network. One that Cash Flo was determined to forget.

Then William "Won" Hunter was shot and killed by Patrick "Pitt" Thomas because Pitt figured out that Won had been conspiring against him and Cash Flo to take over the top spot of the Network. Won, who was known as a tactician of a high order, had been prepared for Pitt and anticipated his moves against him, so before his murder had taken place he devised a plan that would place his protégé in the top spot of the Network in case he failed. Before Won was murdered by Pitt, Cash Flo had been assassinated in his home by one of Won's trusted comrades. That same comrade also made sure that Pitt would meet his untimely demise.

The Network's ten-man council had a new leader now and Won's protégé position carried an extreme amount of pressure and responsibility. The ten-man council that Cash Flo, Won and Pitt helped originate after the deaths of the Flintroy brothers and Mack Brown was designed so all the territories across the U.S. would have a proper representative within the Network. The top man of the Network possessed total control over all decisions made concerning the Network. Each member had a vote on decisions and how the money was to be earned or any other business ventures, which included drugs, prostitution, gambling, and murder. Discipline was a must; if any rules of the Network were violated there would be no hesitation when it came to dispensing the proper punishment for wrongs committed. The ten-man council consisted of eight men and two women. Each was highly respected within their home state and communities, was rich and held stellar positions legally and owned several successful businesses. Being 100 percent legal in all aspects of business if anyone cared to take a close look at their financial status kept their business with the Network hidden very well. Each member ran their respective criminal activities with an iron fist. An iron fist backed with the support and power of the one and only all-black criminal organization, The Network.

Piper Dixon ran Seattle, Colorado, and with Pitt's demise she inherited his Northern California operations in Oakland and San Francisco as well as the entire Bay area. She wasn't a fan of Taz's, but she did respect him for the positive moves he'd made thus far as their new leader of the Network. She continued to watch his every move though. She knew that somehow Won had had Pitt killed and for that she felt a personal grudge against Taz, respect or not.

Jay Bogard ran Detroit and all of the state of Michigan from Flint to Kalamazoo. He was a longtime gangster from the Michigan streets and for years ran the drug trade with heroin, pills, and cocaine without anyone ever knowing of his notorious ways. Real low-key, an intense businessman and even more loyal friend, Taz appreciated Jay for the way he stood by his side from the start of his reign over the Network. Jay was definitely a Taz supporter mainly because he trusted and loved Won totally.

G.R., another highly successful businessman, ran St. Louis and Kansas City and was also a Taz supporter. He had been good friends with Won for years and may have been the only man on the council who knew of Won's plans to take over the Network. When he heard of Won's death he had been deeply saddened because for the first time in all of the years he had known Won it seemed his good friend had finally lost. He laughed with pure joy and admiration when he heard of Pitt's and Cash Flo's demise because he knew then without a doubt that his longtime friend had indeed achieved the goal he set out to do. That was to be the top man of the Network. He may not have been the man actually running it, but he placed the man he wanted to run the Network in the top spot and that was the same thing in G.R.'s eyes. So in essence his friend had indeed won. Taz would always have G.R.'s support.

Chinaman ran the entire East Coast so incognito that it was thought that he was a mythical figure. Then money earned from up top was so stupid at times that a member of the Network felt that they were underachieving in comparison to Chinaman. Everything he touched made profits whether it was drugs, robberies, or whatever. He was a cash cow for the Network. His primary focus was money and more money. So as long as Taz continued to help the Network remain in the position to make the money he couldn't care less about the politics within the Network so his position was considered to be neutral within the council. Most times when the voting wasn't flat-out overruled by Taz, which wasn't often, Chinaman's vote would be the deciding factor.

Chill Will was one of the two men who ran parts of the Lone Star State. Texas was so large that it had been broken down into two parts. Chill ran Dallas and East Texas as well as Houston. He was a savvy and shrewd businessman as well as a deadly gangster in his own right. He had been loyal to Pitt for years so it was a no-brainer that he was not one of Taz's fans. He did admire the young man

though and that said a lot in Taz's favor because Chill
Will rarely gave praise for anyone.

Snuffy had been loyal to Won for years and for his role
in taking care of Cash Flo and Pitt once he got the call
from Won he had been awarded a spot on to the council.
Snuffy ran Austin, San Antonio, and Corpus Christi,
Texas, along with his wife and confidante Charlene.
Charlene was his right hand in everything that he was a
part of. She was an unofficial member of the council because she couldn't attend the quarterly meetings, but Taz
knew and accepted the fact that Snuffy shared everything
with her. That didn't bother him at all because he knew
without a doubt they were on his side on whatever he
chose to do even if they didn't agree with him. They were
loyal. Snuffy owned several successful luxury car lots
throughout Austin and San Antonio. He lacked in certain
areas when it came to his legal businesses but Charlene
was there to pick up the slack. Together they were one
hell of a team both legally and illegally.

Snack was the Southern gentleman of the Network. He
ran parts of the South and was well known in the South's
dominance with the rap game. A mainstay with many successful Southern rappers. Snack was a popular club owner
and promoter for concerts in his Southern region as well
as abroad. His businesses were successful because he was
an admirable man but more so because of his laidback
demeanor. Everyone loved dealing with him. Nothing
seemed to faze him. He took everything good or bad with
a smile on his face. All he wanted to do was make money
and enjoy the very best of everything in life as he had the
last twenty-plus years. Snack loved his life and how he remained in control and he owed that to the Network. He felt
as long as Taz continued to keep the Network headed in the

right direction he would support him. He also felt that if he had any say in the young man that decision could change at the drop of a dime. Atlanta, Alabama, and Arkansas as well as parts of Mississippi belonged to Snack. His parts of the South never failed to meet its quarterly quotas because the man known on the council as the Southern gentleman always handled his business.

Malcolm Brown inherited his position and territory from his uncle, the late Charles "Mack" Brown. He was determined to correct the legacy of his late Uncle Mack. He was also considered a ladies' man like his uncle had been, but he never let pussy sway his judgment or dictate his get down like his uncle did. He ran Chicago, Milwaukee, Minnesota, and Indiana so efficiently and effectively that no one on the council doubted him in the slightest. He was his uncle's nephew for sure because he loved gorgeous women, but he would never do anything as stupid as fuck a business associate's wife. He was also totally loyal to Cash Flo and had been devastated when he found out he had been murdered. Though no one knew for certain how Won had put everything together, the whispers within the Network were however it had been put down Won was the orchestrator of it. For that reason solely he couldn't stand Taz. Like the rest of the council he had to respect him for the good he had been doing at the top spot thus far. One day though he hoped to be the man to either replace Taz at the top spot or at least be able to avenge his mentor and friend Cash Flo.

By Taz holding the top spot there was one last member he had to worry about. That council member was a beast in every aspect of the word. She was not to be taken lightly, never, and she let it be known every chance she could that she would one day be the person to rid Taz from the

Network. Not only the top spot but the entire organization entirely. She felt he wasn't worthy to hold that position let alone to even be associated with them in any way shape or form. She felt he was inferior and beneath them all, not only because he was at least fifteen years their junior, by far the youngest member on the council, but because he gained the position of power in such a despicable way that she refused to accept him. She reluctantly gave him kudos for the achievements he had earned thus far. He had leadership potential, yes, but in her eyes he hadn't earned that position and for that should be removed. That accompanied with the fact that she had been off and on–again longtime lovers with Cash Flo for years made her detest Taz greatly.

Saint Tramon ran New Orleans and Shreveport as well as Tennessee and was considered to be a voodoo believer who once was said to have had a hex put on all of the men who were against her. Though Taz didn't believe in any of that mess he refused to be alone in a room with Saint Tramon. He watched her warily and was always surprised at how pleasant she could be when they were speaking outside of their quarterly meetings. As soon as the meetings began she wasted no time starting her rant about how he should be replaced as the leader of the Network for whatever reason she chose to use. Four times a year he had to deal with her and so far every time she had been outvoted. Even though if the votes did come in her favor Taz had the overruling say-so because he had the keys to the entire fortune of the Network.

Everyone was eating good, but Taz held the power to destroy each and every member on the council. He knew that one day an attempt would be made on his life. He hoped and prayed that he would be able to find out the person who gained enough courage to go against him because they would surely die a painful death.

Taz, Piper Dixon, Jay Bogard, G.R., Chinaman, Chill Will, Snuffy, Snack, Malcolm Brown, and Saint Tramon made up the eight-man and two-woman council of the notorious Network. A force to be reckoned with, a group of men and women who were highly respected by their peers, the group who had successfully maintained their existence for over three decades. The group was divided evenly, with a young leader who was not to be underestimated in any way. Taz was determined to do things how he wanted to, because he felt in his heart that his best interest was for the Network's overall longevity. Drugs would be their downfall and that was something he was not going to let that happen. His decision was going to either take the Network to the next level or destroy them totally.

# Chapter Five

Taz was seated in the living room of his mother's home totally stuffed. Mama-Mama had outdone herself yet again. She cooked a feast for everyone when they arrived in town the night before. Now here they were stuffed to the max and waiting to do nothing but relax and chill. The kids were around playing and all of the grownups were sitting around the house relaxing.

Taz noticed how Red and Paquita, his longtime girlfriend, remained in a close huddle having what looked like an intense conversation. He hoped everything was good between them because he knew how much Red cared for her and her two kids. He thought back to a time when they were at a club when Red was first getting with Paquita and he got into it with her kids' father. That had not turned out good for her baby daddy at all, Taz remembered and smiled.

He turned and watched as Katrina, his man Keno's girlfriend before he was killed, was talking and laughing with Gwen and Sacha. He was happy that she had been able to move forward with her life after such a devastating loss. Especially knowing how Keno had just asked her to marry him the same day he had been murdered.

His mood was slowly turning dark so he tried to shake those thoughts from his head. He placed his right palm across the right side of his chest as he always did to show

love to his fallen homey, Keno. He noticed Tazneema
sitting down on the other sofa playing with her brother Li'l
Bo-Pete and that instantly brought a smile to his face. He
loved his children with all that he had in him and there was
nothing he wouldn't do for them. He stood and stepped
over to Neema and Li'l Bo-Pete and asked, "What you two
knuckleheads doing?"

"Knuckleheads? If me and my little bro are knuckleheads then that means you're a knucklehead too, Daddy,"
Neema said affectionately.

Too affectionately for Taz. *Uh-oh. Neema has something on her mind. Either she has done something she
doesn't think I will like or she wants something,* he said
to himself.

"Yeah, Daddy, you a knucklehead too," Li'l Bo-Pete
added and started laughing as his father grabbed him and
playfully roughed him up.

"Boy, you better not be over there hurting my g-baby!
Come here, Li'l Bo-Pete," Mama-Mama said with a
smile on her face. Li'l Bo-Pete was all smiles as he ran
from his father's grasp into his grandmother's loving
arms. Mama-Mama loved her g-babies to death. She
lovingly referred to Li'l Bo-Pete and Li'l Keno as her
g-babies and the twins adored her. "Now are you okay,
baby? That Daddy of yours ain't hurt you none did he? If
so you know Mama-Mama will get his butt for messing
with my g-baby."

Laughing, Li'l Bo-Pete said, "He called me a knucklehead, Mama-Mama!"

"He did what? Do you want me to get him? If so go
outside and find me a big switch so I can take it to his tail."

Li'l Bo-Pete stared at his father for a few seconds and
then said, "Uh-uh, Mama-Mama, my daddy was just

playing with me and my sister. Don't whoop his tail this time 'kay?"

"All right, if you say so, baby," Mama-Mama said and everyone listening started laughing.

Tazneema turned toward Taz and said, "Can we step outside, Daddy? I have something I need to talk to you about."

*Here we go,* Taz said to himself as he shot a look toward Tari to see if she would reveal anything to him 'cause he knew she knew something. Especially after the way she quickly dropped her eyes when he looked her way. *Should have known,* he thought and said, "Sure, babygirl, come on."

Once they were outside in the front yard Taz stopped by the rose bed and said, "Please tell me you're not preggo, Neema."

She slapped his arm lightly and said, "You need not worry about that at all, Daddy. I'm good. I'm not seeing anyone for any of that to be happening anyway."

"Good. But why aren't you dating? You got to move on with your life, Neema."

Laughing, she said, "How do you want it? Do you want me to tell you I'm preggo or I'm seeing anyone?"

Taz raised his hands in surrender and said, "You already know I'd rather the latter. But for real all I really want is for you to be happy."

"I know. Anyway, what I have to talk to you about is business related."

"It can't wait until we all get together for the Good Investments Inc. meeting before we leave?"

"I kind of want your input on this before we get together with everyone."

"All right, talk to me."

She took a deep breath and then went into her spiel that she'd practiced over a hundred times. When she was finished she smiled at her father and gave him that pouty brat look that she knew he would never say no to and kept her fingers crossed.

After Neema finished Taz smiled and said, "I like your passion for this, Neema, but I do have some concerns. The Bricktown location sounds like it'll cost a grip."

"It may be costly, but I know this restaurant will prove to make a nice profit. They're already finishing up Kevin Durant's restaurant out that way and it's going to be a kicking it spot, real upscale like. We won't lose on this, Daddy, I'm sure of it."

"Chicken and waffles huh? You really think Oklahoma City would take to a chicken and waffle restaurant, Neema?"

"I know it will, Daddy. Atlanta has Gladys Knight's Chicken & Waffles and Cali has Roscoe's Chicken & Waffles. We need to make this move and be the first to bring that to our city. O City is steadily growing and that's something we can definitely take advantage of. If this works like I know it will we can open up at least two more around the city."

"Have you chosen a name for this restaurant?"

Neema was ready for this question because she felt this would be the deal clincher for her. She hated herself in a way for being so manipulative, but she really, really wanted to open up this restaurant. She smiled at her father and stared into his intense brown eyes with her intense brown eyes and said, "I want to call it Keno's Chicken & Waffles. I want to name it in memory of my uncle Keno. Then when it's proven to be a success we can open another and name that one Bo-Pete's Chicken & Waffles. I want to do that and honor my uncle's memory."

"You are too damn good, Ms. Good. How in the hell can I turn you down? Okay, babygirl, run with it. I'm going to green light this at the meeting. This is your baby, but I want to remain aware of all the money that has to be invested into this project. I want Tari on board with you on this, cool?"

"Cool. Tari is already on board with it. We just needed to run it by you first to get your approval."

"Humph. All right then is that it? We good?"

"We're great! Thanks, Daddy," Tazneema said and gave Taz a tight hug.

Taz pulled from her embrace and stared at her. "You do know that there is nothing that I wouldn't do for you, Neema?"

"I know, Daddy."

"I know since I've moved west I haven't been around for you, but you know I'm a text or a call away. I'm never too busy for you, Tazneema. Never forget that."

Tears came to her eyes as she said, "I know, Daddy, and I will call if I need you, promise."

"Good. Now come on, let's go back inside and finish enjoying this Good family day."


Taz and Sacha were lying side by side after sharing several intense orgasms from their lovemaking for the last thirty-five minutes. "Mmmmm, glad to see you're still turned on by your old wife, Mr. Good," Sacha said with a smile as she laid her head on Taz's chest.

"You know I will always be turned on by you, li'l mama. I love me some you, girl."

"I love you too, Taz. It feels funny being back in this house after being gone for so long. I realize how much I've missed this place."

"Me too. This was the first expensive purchase I ever made for real. I had to have a home far enough away but close enough to the city. When I had it built it was my dream come true. I remember when Won told me that building your dream home was like creating the perfect woman."

"Now how in the heck can building your dream home be considered like creating the perfect woman? That don't make no damn sense."

Laughing, Taz said, "Won said that when you build your dream home it's perfect for you and only you. Just like the perfect woman. If a man could create the perfect woman she would have the body of a goddess, the looks of an angel, and the sex drive of a whore in a brothel."

"And like I said, how does that compare to building your dream home?"

"Your dream home is yours forever and so is your woman. The one thing you would never have to worry about is your home talking back or spending all your money."

"That doesn't make any damn sense, Taz Good. Won was crazy!"

Taz laughed and said, "It may not make any sense, li'l mama, but one thing for sure, Won was far from crazy."

"Now that, I can agree with." Changing subjects Sacha switched to business. "I've made my decision on which resort we will stay at for the first quarterly meeting for the council, baby."

"Yeah, which one?"

Sacha jumped off the bed naked, grabbed her iPhone off the dresser, came back and got herself comfortable next to Taz as she quickly found what she was looking for on her phone. She then started reading to him. "I found this on Google and decided that this had to be the one for the meeting as well as the mini vacation. It's perfect:

*"Forbes magazine recognized the St. Regis Bal Harbour Resort as the most anticipated hotel opening of 2012 and they were right to be excited. This AAA five-diamond awarded resort is beyond breathtaking, a true statement of oceanfront luxury. The St. Regis Bal Harbour Resort is elegant and refined, modern and stylish with seductive amenities that will please even the most affluent travelers. It's a peerless haven where you can indulge in life's finest things. Gentle ocean breezes, strolls along the beach, cocktails by the pool, and a delectable cuisine. But your stay at this destination is much more than that. It's about taking your resort experience to another level of luxury. You can step into the Reméde Spa where you'll be able to enjoy exclusive treatments in an atmosphere that is inviting, soothing, and sumptuous. Other unparalleled amenities include two spectacular tropical infinity pools with private cabanas, a state-of-the-art athletic club, and three top-of-the-line dining options. And if there is something that you can't find during your stay, your St. Regis butler is always on call offering meticulous and discreet personal service. The accommodations at St. Regis Bal Harbour Resort takes Miami beach luxury to another level. The resort's elegantly appointed*

*ocean view rooms, studios, and suites were de-*
*signed by the award-winning interior design firm*
*Yabu Pushelberg. All accommodations have private*
*glass-enclosed balconies with ocean views, refined*
*color palettes, and modern conveniences and*
*technology."*

"Damn, li'l mama, that does seem like a proper spot. I like the part about the cabanas. That's where we can have the meeting for the council."

"I was thinking the exact same thing. This will also make for a nice vacay during the middle of January. I'm sure the other council members will appreciate that gesture by their top man."

Laughing, Taz said, "I doubt it. Don't forget half of them aren't feeling ya man Taz."

"That doesn't matter, for a week's stay we'll be spending a nice amount so I'm positive they'll appreciate the gesture as well as enjoy themselves. Now I'm not so sure how they will feel after you drop the bomb on them that you're planning on taking the drugs from the Network to replace it with arms dealing. That may cause you more problems from the ones on the council who aren't, as you say, 'feeling Taz.'"

He sighed and said, "Yeah, I know. But it is what it is, li'l mama. I feel in my gut that this is the best direction to take the Network. I am not going back with it. I have to see it through."

"I know, baby, and I know you will win with this. We can't lose. As long as we all stick to the script and watch everything around us we won't slip or miss a beat. We're one hell of a team, Mr. Good. We got this thang on lock."

Laughing, Taz said, "On lock, huh? So when did you become so gangsta with it, li'l mama?"

She stared at her husband and answered him honestly. "The day I said 'I do', that was the day that I vowed to stand by your side through everything from sickness and health, and the good and the bad. I'm with you all the way, baby. Never forget that." They shared a kiss that turned passionate quickly and their lovemaking started all over again.

# Chapter Six

Good Investments Inc. was located on the sixth floor of a downtown office building not too far from the Chesapeake Arena where the Oklahoma Thunder played their home games. For the last six years it seemed that every investment that Good Investments Inc. had been involved in proved to be some very good investments indeed. The team consisted of Taz and the crew along with his daughter. They tried to have a business meeting monthly so everyone could stay abreast of what was going on with the company. This at times proved hard to do because of the schedule Taz had and because of them living in Los Angeles. They weren't able to have the meetings in person with everyone there; they would have a conference call long distance instead. On this day everyone was in town after a weeklong vacation of sorts in their hometown.

Taz smiled at everyone as they made themselves comfortable around a long conference table inside of their conference room. Taz sat at the head of the table with Sacha to his right and Tazneema to his left. Red and Wild Bill sat next to Sacha, and Tari and Bob sat next to Tazneema completing the seven-member board of Good Investments Inc. Each member on the board was an equal partner within the company and all decisions were decided by vote. Even though Taz was considered the head of the company, they each had equal say in whatever business decisions were made; but just as they did with their other forms of business, Taz was the man making the final decisions. When it came to business Taz valued all of their opinions and chose to make sure everyone's voice was heard.

After Sacha finished giving a complete update on the financial status of the company for the last few months everyone had a smile on their face because the profits were good and the money seemed to continue to pour in from all of their business ventures.

Sacha smiled at her husband and said, "Well, that's all I have. Looks like we've had a good few months."

"That's what's up. Now I have something I want to discuss," Taz said as he smiled at his daughter. "Tazneema here has come up with an idea that I think may turn into one of our most profitable investments yet. She wants to invest and bring a chicken and waffle restaurant out here to the city. I personally think this may work so I am proposing that we support her on this and we make the necessary moves to proceed with Neema's project."

"I like it. It makes a lot of sense. We could definitely win with a move like that," said Bob.

"Yeah, I'm with it too. Let's do it," said Red.

"Count me in," said Wild Bill.

"I'm in," said Tari.

Sacha frowned and then asked, "Where would the location be for this restaurant?"

"In Bricktown," answered Neema.

"That could get real expensive. You know Bricktown property has shot up since it has became such a hot spot for the city. Getting some prime real estate like that would make figures steep."

"I'm aware of that. Tari and I are looking into finding the best deal we can. Though it may be costly it's the most logical move to make. I mean Bricktown is the hottest place in the city. All of the Thunder hang out down there and everyone in the city loves going to eat and drink and chill in Bricktown. Why not bring the first chicken and waffle joint down there? That's the place to be."

Sacha heard the passion in her stepdaughter's voice and smiled. "Please don't think I'm against this because I understand exactly what you're saying, Neema. As the financial supervisor of the company it's my duty to point out what type of money may have to be spent on all investments. I'm in too. I agree that we should be able to make some good money with this venture."

"It's agreed. Good Investment Inc. will bring Oklahoma City its first chicken and waffle restaurant. What I like most about this idea is that my lovely daughter here has chosen to name the restaurant after the homey Keno."

"What? Aww hell nah!" Wild Bill laughed. "You mean to tell me that we're going to call the spot Keno's Chicken & Waffles? That's some funny shit right there, dog. I can see that cocky-ass nigga smiling down at us right now!"

Everyone started laughing.

"That means that if this investment is a success we're going to have to hurry and open another spot and name it after Bo-Pete," said Bob with a smile.

Taz smiled also and said, "Exactly. Okay, let's move to the next order of business. Red and Wild Bill's idea on opening a strip club in L.A. The floor is yours, guys."

Wild Bill started laughing and said, "I'd prefer you to call it a gentlemen's club, my nigga."

Taz rolled his eyes at his longtime friend and said, "Whatever, nigga. Get on with it."

"Seriously, me and Red have been looking at a few different locales around North Hollywood. We want this to be an upscale type of club all the way, not no normal booty club. Our aim is to get the high-class type, not the d-boys or the suckas."

"Exactly. No weak shit and no forms of prostitution at all. Straight up and down all the way. We will have the exclusive table dances or a room set up for private sessions, but nothing that will be illegal," Red said seriously.

"I like that. It shows me you guys will be respecting the women who work for you," said Sacha.

"For us, Sacha. Yeah, me and Wild Bill will be running thangs, but this move is just another one for Good Investments Inc. I think as long as we stick to the script that we've made it can work and be a breadwinner for us. The women we choose will be top of the line all the way. A nice variety of different nationalities, too. Not just a black club, a well-rounded and diverse one."

"I like the sound of that. Why does it have to be just for men? Why not have certain nights of the week for women and have top-of-the-line male dancers as well?" asked Tari.

Red looked at Wild Bill and said, "We've never gave that any thought for real. Shit, I don't have a problem with that. As long as it makes money it makes sense to me."

"Okay, before we go any further is it agreed that Good Investments Inc. will go ahead and pursue this venture with Red and Wild Bill for their, excuse me, for our gentlemen's club in Southern California?" asked Taz.

In unison everyone in the conference room said, "Agreed!"

"I have one question."

"What's up, Neema?"

"What is the name of this club going to be?"

Red and Wild Bill smiled at each other and Bob thought, *oh shit.*

"Heaven On Earth," both Red and Wild Bill said simultaneously.

Bob thought about that name for a minute and grinned. He wanted to see if anyone other than himself figured out what Red and Wild Bill were up to by naming the club Heaven On Earth. He waited a couple more minutes and then said, "So, we're going to name the club H.O.E., huh?"

Tari who was sipping some orange juice almost spit her drink all over Taz when she heard Bob. She turned toward Wild Bill, squinted her eyes, and asked, "You can't be serious, Wild Bill. Heaven On Earth or H.O.E. Stop fucking playing!" Everyone inside of the room started laughing, everyone except for Red and Wild Bill that is.

"Why not? It's like a double entendre," said Red.

"A double what?" asked Bob

"A double entendre, fools. Like a double meaning of sorts."

"Kind of like an acronym but it's not because we won't have it spelled H.O.E. Instead it will be spelled how it sounds, Heaven On Earth. The double entendre is the double meaning we're slipping in and that's the H.O.E.," Wild Bill said and smiled.

"Whatever," said Bob.

"Okay, is there any other business we need to discuss for this quarter?" asked Taz. After no one said anything he continued. "All right, I got the green light from Akim and his private jet will be here this evening so we're out of here tomorrow afternoon. We'll spend a day or two in Colombia meeting with Jorge and then we'll fly back west and get things prepared for the meeting with Danny Orumutto. After that it's off to sunny Florida for the quarterly meeting for the council."

Tazneema became uncomfortable whenever her father began discussing what she chose to call "the other business" so she stood and excused herself from the meeting.

After Neema left the room Tari glared at Taz and he said, "Oops."

"You know better, Taz," Sacha said and frowned at her husband.

"I know. But shit she needs to be aware of everything. I mean if something ever happens to me I want her knowing what is what."

"It's not always about what Taz wants. You have to understand that though she knows what we're a part of she doesn't totally understand it," said Bob.

Taz frowned at him and said, "Whatever. Like I was saying, then it will be off to Florida so we can handle that business as well as kick it a little bit. Once I drop that bomb on the council I'm going to want to tighten things up. I'll get at Snuffy and all I feel are supportive of my decision so no one will be slipping."

"Do you anticipate any trouble from the council members?" asked Tari.

Taz shrugged and said, "You never can tell with something like this, Tari. I'll try to check their temperatures as best as I can during the meeting. If no one blows their cool it'll be on some wait and see type shit. And I'm not trying to wait for any weak shit to pop off. If it's going to be on, it will be on and we will play offense before we play defense."

"That's real," said Wild Bill.

"I want to go to Colombia with you guys. I'm tired of being left out all of the time," said Tari.

"I don't have a problem with that, Tee. If you want to roll then you can."

"That's cool. 'Cause for real, Taz, I need to skip this trip. I have some things I need to get worked out with Paquita," said Red.

Taz gave him a nod and said, "Cool. Me, Tari, Bob, and Wild Bill will make the trip to South America and then meet y'all back in the West. When do you want to fly back, li'l mama?"

"Since the boys are having such a good time I thought we'd stay another day and give Mama-Mama some more times with her g-babies. We'll fly back the day after to-morrow. Will you have your business done by then, Red? If so then we can fly back together. You know Gwen and I will need your help with the kids and stuff."

"Yeah, that's fine," answered Red.

"All right then this meeting is officially in the books. Sacha, make sure you go over all financial moves for the next two investments we're going to make so everything can be cleared on the books."

"Gotcha."

"Good. Now let's get packed and get ready to go holla at the Colombian boss," Taz said seriously.

# Chapter Seven

For over four decades Jorge Santa Cruz ran the Buenaventura cartel with an iron fist. His enemies hated him but respected him as the ruthless leader he was known to be. Yet they still tried to attack him at least three times a year. What frustrated them most was he always seemed to find a way to escape death. It has been rumored throughout Colombia that he had protection from the spirits. Whatever it was, Jorge Santa Cruz took such full advantage of its existence that it amazed the public that anyone would still continue to try to murder such a dangerous man. Buenaventura was Jorge Santa Cruz's to control and he would never relinquish his position without a fight. The number one port in South America's drug trade belonged solely to him. Tons and tons of coca was shipped to Europe as well as the United States through this port. His position remained important to most cartels in South America because if he didn't approve or have a piece of what was being shipped through his port, wars erupted immediately and most times he came out unscathed and victorious.

When Taz and the crew stepped off the private jet Jorge Santa Cruz had two Range Rover stretch limousines waiting for them. They were quickly led inside of Palmaseca Airport so they could be cleared through customs. They then were escorted to the stretch limos so they could be transported to Jorge Santa Cruz's vast estate. Tired from their four-and-a-half-hour flight from Oklahoma City, Tari sat back and relaxed as the SUV limousine rolled smoothly through the city of Cali, Colombia. As they rode through some extremely poor-looking neighborhoods Tari felt saddened as she stared at dirty children playing in the fields kicking soccer balls around. She once again realized how good they had it in America.

A little over an hour the areas slowly transformed from poverty stricken to some very expensive-looking homes. Tari was amazed at how quickly they went from such a grimy looking area to some of the most beautiful landscapes she had ever seen in her life. When she asked the driver of the SUV about this he told her that the neighborhoods they passed first were called *La phallia* and was considered a ghetto and low-income neighborhoods. Whereas now they were entering the neighborhoods called *La primera.* This neighborhood housed the wealthy and the blessed. Tari shook her head from side to side and Taz started laughing.

"Come on, Tee, you act like this is new to you. It's just like back home, you got Nichols Hills and you got the east side, the only difference is we're now in South America instead of the good old U.S.A."

"Still is some sad stuff to be looking at."

"It is what it is though."

Twenty minutes later the driver pulled the limo into what looked like a castle to Taz. A huge wrought-iron gate opened and they entered a large compound-like area. When the limo came to a stop in front of the castle Taz saw Jorge Santa Cruz standing in the doorway with a huge smile on his face. *Wonder if he'll still be smiling after I drop this bomb on his ass,* Taz thought as he got out of the limo and stepped toward Jorge Santa Cruz with his hand outstretched for a handshake with the cartel leader. They shook hands firmly and smiled at one another. "You look good, Mr. Santa Cruz."

"You know better than that, Taz; call me Jorge. Come, you and your associates must be tired from your flight here. Come and we shall eat a nice lunch before we get to the business, *sí?*"

"*Sí,*" Taz said as he followed Jorge inside of his home followed closely by Tari, Bob, and Wild Bill.

One hour later they were all full from a hearty lunch of fish, rice with yucca, a potato-like vegetable that Columbians like to eat with their seafood dishes. Crabs, whole lobsters, several different types of shrimps and *platano,* basically a green banana mixed with their food for added flavor. They all wore content smiles as Jorge Santa Cruz led them out of the dining area to a huge sitting room. He told one of his security detail that they were not to be disturbed and had him close the door. He then turned and went to the bar to pour them all something to drink.

Jorge Santa Cruz was a relatively small man. He stood close to five foot nine, was slim and in very good shape for a man in his mid-fifties. He had brown eyes and a salt-and-pepper mustache that reminded Taz of Won. After pouring everyone a glass of wine he raised his glass in the air and said, "A toast. To good business and long-lasting relationships in a business where friends shouldn't become enemies. Cheers."

As Taz sipped his drink he couldn't help but wonder if Jorge knew something about what he'd come to discuss with him. He watched as Jorge made himself comfortable on a soft leather sofa then wasted no time in getting straight to the point. "Jorge, we're here because I have some very important things to discuss with you."

"But of course, Taz. I knew once you requested my permission to come to my lovely country that it was of serious importance. So please do not mince your words; speak to me, my friend."

Taz gave a slight nod and said, "This will be the last year that the Network will be doing business with you for the coca. At the end of the year the Network will no longer be purchasing any forms of drugs. I am about to end all ties with drugs and move in a totally different direction. A direction that I feel will not only be beneficial for the Network long term but also for you if you wish to continue to do business with me."

Jorge frowned and asked, "And what business is that, Taz?"

"Arms. Everything from guns such as automatic assault rifles, missiles, RPGs, hand, everything. It is well known throughout our peers that you are always in need of some serious artillery. Though I'm quite sure you're already well equipped, I'm positive that with the moves I'm about to make you will have the very best prices on whatever you need as far as weapons are concerned."

"Is this generosity because I'm going to lose you as a client for my coca or because of our friendship?"

"Both. My decision to stop all drugs trafficking within the Network is something that has been in the works for some time now. I feel that in the long run things will become wicked in America with the narcotics and I think now is the time to make the exit and move into something that can be just as profitable for the organization. This decision, I know, affects the men I deal with and by that I want to make sure that I do right by each."

"So I won't be the only man receiving these benefits?"

"No, you won't. I will offer the same to Danny Orumutto in California and Señor Suarez in Miami. I respect each of you for the good business we have been able to conduct over the years and I hope that we will still be able to conduct even more good business with this new venture."

Bob, Tari, and Wild Bill watched the small Colombian, trying to gauge whether he was feeling what Taz just told him. Taz sat there silently wondering if their lives were in any danger. *Damn, I hope I haven't gotten us all murdered way the fuck out here in Colombia,* he thought as he continued to wait for Jorge to speak.

Finally, after a few minutes of contemplating, the Colombian drug lord smiled and said, "Well, I think we should have another drink and toast." He stood and went back to his bar and grabbed another bottle of red wine then stepped back and refilled everyone's glass. He raised his glass in the air and said, "To the future. To new business and to more good business." He downed his drink in one gulp and sighed. "Yes, I think we will be able to do some good business with the arms dealing, Taz. I respect you and I think your visions are admirable. I do have some reservations, but that's only because of the major deductions I will have taken by losing your business with the coca. I appreciate you giving me a year in advance; that helps me tremendously. You are a fair man indeed, Taz."

"Thank you, Jorge."

"Also, I love the fact that I can do business for weapons with someone I can trust. My current situation concerning weapons is, as you say in America, dicey. So this will be an added benefit to me."

Taz sighed with relief and wanted to smile but instead kept his face neutral. "I will make sure that you have the first action at the best that I have to offer as well as the best prices, Jorge."

"Good, very good. If I may ask you, has this decision been approved within your organization? I ask this because I know some of your colleagues within your council very well and I don't think they would be too excited about ending their careers as distributors of the coca."

"As you well know I am in charge of the Network and all decisions are made through the council with my vote being the determining factor. I haven't brought this to the table yet because I wanted to make sure that I would not be offending any of our business associates with the decision to end all ties with drugs."

"Smart. Do you think each man will understand this as I have?"

"I'm not sure. I can only hope that each one respects me enough to understand my position and my decision and accept what I have to offer them."

"And what if they don't?"

Taz stared at Jorge, smiled that faintly mocking smile of his and answered him honestly. "Then things will get dicey."

Jorge started laughing loudly and slapped his legs. "You are a gangster, Taz! I love it! Now, let's go and enjoy some of my country's entertainment. I want to take you and your team out to dance the night away. Let me have my men show you to your rooms so you can have time to get some rest. Then this evening we are going to go out and do some heavy partying, Colombian style. You do know how to salsa don't you, Taz?"

Laughing, Taz said, "I don't, but I have a feeling before we leave your country me and my crew will."

Laughing, Jorge said, "That is a fact!"

# Chapter Eight

Every last member of the crew had a hangover and a monster headache as they boarded the private jet for their flight to Los Angeles. Once they were settled on the plane they all fell into a deep sleep. After a couple of hours into the flight Taz woke to use the restroom. After he was finished he sat back down and thought about how smoothly things went with Jorge Santa Cruz and wondered if things would go as smooth with Danny Orumutto.

He was more than relieved that the drug lord had chosen to accept his offer because out of the three associates the Network conducted their business with, drug-wise Jorge was by far the most ruthless. Even though each man was ruthless in their own right, Taz felt he could deal with the others easier than he could if he had to take Jorge to war. Even with the Russians backing him it would have been an ugly war. War wasn't profitable and if it could be avoided that was the way he would go. If it couldn't then he would do what he had to do in order to make sure that the war didn't last too long. That meant going all out, fast and hard until his adversaries were no more. That was the only way he knew how to war: hit them hard and hit them fast. If he even thought for a second he was going to be challenged aggressively by anyone for the decisions he made for the Network then he wasn't going to waste any time removing whoever chose to go against them.

He sighed and tried to get comfortable so he could get some more rest. Two days in Colombia partying with Jorge took a lot out of him. Jorge partied just as hard as the Russians; instead of vodka his drink of choice was expensive vintage wines, and they had a powerful kick when a lot was consumed. *Damn, my head is killing me,* he said to himself as he closed his eyes.


Saint Tramon was sitting on her bed stroking her latest boy toy's broad shoulders, smiling lovingly at him when her cell phone rang. She sighed annoyingly as she reached and grabbed her phone. "What is it, Damon?"

Her personal assistant hated disturbing her, especially whenever she was entertaining one of her many boy toys. Saint Tramon was not to be messed with whenever she was in one of her horny moods, but he knew she needed to know about the call he had just received. He inhaled deeply and said, "Forgive me, Saint Tramon, but I have received a call from some associates of yours and they have informed me that Taz and a few of his people spent the last two days in Colombia with Jorge Santa Cruz and are now on their way back to L.A. I thought that you would want to know about this as soon as possible, ma'am."

"Colombia? What is that little boy up to flying out to see Jorge?"

"I have no clue, ma'am. Is there anything you would like for me to do about this matter?"

"No. Keep your eyes and ears out in L.A. on alert and let them know I want to know all that our little young leader is up to out that way."

"Yes, ma'am," Damon said as he hung up the phone grateful that Saint Tramon didn't give him one of her fits she was well known for throwing when disturbed.

After she hung up the phone she smiled at her boy toy and said, "Okay, darling, I've just became slightly stressed. I need to relive some pressure. Are you ready for round four?" Her boy toy gave her an enthusiastic nod and smiled as he rolled over and put his head between her legs. She sighed loudly and said, "That's exactly what I had in mind, darling. Mmmmm, you are so good with that wicked tongue of yours!"

It was a bright and sunny day in California when Taz made it to the Winners Circle. Tari, Red, Wild Bill, and Bob were all relaxing in the media room watching television when he entered the room. "Damn, y'all look like some lazy, rich fuckers."

"Yep. We're having him over for lunch. He'll be here at one. I've told the chef to make your fave, Red."

"You're kidding. Taz, man, you be tripping. Ain't no way in hell I'm in the mood to be eating none of that nasty-ass Italian food," complained Wild Bill.

Red shook his head from side to side and laughed. "You are one lame and classless-ass li'l nigga. All you want to eat is fried chicken and hamburgers. That's why your growth has been stunted."

Laughing, Bob said, "Damn that was a good one, Red."

"Fuck both you niggas! And I told your yellow ass about that li'l nigga shit, you big soft-ass super sprung nigga. Keep on and I'll tell Taz about you being so stressed because Paquita doesn't want to move out here to L.A."

Taz stared at Red and could tell that Wild Bill hit a nerve and decided to dead this playing before they really got into it. "All right, G, cool it. We need to get this business out the way with Danny Orumutto and then maybe we can all go ride around and check out some buildings for Heaven On Earth. I mean this you guys' project and y'all acting like y'all ain't ready to make it happen for real."

"Damn, nigga, we just got back from Colombia! It ain't like we lollygagging, dog. We've been making calls trying to get some plugs on the type of sound systems we want to use," said Wild Bill.

"That's cool. What up with you, Tari, you good or are you ready to head back to the city?"

"I'm good. I think I'll chill out here a few more days before heading back home. It's been too cold out there. I like all of this damn sunshine. I might have to come out here and move in here at the Winners Circle with Red and Wild Bill."

"For real, they need you out here to keep they ass from killing each other when me and Bob ain't around."

"I may just do that, but right now Neema needs me to help her with the chicken and waffles restaurant. After we get that off the ground I'll think about it some more. Speaking of Neema she asked me to ask you how would you feel if she moved into Keno's place? No one has been there since you know, and she says she has to get out of Mama-Mama's home because she is finally starting to feel claustrophobic with all of Mama-Mama's love."

Taz started laughing and said, "Finally, huh? I thought she would have wanted to get out of there sooner. It's cool with me. What about y'all? Do y'all have a problem with Neema moving into Keno's place?"

"I'm with it too. Just don't think I'll be visiting too often. That shit would get me all choked up. Damn I miss that nigga," said Wild Bill filled with emotion.

The room fell silent as each member of the crew was thinking about their fallen homeboy. The silence was broken by Taz's cell phone ringing. He checked the caller ID and saw that it was Snuffy from Texas. "What it do, country boy?"

"Country boy? Nigga, I'm from Texas! Your ass is from Oklahoma City; who the hell you calling country?" Snuffy started laughing.

"Whatever. What's up with you, my nigga?"

"Same old shit. Just got the text from your wife informing me about the Miami trip. Loving that choice, dog. I see Sacha is still on top of her game 'cause no way in hell would you have chosen such a fly-ass spot like the St. Regis Bal Harbour Resort. That shit is top flight all the way, dog."

"What makes you think Sacha chose that spot, fool? You think I don't have the taste to make some move like that?"

"Nope, I sure don't!"

"What you know about the St. Regis Bal Harbour Resort anyway?"

"I'm sitting here reading up on all of the shit they got now on my phone, nigga, so I know everything they got popping out that way."

"Should have known. Anyway, did you call me to bust my chops on this weak shit or what?"

"Nah, me and Charlene have been wondering when you gon' get back at us with that business you was talking about. How did thangs go when y'all went to Russia?"

"My bad, dog. Shit has been hectic. We've been to Colombia and back since then and I haven't had time to get at you and break everything down to you."

"Colombia as in Jorge Santa Cruz's Colombia?"

"Yep."

"Is the shit thick or is everything good?"

"So far so good. We're about to meet with Danny Orumutto in a couple of hours. If things go well then the last meeting will be the week after next when we're in Miami for the quarterly council meeting. I'm setting a meeting up with Mr. Suarez before the Network's council meeting. I'm hoping everything goes right; then when I bring it to the table there won't be that subject that can be used to try to change my mind."

"I feel that, dog, but you do know you will meet a whole lot of resistance on this get down, right?"

"No doubt. As long as I have your vote along with the others on our side then my veto power will be intact."

"You know damn well you got my vote, my nigga. I'm rolling with your ass until the wheels fall off."

"Me too, Taz!" Charlene, Snuffy's wife and confidante, yelled in the background.

Taz smiled and said, "Tell your better half I said thanks. All right, my nigga, let me go. I'll give you a text after we're finished meeting with Danny Orumutto."

"That's right. Tell the crew I send mines. Out!"

"Out!" Taz said and ended the call.


Tazneema was sitting inside of her office going over some of the floor plans she had drawn up for how she wanted the new restaurant to look. So far everything was going according to her plan. Even though she hadn't found the right building down in Bricktown she was confident everything was going to work out just fine. She had Lyla whose boutique was in Bricktown keeping her eyes and ears open for any news that she could use to help her acquire the building she wanted. She knew she was going to have to be patient with this. As if reading her mind Lyla called Neema just as she was reaching for her cell to give Lyla a call.

"What's good, crazy white girl?" Neema asked when she answered her phone.

"Nothing much. Slow at the shop right now so I wanted to check on you to see what you were up to."

"Shoot, I was hoping you had some news for me on a building down there."

"You're going to have to be patient, Neema. Something is going to come up. Businesses down here are opening and closing all the time."

"I know, it's just I have to have the perfect location in order for this to work the way I want it to. Anyway, I was thinking, it's time for me to leave the nest. Mama-Mama and I have outgrown one another. Even though we love each other to death it's time for me to get my own place."

Laughing, Lyla said, "Don't tell me you're ready to move back in with me, honey, because I don't have the room in my little place."

"Ha. Ha. Seriously, I was thinking about us getting a place together, though definitely not your place. I have a tad too much money to be living in a one-bedroom condo don't ya think?

"Mm-hmm, yeah, you're really loaded, so what you want to do, big time, get a mini mansion like your dad's?"

Tazneema smiled into the receiver and said, "Actually, that's exactly what I had in mind. I had Tari ask my daddy would it be all right if I moved into my uncle Keno's mini mansion out north."

"You are kidding me right? The same mini mansion he was murdered in? Don't you believe in haunted houses, Neema?"

"No, and neither does your ass, so don't even try to go there with me, crazy girl."

"What did Taz say?"

"I don't know. Tari hasn't gotten back to me yet. Hold up, let me send her a text real quick to see if she has had the time to ask him." Neema quickly tapped on her cell and sent Tari a text asking her if she had asked her father about her moving into Keno's home. "Okay, girl, I'm back. So, will you be with it?"

"With what, Neema?"

"Ugh! I hate when you act blond, girl. With moving in with me into my uncle Keno's place? There's plenty of room there for the both of us. Shoot, that place is just a little smaller than my daddy's. The indoor pool and indoor gymnasium are the only things that Taz has and we won't."

"Trust, you don't have to do any convincing here, I'm in! I can save me a nice piece of money by selling my place or renting it out. Wait, what do the utilities cost for a place as big as that? Shit, we may be paying more than I can afford."

"I'm sure it may be a tad high, but split between the both of us it should be all good. That's all we'll be paying other than insurance. Come on, Lyla, let's go for it. We can redecorate it and give it that woman's touch and be all the way live," Neema said with excitement in her voice.

Laughing, Lyla said, "I'm in! Now all you have to do is get the yes from Taz."

Just as Lyla was speaking Neema received a text from Tari telling her that Taz and her uncle said it would be fine for her to move into Keno's place. Tazneema smiled brightly and said, "Okay, crazy girl, you need to get to packing because Tari just hit me and told me we're good. We're about to have our very own mini mansion. Yay!"

"Yeah, yay! I knew having you for a besty would come with a lot of perks, but never would I have thought we'd be able to come up on our very own mini mansion! Damn, girl, we're big time now!" They both started laughing and then started discussing their plans to redecorate Keno's place.

# Chapter Nine

Danny Orumutto was a tall and slim man with a long ponytail. He looked nothing like one would imagine the leader of a ruthless Japanese drug ring to look like. He carried himself with the swagger of a famous rapper. He was much younger than people thought and had such a carefree attitude it was hard for his peers to take him seriously at times. The rumors surrounding his name and how he came to power of his family's ring made him a man not to be tried no matter how he acted or looked.

Danny Orumutto entered the Winners Circle with his lovely wife, Michelle, and one member of his personal security who refused to leave Danny's side. Taz led them into the dining room and they all enjoyed an extremely large Italian meal prepared by Taz's personal chef, who he inherited from Won. The entire staff of the Winners Circle included three maids, a chef, and a four-man security team who made sure that the Winners Circle was properly protected twenty-four hours a day.

Though this wasn't Danny Orumutto's first visit to the Winners Circle, this was his first time dining with Taz. He was surprised to see that Taz knew of his love for Italian food; not too many people knew this. He appreciated the gesture and told Taz this as Taz led them into the living room so they could have their meeting.

"Thank you for a scrumptious meal, Taz. I do love me some Italian food. Every time I'm out East having business sit-downs with the dagos they go out of their way to show off for me by stuffing me with some of the finest Italian foods I've ever tasted. I must say that your chef has kept pace with them."

Taz gave him a nod and said, "I'll make sure to relay your compliments and let him know that you enjoyed his meal, Danny."

Danny checked his watch, an expensive Audemars Piguet, and said, "I am in no means trying to rush this meeting, Taz, but I do have several pressing matters that need to be tended to today. My people in Detroit have been sweating me real tough for those thirty MG roxicodones. It's like all of a sudden the demand for them that way has increased and I need to make the necessary adjustments to get them out that way. I'm sure your man Jay Bogard has informed you of this already."

"No, he hasn't. We only talk during our quarterly meetings. I don't get into the day-to-day running of their business operations. I only deal with matters of the Network in our meetings. I respect your time schedule so let me get straight to the point. First, thank you for letting us have this sit-down on such short notice. This is very important to me and I hope after this meeting we will still be able to conduct some very good business for a very long time."

"Uh-oh. That sounds like I'm not going to care for what we're about to discuss."

Taz shrugged his broad shoulders and said, "Maybe you will and maybe you won't."

"Please, proceed," Danny said with all trace of humor now gone from his voice. It was strictly business now.

Taz then went on to explain how he was in the process of removing the drugs from the Network and after one year they would sever all ties with everyone whom they were dealing with for drugs. He also explained his reasons for doing so; though he didn't have to do this he felt it would be best to give Danny some form of an explanation. He hoped that tactic would take some sting from his words because he was in no way trying to insult or anger the drug kingpin. He merely wanted to sever with his drug business so they could do some even better business with the arms dealing he was about to embark on. As Taz did with Jorge Santa Cruz he gave Danny Orumutto his word that he would give him the very best prices on any and all weapons he chose to purchase from him if he chose to do business with him after everything was all said and done. After Taz finished he sat back in his seat and waited for Danny Orumutto's response.

Danny waited a few minutes as he processed everything Taz had told him before speaking. When he did speak it was in a low and measured tone that spooked the hell out of Taz.

"I don't know the exact figures, Taz, but I do know that you will be taking a substantial amount of money out of my pocket by removing the business we conduct. Though there has never been a signed contract with the business we've done, I've always assumed that we were locked in for the long haul. To hear you speak on this is shocking, yet I do understand your point as well as your views about drugs. I've always known how you felt about drugs and I respect that. I am not a part of your organization so cannot force you to continue to do business with me. As a longtime associate of the Network I would like to ask you to reconsider this. Why? Because if you take away the business that we do I will be forced to find a replacement for the Network and that won't be an easy task at all."

"I understand that, Danny. That's why I'm giving you a year before we pull out. That should give you the necessary time to find a replacement. I am not going to let anyone on the council of the Network continue to deal with drugs after one year from our first quarterly meeting next week. Out of respect for you and the business we've done over the years I am getting at you now. If any member of the council wishes to continue to do business with you, I will not interfere with them at all. That will be cause for their immediate removal from the council as well as the Network and everything that comes with their affiliation with the Network. It's time for a change, and I have made the decision to make that change now," Taz stated firmly.

Danny Orumutto gave a nod of his head and said, "I understand, Taz, and I am grateful for you getting at me with this. I assume you've met with others concerning this business?"

"Yes, I've already met with Jorge Santa Cruz. I'll be getting with Mr. Suarez in Miami next week."

"If I may, can I inquire what old Jorge had to say about this decision of yours?"

Taz laughed and said, "No problem, Danny. Jorge was with it and basically gave me his blessings as long as I promise to give him first dibs on all weapons."

"I should have expected that. That old fool has to remain prepared for war at all times with all of the attempts made on his life yearly. It's like this, Taz: this move you're going to make will hurt me and I'm not with it. Is there anything that I can do or say to get you to change your mind on this?"

"Come on, Danny. You know better than that."

"I had to ask, Taz," Danny said as he stood and reached out his hand toward Taz. "Well, I guess we'll bring one form of business to a close then."

"And hopefully a new form of business can begin, Danny?"

Danny smiled at Taz and shrugged. "Maybe we will and then again maybe we won't. Time will tell."

After they finished shaking hands Taz led them toward the front door and said, "I'll keep my hopes on us doing some good business, Danny."

"No one can predict the future, Taz. Take care of yourself." They shook hands again and Taz watched as Danny, his wife, and his security man got inside of his armored Rolls-Royce Phantom and left the Winners Circle.

Taz returned to the living room, sat down, and asked the crew, "Well, what do you guys think?"

"Trouble is about to head our way behind this shit," said Tari.

"Yeah, we need to start putting security measures in place for everyone. And I do mean everyone. Out here as well as back home," said Bob.

"Yep, we're going to war with that fool, dog. I can peep it in his eyes," said Red.

"This is real. The only question that needs to be answered now is, do we wait and play defense or do we take the offense?" said Wild Bill. "Me personally, I feel we need to go on and take it right to that chink mothafucka right now. That way we won't have to worry about shit later, Taz."

"I feel that, G. But I need to see how this flies with the council before I make that decision. Their lives are wrapped in this too tough for me to move like that."

"Well, that doesn't make too much sense, Taz. You've already made the decision to affect their lives when you decided to remove the drug dealing from the Network," Tari stated logically.

"I know, Tee. But going to war is totally different. It means everyone is in jeopardy, and I want to see how the council feels about what I'm bringing to the table. Also I want to see how Mr. Suarez reacts. Right now we got the Russians behind this play as well as Jorge Santa Cruz. If the Cubans back the play then there is no way Danny would even think to attempt war. He would lose and then lose even more money."

"That makes sense because that chink is all about the dollar. He's more concerned about his money than anything else," said Bob.

"We wait. We wait for the meeting with the council and the meeting with Mr. Suarez before we make any aggressive moves toward Danny Orumutto."

"I'm with that," said Red.

"Me too," said Bob.

"Makes sense," added Tari.

"I'm always with you and never against you, G. I just hope and pray that we won't wait too damn long. I'm not trying to bury any more friends. That shit hurts too much, real spill," said Wild Bill.

"I feel you, dog. In the meantime we do like Bob suggested. We tighten everything up around everyone. Tari, you get a flight booked and get back to OKC. I want you to go out there with her, Red. You can keep an eye on her and Neema. That way you can also handle your personal business with your girl, dog." Red gave him a nod of his head. "Bob, I think you should take two of the security team with you out to your spot and I'll take the other two. Wild Bill, you good or do you need someone here with you to make sure everything is straight?"

"I wish they would move on me. I got something for they ass. Y'all just make sure them kids are safe. I'm straight. When I go out and about I'll get at Mack or one of the fellas and not roll out alone. One thing I learned from that beef with those Hoover niggas back home, I'll never slip or take anything or anyone for granted. I remain on point at all times."

"Hopefully all of this will be for nothing, but I'm with you, Wild Bill. I too learned from that war with those Hoover niggas and I'll be damned if I ever let anything happen to any of us. Danny Orumutto and his entire family will be wiped the fuck out before I let that happen," Taz said in a deadly tone.

As Danny Orumutto's Phantom rolled smoothly on the freeway toward his home his mind was on what he had just discussed with Taz. As if reading his mind his wife Michelle asked him, "Are you going to take the Network to war behind Taz's decision, baby?"

Shaking his head no, Danny said, "No. The Network is about to have its very own personal war within. I'll sit back and wait for now. If Taz wins that war then I'll do what needs to be done. No way in hell will this year end with our business with the Network being over. That's way too fucking much money to be losing. Either way I don't think Taz will be alive once everything hits," he said seriously.

# Chapter Ten

Often when men achieve huge successes in their life they change either positively or negatively. Taz's changes were so obviously for the better that Sacha smiled inside every time she thought of her husband's transition over the last six years. From cutting his hair to dressing more stylish every single day. She was so happy he let her convince him to give up the Dickies and Timberland boots he was accustomed to wearing daily. Though he could clean up nicely when he wanted to, she was satisfied with his new style even though it was rather simple. Expensive black designer slacks, crisp white dress shirt, tie, and comfortable Italian loafers were his choice of clothing daily. When at home though, he would dress down in a pair of sweats and some Air Force Ones.

Taz's style of dress wasn't the only change made in his life; his way of thinking and dealing with things from the business side to family matters changed as well. His thought process was totally different now. His family and crew depended on him and his decision making so he became more analytical and less emotional when making serious decisions. He took his time and made calculated decisions so that every move he made he was confident that it was the right move to make. He knew that Won was smiling down on him for finally being able to keep his emotions in check and reaching this point in his life.

He was a boss now and he made moves like a boss was supposed to. Cunning, calculated, and decisive was how he would remain. No matter what he would make sure that he ran the Network and continued to make positive moves to push them forward.

That's why he was so stressed as he entered his home. The upcoming council meeting was going to be crucial to the future of the Network. A war with Danny Orumutto could set them back and hurt his position in ways he didn't care to think about. He smiled when he saw his wife sitting in the living room going over some papers. *Damn, I love that woman,* he said to himself as he stepped to Sacha and kissed her on top of her head.

"What's good, li'l mama?"

"Nothing much, going over some figures while those boys are napping. What's up with you?"

After sitting down next to her on the couch Taz sighed and said, "Running things over and over through my head on this move we're about to make and wondering if it's going to be worth all the drama that may come with it."

"Don't. Don't you start second-guessing yourself, baby. You've been over everything and it all adds up to what you want. Trust your gut and roll with it. If there's going to be some drama behind your decisions then we'll deal with whatever comes our way."

"I feel you. You know what, I got an idea. Go get Christina and tell her to watch the boys. We're going out to eat.'"

"Where?"

He held up his hand and said, "It's a surprise. Go get ready, li'l mama. I'm about to make this a night to re-member."

"Mmmm, and what did I do to deserve this special night?"

He gave her a soft kiss and said, "You deserve way more than a special night, li'l mama; you deserve the world. Tonight is something I've been wanting to do for you. I just haven't had the time to put it down." He slapped her on the ass and said, "Now hurry up with your fine ass." He was laughing as she left the room switching her firm rear end hard for him.

Bob and Gwen were sitting on the deck looking out toward the ocean with Gwen sitting on his lap. She gave him a kiss on the knot on his forehead and said, "Mmm, you know how bad this damn knot turns me on, baby?"

Laughing, he said, "Yeah, I know, but why don't you tell me anyway. Tell me what the knot does to that pussy, baby."

"When I kiss it like this . . ." She kissed his knot and ran her tongue slowly all over it and continued. "It makes my pussy tingle, tingle like it does when you're licking my pussy. I don't know what it is, but when I touch it I want you so damn bad. Like right now all I want to do is pull you down to the floor and put this pussy on the knot so I can cum real hard."

"Do it."

She smiled at her husband, the father of her children, the man she absolutely adored, hopped off of his lap and pulled him to the floor of the deck. When he was lying flat on his back she pulled down her shorts, climbed on top of Bob and put her pussy right over his face. She sighed as he began to lick her slit slowly. As it started to get intense she moved up, placed her pussy right on top of the knot and began to gyrate her hips hard on it causing an extreme amount of pressure on her clitoris. Before she realized what was happening she began to come so hard that she barely could breath. "Oh! Oh! Damn! Bob! Damn! I'm cumming!" she screamed.

With her cum sliding down his face Bob smiled as his wife rolled off of him. She was lying beside him panting trying to catch her breath while he unbuckled his belt, pulled down his pants, rolled on top of her and eased himself inside of her soaking wet pussy. She was so warm, so wet that he felt as if he was going to explode after only being inside of her for a few seconds. Gwen wrapped her legs around his waist and used the heels of her feet to try to push him even deeper inside of her sex.

"You like this dick, baby? You like how this dick feels inside of that good pussy?" Bob asked as he humped her harder and harder with each stroke.

"Yessssss! I love it! I love this dick, baby! Give it to me! Give it all to me! Don't stop, Bob! Don't you fucking stop!"

They came together, screaming each other's name as their orgasms rocked through their bodies. Both felt relaxed while they held on tightly to one another. "Damn, baby, I don't think I'll ever get tired of fucking this good pussy."

Gwen slapped him lightly on his chest and said, "You better fucking not, mister. I'll hurt your ass if you ever even thought about leaving me, Bob. I love you too damn much for any of that shit."

"Baby, there is nothing in this world that I wouldn't do to make sure we're going to be together forever. You're my everything, Gwen. Now and always. I love you, baby."

"Good. Now. Round two?" she asked with a mischievous smile on her lovely face.

"If you can wake the monster back up, it's all good with me."

She smacked her lips loudly and said, "No problem, dear." She then slid down toward his crotch and wrapped her warm mouth around the head of his dick. He moaned. She licked down the sides of his shaft. He groaned. She smiled as she put his nut sac inside of her mouth and began to hum softly. His dick grew to its full length. She looked up at him and said, "It's definitely time for round two!"

Smiling, he raised his right hand in the air and rang the bell for round two to begin. "Ding. Ding."


Taz and Sacha drove around for almost an hour listening to some slow jams after they left their home. Sacha knew he had something planned, but he refused to tell her what it was. She sat back in the comfortable leather seats of the Bentley and enjoyed the ride and the music.

Taz received a text and smiled. He then made a U-turn and headed in the opposite direction from which he was driving. Ten minutes later they pulled into the parking lot of Aunt Kizzy's Kitchen Soul Food restaurant out in Marina Del Ray. Taz got out of the car without saying a word and went around the car to open the door for his wife.

Sacha stepped out of the car with a puzzled expression on her face. They hadn't eaten here in years. *What is this man up to?* she wondered as he took her hand in his and led her toward the front of the restaurant. When they entered Sacha saw that the restaurant was empty. No one was there except a waitress who was standing in front of a candlelit table in the rear of the restaurant. Taz was smiling as he led his wife toward the table. After they were seated the waitress smiled and opened a bottle of expensive wine that Taz had had delivered to the soul food restaurant while they were driving around listening to slow jams. After the wine was poured the waitress turned and left the couple alone.

"Surprised, li'l mama?" Taz asked as he sipped some of his wine.

"Am I! How in the heck did you arrange all of this in such a short time, Taz?"

He shrugged nonchalantly and said, "I was going to save this for your birthday or maybe our anniversary but decided what the hell, no need to wait for a special day like that when I can make it happen now. I called and told the manager that I would pay to have the restaurant to ourselves for a couple of hours and would make sure it would be worth their while. The manager thought I was tripping until Klayron came and brought the wine I had him go pick up for me along with a substantial amount of ends. When I called back they told me they would text me once everything was ready for us."

"That's why you were driving around wasting time?"

"Yep. You like?"

"Of course! I remember the first time you brought me here, I was so mad at your ass."

Laughing, Taz said, "Yeah, I know. I had to call Won and have him meet us here so you could get the answers you needed after that crazy shit that popped off at the Lakewood Mall."

"This is where I first met Won. Wow, that seems like forever ago. You miss him don't you?"

"More than words can say, li'l mama. I wish he was here to deal with all of this shit for real. This was his dream, li'l mama, not mine. All I wanted to do was finish up our business and live happily with you and the crew so we could enjoy our lives without the stress and the bullshit. By following his dreams it's like I've brought more shit in our lives."

Shaking her head no, Sacha placed her right hand on top of her husband's and said, "That's wrong, baby. You are doing everything that man wanted you to do because he knew you could do it. You are doing everything right, Taz. I'm with you, baby. The crew is with you. Won is with you too. Don't lose faith in yourself because none of us will ever lose faith in you."

Taz smiled at her and said, "I got you, li'l mama." He then gave a nod toward the waitress and Kem's song "I Can't Stop Loving You" started playing on the speakers inside of the restaurant. The waitress brought their food. After the waitress set the plates of steaming smothered pork chops, rice, greens, and buttered cornbread onto the table Taz smiled and stared at his wife lovingly. "I'll never stop loving you, li'l mama. You complete me."

With tears in her eyes Sacha smiled back at her man and said, "I love you more, Taz. You complete me too. You are the most important man in my life. I mean that. I also mean this: you are in some big trouble, Mr. Taz."

"Trouble? What I do? I thought everything was perfect here."

"Oh it is; it's more than perfect. That's why your tail is in so much trouble. Just as soon as I get your ass back home I'm going to punish you so bad in that bedroom you're going to want to do this type of special stuff all the time!"

Laughing, he said, "Well, bring on my punishment, li'l mama!" They both started laughing as they enjoyed their meal.

# Chapter Eleven

The St. Regis Bal Harbour Resort was everything they said it was and some. Taz and the entire crew were enjoying everything the resort had to offer from the private organic spa treatments to swimming to the scrumptious meals at the J&G Grill prepared by the internationally renowned chef Jean-Georges Vongerichten.

After four days of being totally pampered and extra relaxed, Taz decided that it was time for the business to be handled. He was sitting on the bed waiting for Sacha to come out of the bathroom. While she was off to take the twins to her mother and father's home in Tampa Bay, he would be meeting with Mr. Suarez at his home with the crew, getting the last meeting out of the way before the Network's quarterly meeting set up for Friday afternoon in a private cabana he had reserved.

The council had arrived the day after the crew, and Taz took time to speak to each member briefly. As soon as the conversation tried to turn toward the upcoming meeting, he put a stop to that because there was no way he was discussing any of his moves until he had the meeting with the Cuban drug lord of Miami. Today was that day, and Taz's palms were sweaty thinking about going into the lion's den once again. That's what it felt like it would be once he entered Mr. Suarez's home.

Sacha came out of the bathroom dressed casually in some shorts and a T-shirt with some colorful flip-flops on her feet. She had her long hair pulled into a ponytail. Her bronze-colored skin seemed to glow making her already exotic look seem even more exotic to Taz. He loved looking at his wife; she was absolutely gorgeous.

"Damn, li'l mama, you're looking real damn fine. Why don't I put off that meeting with the Cuban and we lie here on this bed and do the damn thang all day and night?"

"Humph. You wish. No way am I denying my parents their grandkids any longer. They have been pestering me and getting on my last nerves to bring the boys to them. They want the last three days of this trip with the twins and I am not getting in their way. So hold it together until I return this evening big boy. I promise I'll make sure you can get these goodies."

Laughing, Taz said, "I can't wait! All right, baby, make sure you give me a call when you're on your way back. Tell your moms and pops that I send my love and that I'll be flying them out to L.A. real soon. Maybe for the summer if they want."

"Okay, you know they're going to love that. All right let me go make sure those boys aren't driving Gwen crazy. I'm glad she's going to ride down to Tampa Bay with me. That's going to make everything easier."

"That's cool. By the time y'all get back everything will be everything with the meeting with Mr. Suarez."

She saw the stressful expression on Taz's face and said, "Handle it, Taz. Handle it so you can move forward with your plans. Everything is going to be fine." She stepped to him and gave him a kiss. She slipped her tongue in his mouth and the kiss went from a tender moment to a passionate one instantly. She pulled back from him and said, "Whew! Damn, we may need to have a little quickie; you done got me all hot with that one, Mr. Taz."

Laughing, Taz said, "Take off them damn shorts then and come hop on this here dick, li'l mama!"

Doing as she was told Sacha started laughing. "You ain't said nothing but a word!" She pulled off her shorts quickly and climbed on top of her husband's lap and got the ride of her life.


Saint Tramon, Piper Dixon, Malcolm Brown, and Chill Will were all having lunch at the J&G Grill. The main topic of conversation was the upcoming council meeting and what Taz had on his mind. Saint Tramon, the more reasonable out of the four, was truly baffled. It bothered her that with all of her connections she hadn't been able to find out exactly what Taz's meetings with Jorge Santa Cruz and Danny Orumutto had been about. Her sources did confirm however that Taz was having yet another meeting, this time with Mr. Suarez, the top man in the drug business here in Miami. This further piqued her interest because Taz was definitely up to something and she had a feeling that they weren't going to particularly care for what their young leader was going to present at the council meeting.

Saint Tramon, at fifty-nine years of age, was still strikingly beautiful. One could tell by her smooth skin that she had been drop-dead gorgeous back in her prime. She was a true red bone, with long silky hair showing her Creole heritage. There had been numerous rumors of plastic surgery, but everyone close to her knew better. Saint Tramon had aged well and was still considered to be more than highly active sexually. The only thing she was guilty of doing was dying her hair. She detested gray hair and refused to let any gray be seen in her long tresses. Her breasts were still firm with very little sag and thanks to a strict seafood diet and regular workouts she kept her body in tiptop condition. She gave women ten to fifteen years younger than her a run for their money. She proudly boasted to anyone who cared to listen that she kept a different boy toy for her sexual pleasures. She was truly a remarkable woman, remarkable in many ways. When it came to running her business in New Orleans both legally and illegally she was not to be taken lightly. The rumors of voodoo also helped her maintain total control of the ruthless streets of New Orleans being how the New Orleans natives believed in that sort of thing greatly. Saint Tramon loathed Taz for many reasons and she would be damned if she didn't run him out of the Network. That was her mission and every person having lunch with her was in agreement: Taz had to go, one way or the other.

Piper Dixon was totally opposite of her female counterpart. Where Saint Tramon was light-skinned and full figured, Piper Dixon was petite and had a dark complexion. She kept her hair cut short and was most known for her expensive style of dress. She refused to be caught in anything that wasn't hand crafted by some top-of-the-line clothing designer. It was rumored that she spent millions on her wardrobe yearly. She had a serious passion for fashion. She could afford it because of the many profitable business ventures she ran in the Seattle area as well as Northern California. Her illegal enterprise made it so there was nothing that she couldn't afford. The one thing she wanted most though was for Taz to pay for what Won did to Pitt. She would go to her grave trying to punish Taz for what Won had done to her longtime friend and confidant, Pitt.

Malcolm Brown was a handsome man of caramel complexion. At six foot one his slim build gave off the track star type look. In very good shape and considered by most women to be "Playboy handsome" he was a man who loved and appreciated a beautiful woman. Business was first with Malcolm and women were secondary. He would never make the same mistakes his deceased uncle made. Yes, everyone knew that if he possessed a weakness it would be women. He was not a weak man and the one thing he wanted more than anything was the top spot of the Network. That meant he wanted Taz out, sooner rather than later.

Chill Will was a small, slim man. He stood a little over five foot eight. He was well known for his blazing temper. He could kill a man or have a man killed for the smallest things. Some considered him to be very petty. Most knew that he was extremely dangerous and not to be taken lightly. He had been totally loyal to Pitt and, for that reason only, he detested Taz.

"Okay, since no one seems to know what our young leader is up to it's safe to assume we're in for some surprises at the council meeting Friday. I suggest we make our pact now that whatever Taz is up to or presents to us we shoot it right down. I mean total nays from each of us," suggested Saint Tramon.

"What if it's something that can be in our favor? We cannot go into the meeting like that," said Chill Will. "I'm no fan of that young man, but I'm no fool either. He has done nothing but make one good move after another for the good of the Network. I say we wait and see what he is up to before we agree to shoot it down."

"Makes sense to me," said Malcolm Brown.

"Me too," added Piper Dixon.

"Much as I can't stand that young man I guess you're right. I still feel we should be prepared to go against him because my gut tells me we're not going to like what he has to say. I mean why would he have to have these meetings with the main suppliers for the Network's drug connections? We all know how Taz feels about drugs. What was those damn meetings about?" Saint Tramon said obviously frustrated.

"There's no need beating ourselves up over something we don't know the answer to. We'll just have to wait and see at the meeting. What I do suggest we do though is have some words with Chinaman and see if we can get him on our side. He can be a deciding vote if need be," said Piper.

"True. But honestly none of that really matters because Taz has the final say in everything," said Chill Will.

"That is something that really irks the hell out of me. That rule applied to Cash Flo and Cash Flo only. It shouldn't be applied to Taz! We have to find a way around that somehow," said Saint Tramon.

"It applies to the leader of the Network and right now Taz holds that title. The only way we can remove him from that position is if we can show and prove that he has been negligent or flat-out fucked up in his decision making concerning the Network's best interests. Taz has his supporters on the council and we all know that they will stand by his side unless we can prove he is no longer worthy of the top spot," Malcolm Brown said seriously.

"This is true. Or we can simply have him killed."

The other three council members sat there silently and stared at Saint Tramon. She finally spoke the words that each of them had thought about seriously over the last six years but never had the nerve to say aloud. Murdering the leader of the Network could cause the demise of what they were a part of or make everything go the way they all wanted it to. It could cause a war within the Network so serious that everything could go ass backward for all of them. Was it really worth the risk? This question was swirling around inside of each of the four council members' minds as they sat there in silence.

# Chapter Twelve

Taz, Tari, Red, Wild Bill, and Bob arrived at the Suarez mansion fifteen minutes late. Taz laughed when Tari told him that they were what was called fashionably late. Once the gate was electronically opened Red eased their rented SUV inside of the massive grounds of Mr. Suarez's home. When they pulled in front of the mansion Taz took a deep breath and told the crew, "Okay, this is for real the one meeting I am worried about. I intend to play this cool, but at the same time remain firm on my stance. In no way though do I want to insult Mr. Suarez so I need y'all to keep your poker faces on even if he says some slick shit. There's nothing we can do if he gets salty at us, so there's no need for any signs of emotions to be shown. If we have to go to war with the Cubans then we'll express ourselves when we get to it. Y'all feel me?"

"Better fucking believe it, dog," said Red.

"One hundred percent, my nigga," said Wild Bill.

"All the way, baby," said Bob.

"I'm good with that, Taz. You just make sure that you stick to what you're telling us," Tari said and smiled.

Taz returned her smile. "I got you, Tee. Come on, there's Castro, Mr. Suarez's number one." They all got out of the car and followed Taz up seven steps of the front door of the Suarez mansion. Taz reached his hand out and gave

Castro a firm handshake. "What's good, Castro, you're looking well."

Castro at six foot three was a mean-looking Cuban who gave the impression that when it came to him handling his business it would be handled very violently. To those who were close to him or considered him a friend he was a calm and cool man. He smiled at Taz and said, "I try to keep myself looking good. You know that, Taz. I see you're looking dapper as ever."

"You know how I do." Taz turned and waved toward the crew and said, "You remember my crew?"

"*Sí.*" He then gave each crew member a nod in greeting. He faced Taz again and said, "I must search all of you now, Taz."

Taz gave a nod and raised his hands so Castro could search him. After he finished searching Taz he quickly pat searched the rest of the crew and smiled. "You good, Castro?"

"Always good when dealing with you, Taz. Come. Mr. Suarez is waiting." He then led the way inside of the mansion followed closely by Taz and the crew.

Mr. Suarez was sitting behind a huge mahogany desk inside of his office looking every bit the boss that he was. When he saw Taz he stood and came from behind the desk smiling. He stepped to Taz and gave him a hug and said, "Welcome, Señor Taz. Welcome to my home." He turned, faced the crew, smiled at them, and said, "All of you look so serious. Smile, this is a beautiful day!" That seem to put the crew at ease as each smiled and greeted the Cuban drug lord of Miami. After telling everyone to be seated Mr. Suarez went back behind his desk and said, "Before we get to this serious business meeting that you suggested we have, Taz, I want to take a moment to share a few things with you if I may?"

"I have no problem with that, Mr. Suarez."

"Good. Because when I'm finished I'm positive all of the seriousness concerning your reasons for this meeting will vanish. Let me start by saying I already know about your plans to end our business with one another as far as the purchase of the yay-yo from me."

Taz's face remained neutral as he asked, "And may I inquire as to how you came up with this information, Mr. Suarez?"

Mr. Suarez laughed and said, "From a very reliable source. So reliable in fact that I felt he was needed here today for this meeting."

As if this had been rehearsed, Castro entered the room followed closely by none other than Akim Novikov and Alexander Sokolov. Taz was no longer able to maintain his poker face. The shocked expression on his face brought a smile to Akim's. "Ah. I see that my American comrade is shocked to see me."

"Very shocked. What's the business, Akim?"

Akim and Alexander took seats next to Taz and waited for Mr. Suarez to speak.

"Taz, you have to understand that the business moves you're about to make will affect a lot of different organizations. You are taking a lot of money out of people's pockets by pulling the Network from the drug trade. No one can make you spend your money, but that won't stop some from being disgruntled with you."

"Are you one of the disgruntled people, Mr. Suarez?"

Laughing loudly, Mr. Suarez said, "By all means no! Next to Akim here I'm one of your biggest supporters. Your biggest problem lies within your very own organization.

There will soon be a strong dissent within the Network that will either destroy your organization or remove you from your position at the top spot. The only way you will be able to maintain your position of power will be by being smart, shrewd, and extremely violent. That added with your ace in the hole you should come out of this situation unscathed and remain in total control."

"My ace in the hole. What's my ace in the hole, Mr. Suarez?"

Mr. Suarez stared directly in Taz's eyes and smiled as he answered his question. "Me. I'm the man who will make all of your problems seem simple to deal with."

"How?"

"May I take it from here, Mr. Suarez?" asked Akim.

"Please," said Mr. Suarez.

"At the time of our last meeting I hadn't had the privilege of meeting Mr. Suarez here; that is why you weren't informed. Since then I've met and have had several serious discussions with Mr. Suarez. He knows of our plans and agrees fully with the moves we are planning to make. The loss of the Network's drug purchases from him are minor compared to what he will gain by dealing with us in the arms dealing ventures we've discussed. More important, Mr. Suarez has a friend within the Network who is currently not one of your biggest fans, Taz." Akim saw anger flash in Taz's eyes and smiled. "Be calm, my friend, this is to our advantage in every way."

Through clenched teeth Taz asked, "Who is this person?"

Shaking his head no, Mr. Suarez said, "You are not ready for that information just yet, Taz. Please be patient and understand my position with this. If I exposed my associate then you would do something that would destroy our position. Patience is key with this; let it play out the way we all want it to. This way you will be able to remain two steps ahead of your opposition."

Taz sighed and nodded at the logic that was spoken by Mr. Suarez.

"The council right now is in total confusion trying to figure out why you have had meetings in the last month with Akim here, Jorge Santa Cruz in Colombia, Danny Orumutto in California, and now myself. They don't have a clue to what your intentions are, yet they know it's something major and you have them somewhat scared. Though you are the youngest member of the Network, they respect you greatly for what you have accomplished thus far. Your supporters on the council are behind you one hundred percent. But your adversaries on the council want your head. Each member who is against you has a different reason for being against you; this you already know. What you don't know is that Danny Orumutto is pushing buttons now trying to manipulate certain council members in hopes to stop you from making the changes you plan to make by ending all drug activity within the Network. That's where things get tricky."

"How can Danny Orumutto be manipulating shit and no one knows what my moves are?"

"Because he hasn't tipped his hand to that yet. He's waiting for you to inform the council of your decision to remove the drugs from the equation and then he's going to use his influence with some of your council members to start a war within from the anger he is positive will come from some of them. He hopes to destroy you one way or the other, Taz."

Taz stared at his crew one by one as he thought about what he had just been told. "I understand. So, this member you have on my council informed you of all of this?"

Mr. Suarez waved his right hand from side to side and said, "Some, but most of this is what I've deduced from Danny Orumutto and his actions. He has contacted me and asked me to see what I could do to intervene and hopefully help him with this situation. Danny Orumutto is a shrewd young man and should not be taken lightly, Taz. You are a leader in every sense of the word. Won was one hundred percent accurate by making you the man to take over the Network in case of his demise. I respect your loyalty and rectitude; that is why I have used my inside source to help keep the Network's business with me intact. Akim has given me the opportunity to become a partner with you in this arms dealing venture. I'm a man who will never be one dimensional so this arms dealing venture excites me greatly."

"Your part in all of this is to help me remain in control of my organization so we can move forward and handle our business with the arms dealing?"

"*Sí.*"

"Tell me, Mr. Suarez, what would you say if I told you I didn't want nor need your help in this matter?"

Laughing, Mr. Suarez said, "I'd be totally shocked because I honestly feel you won't be able to pull this off without my assistance. Like I said, Señor Taz, I am your ace in the hole."

Taz gave him a nod and said, "True. But you have revealed things to me this afternoon that have troubled me to the point where I'm on the verge of murdering every member of the council who I feel is against me. If I did that then why would Akim and I need you as a partner?"

Speechless, Mr. Suarez turned toward Akim and shrugged with raised eyebrows.

"Taz, Mr. Suarez is a valuable asset to us, not only because of who he has on your council informing him on matters. He's a key component for the storage as well as some of the transport of a large amount of the weapons that will be shipped to your country. That's another reason why we need him as a partner. Mr. Suarez is demonstrably the most important part of all of our business. We cannot have you go off murdering half of your council because that will draw too much attention toward you and that's something we can ill afford. Remain calm and detached so you can make the right moves for us to win, comrade. I understand your anger, but do not let your emotions override your intelligence here."

Taz gave that smile to each man and answered in a measured tone. "I'm a good pragmatic judge of what I can and can't do, Akim. I respect you highly as I do Mr. Suarez here. I want to take the Network higher than it has ever been. I intend to making Won's dreams become a reality. You have my word that I will not do anything to jeopardize what we have put together."

"But?" asked Mr. Suarez.

"Yes, but, I want to know who the member on my council is who has betrayed an oath that was taken way before I became the head of the Network. That person must and will be punished for violating that oath. If you refuse to divulge that information to me on this day then our business ends today."

Shaking his head no, Taz said, "Never. I would never disrespect you, Mr. Suarez. I am merely stating how I feel and what I must know. If I had someone within your organization informing me of some of your private business dealings would you not want me to give you that person for betraying you?" Before the Cuban could answer Taz continued, "As I stated I will not do anything to jeopardize our business. But I must know who this person is because if he or she has betrayed me once they may have done it with others. When the time is right I will murder this person for the travesties committed against my organization."

"When the time is right? When will that be, Señor Taz?" asked the Cuban drug lord.

Taz again gave that faintly mocking smile and said, "Once our business has begun to flourish and everything is good all the way around for all of us."

"You give me your word this day that you will not expose this person until we have removed all threats from Danny Orumutto as well as your other adversaries within your council?"

"I do."

Mr. Suarez stared at Akim for a moment and then said, "Señor Malcolm Brown is the man who has been keeping me abreast of the Network's business dealings. I have one more request, Señor Taz."

"Yes?"

"When you deem it's time for Señor Brown to meet his demise would you make his death swift? He doesn't deserve to die painfully."

"If a bullet to the brain is okay with you then it's just fine by me," Taz said in a deadly tone.


After Taz and the crew left the Suarez mansion Akim, Alex, and Mr. Suarez continued with their meeting. "Taz took that exactly as you thought he would, Akim," said Mr. Suarez.

"Actually he took it better than I thought he would, and that bothers me."

"Why, comrade? You don't think Taz would go back on his word and put all of our business in jeopardy because of his anger?" asked Alex.

"Taz's anger is something that he will control. The calm demeanor he expressed tells me that we should monitor our colleague's movements very closely because he feels threatened and when a man as deadly as Taz feels threatened there will be more death than what may be called for."

"*Sí,* I agree. I didn't much care for revealing who my contact was within the Network. Malcolm Brown is a greedy man, a power-thirsty man who has always wanted to gain the top spot of the Network. That is the only reason why he chose to betray his associates. Now that I have given Taz that information I feel bad for the outcome of Señor Brown's life."

Akim shrugged his shoulders and said, "This was something that needed to be done in order for our business to progress. Danny Orumutto will have to be dealt with, too, it seems."

"*Sí.* The sooner the better. If he gets wind of any offensive moves being planned against him he will strike fast and hard."

"Do you think he has someone inside of the Network too?" asked Alex.

"I doubt it, but I wouldn't totally disregard that. The hatred for Taz is great in that organization so anything is possible."

"Let's wait and see what the reaction is from their council meeting tomorrow and then we'll decide which way to take this matter."

"*Sí.* My question to you Señor Akim is who has the privilege of taking that young, dishonorable son of a bitch Danny Orumutto's life? Me or you?"

With a deadly smile Akim shrugged and said, "Why not the both of us? We both have longed for the opportunity to dispose of that trash. A man who can kill his own father and uncles to achieve leadership of the family business is a man not worthy to have what Danny Orumutto has. If he invades our moves in any way then he dies slowly and painfully."

"If he doesn't invade our plans with Taz he still dies slowly and painfully. I'm tired of waiting for him to give me a reason to kill him. Osata was a good man and a good friend of mine."

"Yes, the elder Orumuttos were solid men who didn't deserve their untimely deaths. So, it seems that Danny Orumutto's fate has been set!"

"*Sí*. Set in blood."

# Chapter Thirteen

Sacha and Gwen were driving down the highway headed back toward South Beach after dropping the twins off at Sacha's parents' home in Tampa Bay. Both were thinking about the meeting that Taz and the crew were having with the Cubans. Each had their own concerns because they knew that if things didn't go right, their men could soon be caught up in something violent, and that scared the hell out of each of them. Speaking her thought, Gwen said, "Damn, mommy, I sure hope everything went well with the Cubans this afternoon."

"I was just thinking the same thing, mommy. Taz has been really stressing behind all of this. If things went well at the meeting then things should be good tomorrow at the council meeting," Sacha said.

Shaking her head no, Gwen said, "I don't know. Things may get even more touchy when Taz informs the council of his plans. It looks like this year will be a wild one."

"You mean a violent one. 'Cause if things go left then Taz and the crew are going to get back on that murder shit like they were with those Hoovers six years ago."

"Lord knows I am in no way trying to see Bob back in that state of mind, mommy."

"I hear you, but it's almost impossible for it not to happen. This is the life our men lead, and all we can do is support them and stand by their side. At least we won't have to worry about them actually getting their hands dirty. Their murder game now is all about sending out hit squads and shit."

Laughing, Gwen said, "How in the hell did I let you get me caught up with a bunch of serious-ass movie type gangsters?"

"You know you need to quit that shit. Your horny ass chose Bob not me!"

"True. But your hot ass fell head over heels for Taz first, which in turn had me end up meeting Bob. So this is all on you, mommy!"

"You are a mess." Changing the subject Sacha said, "I'm so glad my parents are keeping the twins. I'm thinking about asking them to keep them for a couple of weeks depending on what takes place at the council meeting tomorrow."

"That's smart. I've already spoken to Bob about flying the kids back home so they can stay with my parents for a little while. They love it when they get to be with their grandparents. I feel we need to make sure everything is good all the way around before we bring them back home."

"We have to keep all our kids safe."

"Priority *numero uno*. Tell me something, mommy, why haven't you ever told me about your brothers?"

Sacha frowned and said, "That's a subject I have tried to keep buried real deep, mommy."

"I understand," Gwen said hoping Sacha would dead this conversation. She wasn't that lucky though.

"How did they die, mommy?"

"They were murdered."

"I know that. I saw the sad look on your mom's face when she saw me staring at the picture of your brothers on the mantle. She smiled sadly and told me how she misses her sons every single day. She also told me how she feels so cheated by the murdering bastards who took them away from her. I saw how sad she was and instantly began thinking about the accident. That type of pain never leaves you, mommy, and I do mean never. That's why I'm curious as to how you've been able to suppress those memories of your twin brothers."

"I wouldn't say that I've suppressed the memories of my brothers. I just don't like to talk about them. I miss them dearly and think of them almost every single day. My sons look so much like my brothers that it's kind of scary."

"I understand. I'm not trying to pry here, mommy, just doing my psychological thing here."

Laughing, Sacha said, "Trust and believe I know. But let's change the subject, okay? We're out here in sunny Miami and we still have some time to have some more fun before we get back to the business at home."

"I concur. Shit, I've been trying to get Bob to take me on the beach so we can get nasty with it. His ass is scared we'll get caught."

"You might! You know we're not trying to have to bail you and your damn husband out of jail for indecent exposure way out here in South Beach."

Laughing herself now, Gwen said, "That's what South Beach is for, some damn indecent exposure! Have you paid attention to all of the bad-ass exotic women walking around this place? We're damn lucky to be able to keep our men's attention honestly."

"Oh trust and believe we have their attention all right. I wish Taz's ass would try to stray; then he'd see that he's not the only gangsta in the family."

"I know that's right! Get us back to that resort so we can do the fun thang, mommy!"

Sacha checked the time on her watch and said, "We should make it back right before sunset so it's on!" They were both laughing as they drove toward South Beach.


Taz was furious. He wanted Malcolm Brown's head served to him on a platter. The betrayal he felt by knowing that he had been passing information about the Network's business to Mr. Suarez made him feel somewhat inferior and that was a feeling he wasn't accustomed to. Malcolm's actions showed weakness within the Network, at least that's how Taz was looking at it as Red drove them back to the resort. Each crew member was caught up in their own thoughts and each member knew that Taz was on the verge of going the fuck off. The only solace they had was the fact that Taz gave his word to Mr. Suarez and Akim that he wouldn't handle shit with Malcolm until the business was handled. They were still upset as Taz was. Their crew was based on loyalty and love. Loyalty first. They would never do anything to bring any shame or harm toward Taz. Each would gladly give their life first.

When Red pulled into the parking lot of the resort Taz sighed and said, "Meet me in the cabana we're using for the meeting tomorrow. We need to talk about all of this shit. Give me twenty minutes to get my mind right." With that said he jumped out of the SUV and went to his and Sacha's cabana. He didn't realize that Tari was right behind him until he was sliding his key card into the door of his cabana. "Come on, Tee, save it until I can at least have a drink please," he said as he entered the cabana and headed straight toward the fully stocked bar. He grabbed a bottle of Courvoisier XO and poured himself a drink. After downing the first glass he quickly poured another and sat down on the barstool. "You do know that this is some real fucked-up shit right? How do you think this makes me look, Tee? Like some fuck-up who can't run shit. Won is up there looking down on me shaking his fucking head right about now."

Tari stepped to the bar and sat on the barstool next to Taz and said, "Stop that shit. You know damn well you're hated by Malcolm as well as Saint Tramon. Shit, the council is split when it comes to you so don't even go there. Honestly, this type of shit was to be expected. They dislike you to the point that they are willing to do whatever it takes to get you off the top spot. Why are you tripping so damn hard about something you should have anticipated happening?"

"That's fucking it right there, Tee! I have been so caught up trying to make sure I've been making all of the right moves for the Network's future that I missed that shit. You know I know what's what with the hating and all of that. I never thought anyone on the council would be disloyal to the Network like that. This thing is based on some real live honorable gangsta shit. The oath taken was supposed to never been violated. To know that it has been in the name of hating me pisses me the fuck off. I should have seen this shit coming and been on top of my shit better. I slipped, Tee. But that shit ain't happening no more I tell you that."

"What you got working in that crazy head of yours, Taz?"

"I can't expose my hand yet because I've given my word and I will stand on that. But the degree of the council meeting has just been turned all the way up. I was going to be subtle about the changes I was bringing to the table. Fuck all of that shit now though; that shit is a wrap. I'm giving it to they ass straight the fuck up. The vote shit won't even be spoken on. I'm telling them what it is and how it will be. I'm breaking it down to them and letting everyone know either they will be with it or out of it. One year from tomorrow all drug business will be concluded within the Network. Period."

Tari gave a nod in understanding and then asked, "Are you sure this is the approach you want to take? This could possibly turn a council member who's on your side the other way."

"I doubt it. If it does then so fucking what? After this meeting every single one of those muthafuckas will be under my microscope. I'm putting the feelers on everyone, even the ones I feel are on my side. I trust no one but the crew, period. And I swear to God, Tee, if I find any more disloyalty within that fucking council it's—"

Tari cut him off and finished his sentence for him. "Off with their heads."

Taz down the rest of his drink and said, "You mutha-fucking right."

# Chapter Fourteen

The Network's first council meeting for the year began promptly at eleven a.m. with a healthy brunch served by several maids and butlers provided by the resort. After brunch was finished, a brief break was taken while everyone got themselves together by either taking restroom breaks to fix their makeup or the men stepped out to the living room area of the spacious cabana to have a smoke. Everyone met in the back of the cabana where Taz had arranged for a long conference table to be brought. Each member of the council was seated at the conference table with Taz at the head of it. Tari and the rest of the crew were there dressed in all black. Each crew member wore serious expressions on their faces as they stood at prearranged spots around the room, basically surrounding the council members. This show of intimidation was a move Taz came up with the night before. He was about to flex his muscle and he wanted everyone on the council to know that he was not fucking around with any of them.

Taz was immaculately dressed in a well-tailored black suit, crisp white shirt, and a perfectly knotted tie. He was looking the part of the leader of the Network to a tee. His handsome features were clouded with a determined look on his face that seemed to come out of nowhere. During brunch he had been extremely cordial and pleasant with everyone; now it seemed as if he had become someone totally different than he had been a mere hour or so ago. It was time for business.

Taz stood and got the council members attention by staring at each one of them one by one. The room fell silent as they waited for Taz to begin. He stared to the right side of the table at his supporters on the council but kept the granite rock-like look on his face. Jay Bogard, G.R., Snuffy, Snack, and Chinaman returned Taz's glare with a curious look on their faces, wondering what was wrong with their leader. To Taz's left were his adversaries on the council. Saint Tramon, Piper Dixon, Chill Will, and Malcolm Brown. Taz didn't want to give anyone more attention than needed, but he couldn't help but give Malcolm Brown a few extra seconds of his glare. *You bitch-ass coward, I cannot wait until I take your last breath,* he said to himself as he stared at the man he felt was a traitorous peasant. He then cleared his throat and said, "It's time to get to the business. Before we go over the numbers for the end of the year and other matters there is something that I have to bring to your attention."

"Excuse me, Taz, but shouldn't your team step out of the room for this meeting? This is highly irregular isn't it?" asked Saint Tramon.

"With all due respect, Saint Tramon, I am the head of the Network, I make the decisions. I understand that things have been a certain way years before I became the leader of this esteemed organization. But things are about to change. My team is here and will be here for the entirety of this council meeting. Now, as I was saying, I have something serious that I need to bring to the attention of this council. What I am about to inform you about is not up for debate or vote. I've made my decision and nothing anyone on this council can say will change my mind."

"Wait a minute, Taz, that's not how we've been doing things. What's with this aggressiveness all of a sudden?" asked Malcolm Brown.

With her hands clasped behind her back Tari crossed her fingers, praying that Taz didn't rush Malcolm Brown and start beating the shit out of him. She sighed with relief when Taz smiled and continued talking.

"As I stated, things have changed, Malcolm." He held up one finger and said, "In one year, one year from this very date, the Network will have concluded all business dealings concerning all narcotics. That means that there will be no more distribution of X pills, cocaine, codeine, oxycodone, heroin, or marijuana."

"What!" several of the council members screamed in unison from both sides of the conference room.

"Come on, Taz. You can't be serious about this," said Chinaman. "How do you expect for us to continue to make serious money? Most of our major moves are from the distribution of narcotics."

"I understand your concerns, and if you will let me finish with what I have to say without interruption, all of your questions will be answered and I feel you will be satisfied. If not, then so the fuck what."

The firm and blatant tone in Taz's voice shocked the council as they sat and waited for Taz to continue. Suddenly there seemed to be a tremendous amount of fear in the room. Taz could see it in each of the council members' eyes, and that was exactly what he wanted. He wanted them to fear him. Fuck their respect; he no longer cared whether they respected him or not. Going that route had led to them all being betrayed by that weak-ass Malcolm Brown. It was a new day for the Network, and Taz was about to make sure they damn well knew it.

Taz went on to explain his plans for the Network. He went into a detailed description of each and every move that would be made as far as the arms dealing was concerned. He broke down the numbers so each member could see that they would all be making large sums of money and what would be lost from the ending of the drug moves would easily be made up for within the first year of the deals being made with the selling of weapons. He also explained to them about the meetings he had with each head of the other criminal organizations they were affiliated with. He told them how he had been assured that there would be no ill feelings toward the Network for the ventures they were about to pursue. When he was finished he sat down and said, "Now, I will listen to what you have to say. Again understand that my mind is made up and nothing will change that."

"So, you're saying that you are giving us one year free of any obligations financially to make a full profit on all of our moves with drugs?" asked Chinaman with a smile on his face.

Taz smiled because he knew that Chinaman would love that part of it all. "That is correct. One year, you will owe the Network nothing for the support or use of any of our resources to conduct your business. That is because during that year I will be finalizing everything and making sure that everything is in proper order with the Russians. I am not a man who wants to lose money. I want to make as much as possible. That's why these arms dealing moves will be a go ASAP. Drugs will ruin us one day. That is my stance on that, and that is why I feel the time is now ripe for us to make this transition."

Laughing, Chinaman said, "I love it. I fucking love it! I'm in!"

"Thank you for that, Chinaman."

Snuffy, G.R., Snack, and Jay Bogard each gave a nod in Taz's direction, letting him know that they too were on board with him. Taz waited for the naysayers to speak, and he didn't have to wait long at all. Piper Dixon was first up to bat.

"You always have a choice, Piper. If any of you choose not to adhere to what I am bringing to our organization then you will no longer be a part of the Network. You will no longer have access to any of the Network's resources. Basically you will be on your own to do as you please. You owe us nothing and we owe you nothing. You want to continue to run your drug operations it will be with no assistance from the Network and any of our associates. If I find out that anyone who remains on this council is in fact working with anyone who chooses not to adhere to what I've come up with then things will get ugly."

"Are you threatening me, Taz?" asked Piper Dixon with fire in her eyes.

Shaking his head no, Taz replied, "No. I'm giving you my word; either roll with us or get rolled over. Period."

Next at bat was Chill Will. "You want us to stop doing business like we've been doing for the last three decades just like that?" he asked and snapped his fingers for emphasis.

"Nothing can happen just like that, Chill Will. That's why I'm giving you all one year. One year from this day to bring everything to an end as far as drugs are concerned. That should more than compensate for the time I need to get everything running properly. In one year the arms dealing will be even more profitable than what we are getting from the drug distribution. There will be less risk to any of us getting caught up in some federal indictment for conspiracy with that drug shit."

"Like I said, three decades we've been handling our business so why do you feel we'll get caught up in some drug conspiracy now? Can't you see that we know what the fuck we're doing? Or are you just being an arrogant fuck because you're in the position of power to do so?"

Taz smiled. "I'm making this move because I feel it will be best for the Network and for our future. If you are in disagreement then you can get the fuck out, Chill Will. If you think that I will let you get away with insulting me again please understand that would be very unwise. Arrogance has absolutely nothing to do with my decisions. I am trying to win at this shit and win long term. Yes, you all have been able to move the drugs for a very long time and that is exactly why I feel it's time to switch things up. As the leader of this organization it is up to me to excel at compartmentalizing the rigors of our clandestine operations and I plan to do so at all costs, by protecting our interests and making as much money as I can for us. All I need from each of you is proper storage facilities in your controlled states. Once that has been established everything else will fall right in place. Along the way you will have the authority to make side deals and get the reduced rate on all weapons and make even more money. Not only will your responsibilities be lightened, your pockets will be fattened. What's so hard for you to understand about that?"

"What you're saying makes perfect sense, Taz," said Malcolm Brown. "It's the sudden change that I think has us all wondering. You giving us one year to make as much as we can is very generous. At the same time we're accustomed to doing things the way we have been and that makes us somewhat skeptical with what you've brought to the table."

Already agitated by Chill Will's insult Taz had very little patience for anything Malcolm Brown had to say. "It doesn't matter to me what you think or how skeptical you are about the decision I've made. This is how it's going to be, period."

"I like this and though I may not agree with your tactics this afternoon, Taz, I feel what you are doing will help us all in the long run and you have my support. I'm in," said Saint Tramon and the room fell in silence from the shock of her words. Even Taz was speechless, as he stared at her unbelievingly.

"To say I'm shocked would be putting it mildly, Saint Tramon. But I do appreciate your support on this. Let me make something clear to you all. I have no ulterior motive here. All I want is for all of us to win. I want us to continue to make money and maintain our strengths so that our peers will see that we are still a force to be reckoned with. We won't be losing money; we'll be gaining more as well as positioning ourselves as major players in the game. The Russians as well as a few others are behind us with these moves. Trust me on this, we will win."

"There is no need for you to be shocked, dear boy, I don't dislike you personally. I've grown quite fond of you honestly. I respect how you have maintained the position as our leader. I just don't care for how you got the top spot. That's personal though; this is business. And when it comes to our business it all boils down to profits and losses. I have no time for losses. You've given us the opportunity here to make some very large profits indeed. One year of distributing narcotics without any fees given back is more than generous on your part, Taz. To hear that our responsibilities with the Network's business as far as arms dealing is concerned will be minimal yet the profits will remain just as large as our narcotics sales is basically a win all the way around. We would be fools to go against you on this."

Taz smiled at the sly old woman and wondered what she had up her sleeves because in no way was he falling for her sudden support for him.

"There is one thing that worries me, Taz."

"Yes?"

"Let's say that things don't go as smoothly as you plan. Will you be willing to revisit the drug trade?"

Taz thought about that for a few minutes and said, "Just as I am giving you all one year to get things situated with the switch we're about to make, that's what I will give in return. One year. If in one year you don't see the profits that I have predicted here today then I will grant permission to whoever wants to, as you said, revisit the drug trade."

"That is more than fair of you, Taz. As stated, I'm in," said Saint Tramon.

"So am I," Chill Will said reluctantly.

With a nod of his head Malcolm Brown agreed as well.

Piper Dixon smiled at Taz and said, "I will give this the run you request, but I want it on record that I feel we may be setting ourselves up for something slick to happen. Those Russians are smart as hell as well as crafty. I don't trust them. From the money standpoint its only right that we make this move with you, Taz, it would be stupid not to. I'm in. One more thing though."

"Yes?" asked Taz.

"Don't you ever fucking threaten me again, Taz. Leader or no leader you have no fucking right to think you can intimidate me or threaten me in any way. You do that again and we will have a serious problem on our hands. A problem that will be addressed violently."

Taz raised his hands in mock surrender and said, "I did not mean to disrespect you or your gangster in any way, Piper. But I will not apologize for my statements because when it comes to this organization, I am dead serious, I will do whatever it takes to make us win. If I feel there's an issue or a problem that issue or problem will be addressed aggressively. No threats. I don't waste time giving those. I speak from my heart and I tell no lies. If I feel like any of you will cross me for whatever reason you may have business or personal, I will take your lives without thinking twice about it. That is no threat to any of you here today. That is my word. This meeting is adjourned until our next council meeting in four months. Enjoy the five thousand dollar a night cabanas for the remainder of the week." Taz stood and led the crew out of the cabana.

After Taz and his supporters, along with the crew, exited from the cabana, Chill Will furiously screamed, "What the fuck was that shit, Saint Tramon? You're actually siding with that fucking young prick?"

Saint Tramon smiled as she pulled some lipstick from her purse and started applying some to her pouty lips. When she was finished she smiled at her fellow council member and said, "You really need to become less emotional about these types of things, darling. Taz has made it so we all can make a lot of money for this year. By the year's end when it's time for us to make this switch within the Network's way of business, there will be a new leader at this table. The only question that needs to be answered is who will it be? I for one don't care to take that top spot, but I will make sure whoever does, they will do things the way they should be done."

"Can you tell us how in the hell you know there will be a new leader at the table? 'Cause I know Taz isn't stepping down without a fight," said Piper Dixon.

Saint Tramon stared at the only other female on the council with her and said, "Dead men can't fight, love."

"So, like our colleague here so eloquently put it, our arrogant fuck of a leader Taz has to die?"

"Exactly. Now, let's go finish enjoying our expensive rooms and finish these discussions over drinks." The council members who were all against Taz stood and left the cabana with the same thought in their heads: Taz had to die.

# Chapter Fifteen

Mama-Mama was smiling as she sat and watched her granddaughter load the last of her stuff inside of her BMW SUV. Tazneema came back inside of the house and stared at her grandmother for a few seconds and asked her, "Why are you sitting there with that funny smile on your face, Mama-Mama?"

"Funny smile, humph. This is a happy day for me, child. I thought after you graduated from college you would only stay here for a few months tops; was I ever wrong about that one. Its way past time for you to leave the nest, Neema, and I for one can't wait to have some peace and quiet inside my home."

With a frown on her pretty features Neema said, "You know you need to quit it, Mama-Mama. You know you're going to miss me and expect for me to be here every Sunday for dinner. I miss one Sunday and you'll throw a fit."

Laughing, Mama-Mama replied, "This is true. I will miss you dearly. And your tail better not miss one Sunday meal, I mean that. It's bad enough your daddy done left us for the West Coast. Sunday is our family time and you might as well let that fast little white girl Lyla know she had better be here too. Seriously, Neema, I want you to start living your life and enjoying yourself more. Ever since that incident with Cliff you haven't seemed to bounce back to your normal upbeat self. You act like an old woman instead of a young twenty-four-year-old woman with plenty of life to live. You moving out shows me that you realize that, too. That and the fact that I have been purposely getting on your nerves here lately."

"Ooooh you are so wrong for that, Mama-Mama!"

"Neema, you act like I don't know you, girl. I knew the minute I started fussing about every little thing you would get tired of me and be ready to move out of here with the quickness. You needed that from me or your tail would sit here with me and be miserable trying to act like everything was fine and stay engrossed in your work. I love you too much to let you waste your life like that. Now that you and Lyla are living together in Keno's place I expect for her to help you get back to enjoying your life. That doesn't mean to turn into no damn fool, girl. Live and enjoy these days the Lord has blessed you to see. I mean that, Tazneema Good."

With tears in her eyes Neema stepped to her grandmother and gave her a kiss and a tight hug. "I love you so much, old woman, you know that?"

"Yeah, I know. Just like you know I's loves me some you! Now g'on, girl, Mama-Mama has a dinner date with the reverend this evening and I'm trying to get me some rest before I pamper him with one of my special meals."

"So that's the real reason you wanted me out your house, so you could get nasty with the preacher man! I'm telling Taz on you, Mama-Mama!"

They both started laughing.

"The last time I checked I'm Taz Good's mother. That boy don't run me! Now get, girl! And make sure you have your tail here by three p.m. come Sunday."

"I will, Mama-Mama. Love you."

"Love you too, Neema. Remember what I said, girl: live your life and enjoy it."

"Okay. Bye, Mama-Mama," she said as she turned and left the house. Once she was inside of her truck and headed toward her new home she thought about what her grandmother told her and realized that she was right. Ever since her relationship with Cliff went straight to hell she left men alone and got all caught up in her schoolwork. After college she had been grateful that Taz started the company so she could use her job there as another outlet to keep herself busy. It wasn't that she didn't like men. She realized she doubted her decision making when it came to them, so she thought going the celibate route would make things easier. So many lonely nights with her vibrator and all because she was afraid of meeting the wrong man again. All because of that bastard Cliff.

*I hope he's burning in hell for what he did to me. I'm glad I killed his ass,* she thought as she drove on. Her grandmother's words kept ringing in her ears. *It's time to live. I got money, I'm young, I look damn fine, yeah, it's way past time for me to get back in the dating game. I'm done letting what that man did to me ruin my life with all of his lies. He got what he deserved and now I'm going to give myself what I deserve and that's some good dick!* She started laughing at that thought as she grabbed her cell from her purse and called Lyla. When her best friend answered the phone she told her to pick a cute outfit; they were going clubbing tonight!

Taz was pissed, but he didn't show it as he played with his sons. He loved spending as much time as he could with Li'l Keno and Li'l Bo-Pete. His sons were his world and every minute he was with them gave him a pleasure that words couldn't begin to describe how he felt. Even as he was playing with the twins he couldn't shake the infuriating thoughts going round and round inside of his head. *I know that bitch Saint Tramon don't think she is rocking me to sleep so she can try to get me to slip up. If she even thinks she can make a move against me or my people I'll chop that voodoo bitch's head off of her fucking shoulders,* he thought as he playfully roughed up the twins.

"Okay, you two, y'all done wore your daddy out. Go get your mother for me and tell her I said I need some help with something real quick."

"Is it time for some business, Daddy?" asked Li'l Keno.

"Yep. It's time for Daddy to take care of some business."

"Can I help you? I like taking care of business with you, Daddy."

"Not me. I wanna play some more," said Li'l Bo-Pete.

Taz smiled at his sons and said, "Go on and get your mother for me and after I'm finished handling this important business you and I will take care of some other business I need to take care of, Li'l Keno. Then when we're finished we can get our play back on; is that cool Li'l Bo-Pete?"

"Yep, it's cool, Daddy. Come on, Li'l Keno, let's go!" The boys then raced away to go get their mother for their father.

Taz sat back on the sofa and thought about Saint Tramon, Chill Will, Piper Dixon, and that scum fuck Malcolm Brown. He wondered if he should go on and give the order to have them all slaughtered and get it the fuck over with. *Why wait and let them try some weak shit? Take the offense with this shit and move on them first and let everything be everything.* He shook his head at those thoughts because he knew that wasn't the way to move with this. He had to remain calm and not let his emotions make him make a hasty decision. *Be calm and cool like Won would be and continue to outthink they ass.* Thinking about Won put a smile on his face as he sat back on the sofa.

Standing in the doorway of their media room with one hand on her right hip Sacha asked, "What you got that smile on your face for, Mr. Taz? Please don't tell me you sent the boys to get me because you're sitting in here horny. I was working on something important."

Taz turned and faced his lovely wife and said, "You know damn well I'm always horny for you, li'l mama. The reason I sent for you is because we need to talk. I need to run some shit by you to see how you feel about it."

She came all the way inside of the room and sat next to him and asked, "What's up, baby?"

"Been thinking about Saint Tramon and those other wannabe slick-ass council members. They're up to something and that bothers me, li'l mama. You and I both know they want me gone and I'm starting to feel like I may need to go on and smash they ass before they try to make a move on me first."

"For any of them to make an aggressive move like that against you they would have to have a majority vote within the council without you knowing. That's basically impossible, baby. You know your supporters on the council would tip you off to something like that before anyone world be able to make a move against you."

"True. What if they're on some other shit though?"

"Explain."

"Come on, li'l mama, you know what I'm saying here. Won didn't seek council approval when he made his move. He did what he did with one long detailed plan of action."

"That's true, but he also made sure that he had the support of several key members on the council so in case of his demise you would be able to be put in play as the leader of the Network, which has given you your supporters now. What do you want to do, Taz, murder half of the council because you're somewhat paranoid?"

"Paranoid? Is that what you think I am with this, li'l mama? Paranoid?"

She shrugged and said, "If it's not paranoia then what is it, baby?"

"It's called staying ready so I won't have to get ready. If I move first I won't have to worry about any weak shit later. If I let them move first and they move correct then I'm done. I don't think they would go after anyone but me but it ain't no telling with that slick bitch Saint Tramon."

Sacha sat back next to her husband on the sofa and thought about what he told her for a moment. She then said, "Killing them I feel would do more harm than good within the council. The rest of the members would be your supporters, but how long do you think they will give you their support after seeing you murder the other half of the council? The respect would be lost."

"Maybe. I know one thing though."

"What's that?"

"They may lose some respect, but they will have a whole bunch of fear because they will learn for sure that I am not to be fucked with."

"That's what you'd rather have, fear over respect?"

He thought about that question for a minute and answered honestly. "I don't know. I mean I would love for all of them to respect me; shit that is what I have been striving for since I took the top spot. To learn now that someone has basically crossed us all just for the sake of not liking me makes me feel like I need to instill some serious fear into they ass."

"Even the people who have your back on the council? That makes no sense, Taz."

He sighed heavily and asked, "Okay, what do you suggest, li'l mama?"

"To give you some peace of mind I think you should put some eyes on whoever you feel is your biggest threat."

"That's easy, Saint Tramon's ass."

"If you say so. But I think the obvious in this case is the wrong way to look at this. Who do you feel is the lesser threat to you out of the four council members who are against you?"

Taz thought about that for a few seconds and then said, "Most likely Malcolm Brown's punk ass."

"Then that's the one I would have watched the most. Saint Tramon is on record as being the most vocal detractor of yours. You told me yourself that she said it's personal with her. She will keep to the business side of things because she sees the profits being huge in her favor. She also understands that you are no fool and will be watching her every move from a distance. Smoke and mirrors, baby, smoke and mirrors. She will try to have you thinking and looking one way while she will have another move coming at you from a totally different direction. A direction you won't see coming. I'd put someone on Malcolm Brown and see what you can learn from him and the moves he's making."

"With him checking in with Mr. Suarez that angle is already covered for real."

"Is it? Are you sure that he is telling Mr. Suarez everything? You can't be sure of that. Cover all your bases, baby. Take nothing for granted."

"You know what, fuck it. I'm putting teams on all of they ass. That way I won't miss shit. I will have them watched as well as under the gun at the same time so if I even think they're about to make an aggressive move against me I'll move first."

Sacha laughed and said, "That's rather barbaric, but at least you'll feel more secure."

"You got that right." Before Sacha could say something they were interrupted by Taz's cell phone ringing. He saw Tazneema's face on his iPhone 5 and answered. "What up, Neema, you good?"

Tazneema paused for a second to try to compose herself then said in a shaky tone, "You need to hurry up and catch a flight out here, Daddy. Mama-Mama has been rushed to the hospital."

"What? What's wrong? What happened to her, Neema?"

"Reverend Collins just called me and told me they were sitting and chatting at the house when Mama-Mama clutched her chest and said she felt some sharp pains. He think she had a heart attack, Daddy," Tazneema said and started crying. "I'm on my way to Spencer Hospital now."

Taz checked his watch and saw that it was a little after five p.m. and said, "Okay. I'm catching a redeye out of here. I'll be there in the morning. Until then you call me just as soon as you know more. Calm down, Neema, I need you to remain in control of yourself right now. Don't panic on me, babygirl. Mama-Mama is going to be all right."

"Okay, Daddy, I will. Just hurry up and get here."

"I'm on my way," he said as he hung up the phone with tears sliding down his face. Sacha saw the tears and tears of her own started falling from her eyes as Taz told her that his mother had had a heart attack. Without another word being said they both jumped up and started moving toward the bedroom to pack. Taz had his cell out and was calling Red, Tari, and Wild Bill while Sacha called Gwen and Bob. Everyone would be flying back to Oklahoma City tonight to be there for Mama-Mama.

# Chapter Sixteen

By the time Taz, Sacha, the kids, and the crew made it to Oklahoma City Mama-Mama had been transferred from Spencer Hospital to Mercy Hospital, a hospital better equipped to take care of Mama-Mama's needs. Taz had been a nervous wreck up until the doctor came and told them that Mama-Mama was in stable condition. That calmed him tremendously but only temporarily because the doctor then informed him that Mama-Mama needed to have heart surgery due to clogged arteries to her heart. A bypass surgery needed to be scheduled as soon as possible.

Taz shook his head and sat down so he could think straight. He knew that Mama-Mama wouldn't want to have any type of surgery. She told him a long time ago that if it was her time to go then let her God take her 'cause she would be ready if He was ready for her. Her words were clear in his head, but he wasn't going to let that stubborn old woman be taken from him. He stared at the doctor for a moment and asked him, "How soon can you schedule this surgery, Doctor?"

"As long as her condition remains stable we can do it within the next twenty-four hours."

"What are the risks involved, Donald?" asked Tari who used to work as a nurse at Mercy and knew that the doctor assigned to Mama-Mama was very competent, which made her feel better about this situation.

"It will be fairly routine bypass surgery. The risks are minimal as long as her vitals remain as stable as they are now. That's why I would like to monitor her for twenty-four hours before proceeding."

Taz was shaking his head from side to side. "What's wrong, baby?" asked Sacha.

Tazneema answered for her father. "Mama-Mama has always told us that she will never have anyone cutting on her. She said if it's her time to go then she will be ready for the Lord's calling. She made us promise to never let anyone do any kind of surgery on her."

"Come on, man, Mama-Mama can't be that stubborn on this one, dog. We can't let her go out like this, Taz," said Red.

Taz sighed heavily and said, "Will she be awake anytime soon, Doc?"

The doctor smiled and said, "Right now she's heavily sedated for comfort and to help her vitals. If everything remains in good condition by the morning I'll ease back some of the sedatives I have her on and she would wake up say around evening time."

Taz returned his smile and asked, "And when would the surgery take place if her vitals are still good?"

"I would schedule it close to ten a.m."

Taz stared at his daughter and asked her, "What you think, Neema?"

"Uh-uh. You ain't putting that on me. I want Mama-Mama here healthy and safe, but I'm running for the hills when she wakes up and finds out you approved having surgery done on her, Daddy. This is your call to make not mine. And I'm making sure she knows it, too!"

Everyone inside the waiting room started laughing because they all knew and loved Mama-Mama. They also knew that she was going to go off on Taz for going against her wishes. But each member of the crew plus Sacha knew that Taz was not about to let his mother die because she didn't want to ever have any form of surgery done on her. Taz took a deep breath and told the doctor to schedule the surgery and he would sign the necessary documents to approve the surgery for Mama-Mama. After shaking the doctor's hand Taz turned toward the crew and said, "Y'all niggas better make sure you help me when Mama-Mama comes to because she is going to kill my ass!" The laughter from everyone this time was more like a tension reliever because everyone knew that Taz had just made the right decision as far as saving his mother's life.

"I've just received word that Taz and his merry crew along with his wife and kids are now in Oklahoma City."

"What made him make that trip so suddenly?" asked Saint Tramon.

"His mom had a heart attack last night."

"Mmmm. Does this mean he will remain out that way for a while?"

"Too early to tell, but I would think so with him being the only child and all."

"How will that affect your plans?"

"It's a setback because I don't have people in place out there like I do out this way. But it's nothing that couldn't be taken care of when the time is right."

"Are you sure? That's his home turf; he may be able to spot any suspicious behavior."

"I doubt it. Like I said I would have to put people in place and look at it closely before I made a move anyway. It's not like I'm rushing with this. We have all the time in the world to make this move on him and his crew."

"Actually we don't. Once Taz is removed from the equation things will get hectic for the Network. Time is important in several ways. Taz should be removed no later than summer's end; is that enough time for you?"

"More than enough."

"Good. You do know that you cannot miss. This has to be as strategic as possible. The entire crew must be handled. If not, everything will blow up in our faces because they won't hesitate to bring everything that they have at us."

"When I get down I don't do misses, Saint Tramon," Danny Orumutto said seriously.

"I hope you won't start either."


Each member of the crew went to their homes in Oklahoma City to get some rest because they would all be returning to the hospital in the morning to wait it out during Mama-Mama's surgery. Taz and Sacha were making themselves comfortable at his mini mansion, waiting for Gwen to bring the twins from her and Bob's place. While Sacha was fussing around the house making sure everything was in order, Taz had a few calls to make. He called back West and spoke with his head of security to let him know that he would be gone for an undetermined amount of time. He wasn't going back to California until he knew without a doubt that his mother was okay. The more he thought about the move, he wanted to make Mama-Mama leave with him when she got out of the hospital. He had to laugh that off because no one made Mama-Mama do a damn thing. The more he thought about things, the better he began to feel. Coming back home may have been a blessing in disguise. He felt more comfortable in Oklahoma City and would be able to spot any bullshit coming his way if Saint Tramon or any of the council members tried to make a move against him and the crew. *Yeah, this may just work out right,* he said to himself as he called his head of security back.

"Say, Mack, I need one more thing from you."

"Holla at me, boss, and you know I'm on it."

"I need you to get my dogs and have them flown out here to me."

"Damn, Taz, you know I do not like fucking with them damn Dobermans when you're not around."

Laughing, Taz said, "Man, come on with that shit. You are six foot six, 275 pounds of solid mass, and you are scared of my babies?"

"You fucking right! I know them dogs are trained to kill, and I swear I'm not trying to beef with you, Taz. If they ever try to get at me, I'm putting two in each of they head!"

Taz stopped laughing and said in a very serious tone, "The day that happens will also be the day your ass dies. Get them on a flight out here to me and let me know when the flight arrives, big scary-ass nigga."

"Will do. I'm telling you now I'm delegating shit on this one. I am not going near those vicious fucking dogs!"

"Do what you gotta do. Just get my dogs to me, Mack."

"Will do, boss."

"One more thing."

"What up?"

"Find some discreet folks on the team and put some eyes from a distance on Danny Orumutto for me."

"Like that?"

"Yeah, like that. That slimy fuck may be on some shit, so I want to keep tabs. Can you handle that?'

"Done deal. Anything else?"

"Not at the moment. Might as well tell the rest of the team they can chill for a minute 'cause I'm out this way and ain't no telling for how long at this point. Stay ready. Never know I may need y'all to hop a bird this way."

"We're always ready, boss."

"I know. Talk to you later," Taz said and hung up the phone. He then called Snuffy in Texas and told him that he wanted him to fly out to OKC and come and meet with him in a few days. After that was taken care of he stretched and yawned loudly. He was dead tired; all he wanted to do was take a long, hot bath and get some sleep.

Tazneema was feeling much better now that her father and play uncles were in town. Their presence gave her instant confidence that everything would be all right. The mere thought of Mama-Mama dying was terrifying and way too much for her to handle. When she stepped into her new home she sighed and thought about all of the work that she and Lyla still had to do and how it would have to be put off until after Mama-Mama's surgery. Lyla was sitting down in the living room when Neema entered and asked, "How's your grandma, Neema?"

"She's in stable condition but needs to have bypass surgery. It's been scheduled for tomorrow morning as long as her vitals remain okay."

"That's good news I guess, huh? I mean she being stable and all."

"Yeah, it's good news, could have been worse. Mama-Mama's going to be so pissed at Taz for authorizing that surgery. She always told us she never wanted to be cut on no matter what."

"I know Mama-Mama is stubborn, but even she wouldn't be that stubborn."

Smiling, Neema told her besty, "You don't know, girl, you really don't know. Anyway, what you been up to?"

"Nothing much, just lugging my stuff over here and now tired from making five trips. Geesh, I didn't know I had this much stuff."

"At least we won't have to worry about room. We've got plenty of space," Neema said as she waved her arms around.

Laughing, Lyla said, "You ain't never lied, girl. My God this mini mansion is like really not mini at all. Why do they even call a place like this a mini mansion anyway?"

"I don't have the slightest idea. All I know is I love it and I'm glad I decided to make this move. It works out perfectly for the both of us."

"I know that's right. You do know once we get everything in order with our personal touches we're going to have to throw a little something here to break in our home right?'

"You know I don't do parties so you need to dead that one, girlfriend. This is our home, our safe haven. Let's enjoy it together, Lyla."

Frowning, Lyla said, "It's not about breaking in the house. It's more about starting to live again, Neema. It's way past time that you knock them cobwebs off that coochie, girl, and start living again. We need to party more and get out. Shit, I've let you lull me into a damn funk. It's been like three months since I've had me some! I am so sick of my toys!"

"Ugh. TMI, Lyla."

"TMI, my ass, it's the truth! You know damn well I know your freaky ass have plenty of toys your damn self so don't even try that with me, Neema. Seriously, I know what you went through and I understand, but it's time to start living again. You have a great career, plenty of money, and now you got a fantastic home. All you're missing is some fun. I'm not trying to get you all the way out there like I was when we were in school. I'm saying let's enjoy life. Let's get back to clubbing and, you know, doing what it do."

Neema smiled at her best friend and knew that she was right. It was way past time for her to move on with her life, just like Mama-Mama had told her. "This is one of those rare times when you are right and on point, girlfriend. So this is what we'll do. After Mama-Mama's surgery is complete and all is well with her then we can start making some plans on hanging again. I'm dead serious this house is not for everyone to know about. Taz would have a fit and get to preaching to me about security and how I am not the normal type of female because of who he is. So we have to maintain a strict privacy code when it comes to where we stay. Cool?"

"I got you. Are you saying if I meet someone and feeling him I can't bring him here to get my freak on?"

"Yes and no. If you meet a guy at the club or around the way and want to fuck him day one like you have been known for doing then hell no, he can't come here! But if it's something serious and you've taken the time to get to know the man then I have no problem with him coming over here. You just have to be careful is all I'm saying, Lyla. This is not just my place; it's our place. I am not making all of the decisions; we're making them. Being safe is my father's main concern and after looking at my past situation I have learned not to go against the grain when it comes to Taz. Been there and done that and that's not happening ever again."

"I'm with you, girl, and I understand. We got a super place and we will enjoy it together. Can you answer one question for me?"

"What?"

"Why does this place have like four bathrooms? Didn't your Uncle Keno stay here by himself?'

Shaking her head, Neema said, "You are the stupidest smart girl I have ever met in my life you know that?"

"Whatever. I know one thing, we're splitting the bathrooms. I want the one with that huge-ass bathtub; you can have the smaller ones."

"Whatever you want, Lyla. Let me go to bed. I have to get up early to be at the hospital for Mama-Mama's surgery."

"All right. I'm going to do some more unpacking and may make another trip or two back to my old place. Is it cool to store my extra stuff up in the attic?"

"Yeah, that's where I was going to put some of my uncle Keno's stuff, too. I already boxed up his clothes and stuff."

"What about his cars? I like them old school Chevys he has. They are clean, girl.'"

"I'll have Taz or one of my uncles come and get them. I think they may hold some sentimental value to the crew so we better steer clear of them. But if they don't trip we can pull one out and get our roll on every now and then!"

"Ha ha ha ha ha. I love it! That's the Neema I remember. My girl is back! I love it we about to act a damn fool!"

Tazneema rolled her eyes at her besty and turned and left the room thinking, *oh Lord.*

# Chapter Seventeen

Taz and Sacha made it to the hospital a little after nine a.m. and were shocked to see the waiting room filled with their loved ones. Taz was overwhelmed by all of the love, not only from his crew but from the others who came to show their love and support for his mother. There was Bo-Pete's mother, Mrs. McClelland, along with her sister, Sherry, Reverend Collins and a few other people who were from Mama-Mama's church. After greeting and thanking everyone for coming they sat and settled down for the wait until Mama-Mama's surgery was over. Tari seemed to be extra calm and that transferred to Taz because she knew and trusted the surgeon who would be operating on Mama-Mama. He gave her a smile and she smiled, giving him a nod and a wink in return.

Tazneema was a nervous wreck; he could tell by how she kept wringing her hands together. He gave her a smile and said, "I don't know why you're sitting over there all nervous and stuff, Neema. I'm the one who should be scared. Mama-Mama is going to kill me when she finds out I authorized this surgery."

Everyone inside of the waiting room started laughing. Though there was nervous tension in the room, Taz's joke seemed to put everyone at ease.

"I don't know who's worse, you or Lyla. She has been telling me all morning I need to calm down, everything is going to be all right. I know Mama-Mama will be fine. Shoot, I'm more scared she's going to make me move back home. I just moved out!" That got another roar of laughter from everyone.

Taz shook his head and said, "I was thinking about that. Don't worry, babygirl, you won't be having to move back home. I'm thinking about bringing Mama-Mama out to L.A. so I can look out for her properly."

"Good luck with that one! Dog, you know Mama-Mama will not even entertain that thought," said Bob.

"It's either that or I'm staying out here. I will not leave my mother out here living alone with a bad heart. Not gon' happen," Taz said in a serious tone.

Hearing the passion in his voice made Sacha rub his thigh to calm him down some and said, "Don't you add to your stress right now, Taz. We'll come up with something to make everything right." Before Taz could respond he smiled as his man Snuffy and his wife entered the waiting room.

Taz stood and said, "I told you to come out in a few days, clown."

After shaking hands with Taz, Snuffy stepped back and said, "Did you really think we'd wait a few days to come down here when Mama-Mama is lying up in here? You tripping, fool."

"Yes, really tripping," added Charlene, Snuffy's wife and right hand.

Taz placed the palm of his right hand over his heart and told the couple, "That's love. Well, have a seat and join the wait." After they were seated Red stood and asked Taz to step outside because he wanted to talk to him about something real quick. Once they were in the hall outside of the waiting room Taz asked Red, "You good, my nigga?"

"I'm straight. Just thinking about what you said about staying out here. You know me and Paquita been going back and forth about that. She's not trying to move West and that shit drives me crazy. I love her, dog, and I want to put a ring on it, but my loyalty to the crew comes first. So I'm getting at you with it real. What do you think I should do, Taz?"

Without any hesitation Taz said, "I think you should follow your heart, my nigga. You have been with Paquita for a good minute and your heart is telling you to make her your bride, do that. There's nothing that we can't adjust to. You being here will actually make things easier for me 'cause you know just like I do Mama-Mama won't let me take her anywhere."

Red smiled and said, "Yeah, I know. I'll check on her every hour on the hour, dog. Not just to keep you sane but for my sanity as well. You know I love that old lady," Red said sincerely.

"I know, dog, there's more to this though. We'll talk about that later. Right now let's finish sweating this wait out. When Mama-Mama is good we'll have a sit down with Snuffy and Charlene as well as the rest of the crew 'cause we need to remain on point. Coming home for a minute may be just what we needed. The West Coast has been our home for the last six years, but Oklahoma City is our home court for real."

"I feel you. You really think that chink fool will try us?"

Taz shrugged. "He's the only one who's not with it. We have to take Mr. Suarez's words seriously. That fool is a threat. That combined with having to watch that snake son of a bitch Malcolm Brown we can't take anything or anyone for granted. Stay ready and we won't have to get ready."

"Always, my nigga."

"Come, let's go back inside. Call Paquita and let her know that you ain't going nowhere."

Red smiled at his longtime friend and said, "That's right. One more thing, dog."

"What up, dog?"

"Don't let that fool Wild Bill know about my moves yet. I'm really not trying to hear his mouth. Plus, he's going to be salty thinking I'm going to desert him on the strip club move."

Laughing, Taz said, "Don't worry about that clown. We'll delegate him some more control over the strip club thing and he'll be fine. You right thinking he is going to try and clown ya ass! Come on, fool." They went back inside of the waiting room to continue to wait for the news from Mama-Mama's surgery.

Four and a half hours after arriving at the hospital Dr. Porter entered the waiting room and everyone stood anxiously and prayed silently as they waited for the doctor to deliver the news on Mama-Mama. When he smiled at Taz everyone let out a long sigh. "The surgery was a success and your mom is just fine. As long as she can adjust to a proper diet she should be with us for a good lengthy period."

"Praise Jesus!" screamed Mrs. McClelland.

"Amen!" added Reverend Collins.

"Yes!" Bob, Red, and Wild Bill said in unison.

Tazneema, Lyla, and Tari gave each other a hug and continued to listen as the doctor explained the process of the surgery and other specifics to Taz and Sacha. After he was finished Taz asked him, "When can we see her?"

"That's something I'm somewhat concerned about. Though she is fine and her heart is in good condition I was thinking that maybe we should wait until this evening before letting you all see her. My fear is that it may be too soon for her to become upset, especially after what you've shared with me about her not wanting to have any form of surgery."

Taz nodded and said, "I understand that, Doctor, and I appreciate that. But I know my mother and even though she's a stubborn old woman she knows she's my every-thing. She may be mad, but when she opens those beautiful brown eyes and sees my face she won't do anything but shake her head at me and give me the smile I need to see so very much."

The doctor smiled at Taz and said, "Well, in that case you can see her within the hour. But not too long; she needs her rest. We will be keeping her for at least another week or so to make sure everything is okay and she's heal-ing properly. After that I will give you the strict diet that she must maintain."

"Understood." After the doctor left the waiting room ev-eryone started clapping and laughing. Mama-Mama was going to be fine. Taz gave his wife a hug and a kiss and said, "Give Gwen a call, li'l mama, and have her bring the twins so they can see their g-mama. You know that's go-ing to keep her in a good mood."

"Yeah, she love her g-babies," Sacha said as she pulled out her cell and did as Taz told her to.

Twenty minutes later the doctor came back to the wait-ing room and told Taz that they would have thirty minutes with Mama-Mama. Since everyone came and showed their love and support for his mother Taz felt it was only right that he let each person who came and suffered with him during the long wait while Mama-Mama was in surgery go in and have a quick word with Mama-Mama before he had his turn.

"Oh, that's so smooth, Daddy, let everyone soften her up before you go in, huh? Real smooth," Tazneema said with a smile on her face.

"That's why I'm Daddy! You make sure you do your part and help your daddy out." They smiled lovingly at one another.

After about ten minutes it was down to Taz, Sacha, and Tazneema. Taz took a deep breath and was about to say something when Gwen entered the waiting room with his sons. "Perfect timing, Gwen. Li'l mama, why don't you, Tazneema, and Gwen take the boys in to see Mama-Mama while I make a call real quick."

"Yeah, right, slick. Come on, boys. Let's go see your g-mama," Sacha said as she led the way into Mama-Mama's room.

Taz smiled as he watched them enter the room. He pulled out his phone and made a call to kill time while his sons spent time with his mother. After making sure everything was straight with Precious and Heaven's flight plans to come to Oklahoma City, Taz hung up with Mack and took a deep breath. "Here we go." He stepped into the hospital room and couldn't help but smile at the sight of his mother smiling while holding on to each one of his sons' hands. *Thank you, God, for not taking this old woman away from me,* he prayed silently.

When Mama-Mama looked up and saw her son, she frowned for a few seconds and then gave him what he knew she would: that special smile that only Mama-Mama could give. "You do know your tail is in trouble, don't ya, boy?"

"Be nice, G-mama. You sick and you got to get well," said Li'l Keno.

"Yeah, G-mama, be nice to Daddy," added Li'l Bo-Pete.

"All right, babies, Mama-Mama will be nice to your daddy."

"Promise?" the twins asked in unison, looking totally adorable to their grandmother.

"Promise. Now let your g-mama talk to your daddy for a little bit. I needs to get me some rest okay?"

"Okay," they said and gave their grandmother a kiss and let Sacha and Gwen take them out of the room.

After they left, Mama-Mama said, "I'm going to keep my promise to my g-babies, Taz, but I want you to know that I am disappointed in you for not honoring my wishes."

"Noted, Mama-Mama. But you know there was no way I was going to let you be taken away from us without a fight. So if you're going to be mad then be mad. I take full responsibility for that call I made. If I had to make it again I would make the same call. I don't know what I'd do if something happened to you, old woman," Taz said as he grabbed her frail hands with tears sliding down his face. This show of emotion was very rare for him. His tears made Mama-Mama cry, which in turn made Tazneema start crying too.

"Oh, Lord, look at us bawling worse than them babies that just left here." They each wiped their faces and laughed. Mama-Mama was definitely okay. They sat and spoke about the surgery and how Mama-Mama was going to have to stick to the diet that the doctor was going to give her. She fussed a little, but Taz could see that she was going to do whatever it took to get healthy. She wasn't ready to leave this world just yet. After about ten more minutes Doctor Porter came into the room and told them that it was time for Mama-Mama to get some rest. After he checked her vitals and was pleased with what he saw Mama-Mama asked him, "Can you give me ten more minutes with my hardheaded son here, Doctor? I need to speak with him in private please."

"Ten more minutes is about all I can spare for you, Mrs. Good. You need to get some sleep."

"That's fine. Ten minutes and I'll be ready to go back to la-la land believe you me."

The doctor smiled and shook his head as he left the room followed by Tazneema.

As the door closed behind them Mama-Mama sighed and said, "For the first time in your life I am not mad at you for going against me. You being hardheaded on this one was the best decision you've ever made, boy."

With a puzzled expression on his face Taz asked, "What's up, Mama-Mama?"

"Since I only have ten minutes I'll give you the quick version of things. I should have had this conversation with you, but I never thought I'd have a damn heart attack."

"What are you talking about, Mama-Mama?"

"Shh, and listen to me. I have some money put up for you and I have to make sure I give you all them codes and whatnot so you will be able to get a hold of it when the time comes. I'm sure you won't need to for yourself, but it's yours to do what you want. I was just watching over it for you because your daddy didn't want you to know anything about it until I was sure you was okay."

"My daddy? What are you talking about, Mama-Mama? I thought my daddy died when I was a baby? You're not making sense here."

"Your daddy did die, but not when you was no baby, Taz. Won was your father, son."

Taz stared at his mother as if she'd lost her mind and whispered his next question. "How?"

Mama-Mama smiled and said, "Boy, you got three kids so 'how' is something you already know the answer to."

"You know what I mean, Mama-Mama."

"Won and I had been together since I graduated from high school. I loved that man with all of my heart and soul. He was my everything, but I wasn't his everything, money was. Money and power. He chose that life and refused to give up anything that had to do with that illegal life he was leading. When I told him I was pregnant with his child he swore that he would always be there for us, but he wasn't leaving that life. You know me. I'm no punk so I told him if he chose that life over us then he wouldn't be able to see us period. He stuck to his word and I stuck to mine. That is all the way up until Mimi's death. When I saw how you was out there hurting people and on that deadly path of destruction I knew that I had to call your father to save you because he was the only man I knew who could reach out to you and make things right."

"So you're the person who put Won on to me? You're the one who introduced him to Tari, too?"

She smiled at her son and said, "Yes, to both questions. I knew for a fact that Won would be able to take you under his wing and bring the best out of you, even if it was living the same kind of life he lived all of his life. I didn't want that way of life for you, but fate had already been decided. I had a granddaughter to think about as well as my son and I wasn't going to sit there and lose you to them streets because you were hell bent on killing everyone after Mimi was murdered."

"I understand. But why didn't y'all tell me he was my daddy?"

"Won didn't want you to resent him, or think he thought of you as a charity case. You two are just alike and I'm surprised that you didn't figure it out on your own. The passion that man possessed for money has been transferred to you and so has the thirst for power. His thirst for power was what he craved most and he wanted to make sure that no matter what happened if he didn't make it you would make it to where he wanted to be. He was very proud of you and loved you dearly, Taz. He knew toward the end that things weren't going to go the way he wanted them to. He came and gave me a long talking to about what he wanted me to do and how to make sure the money that he had worked hard for his entire life was passed on to his only son. You, Taz. William Bryant Hunter is your daddy."

"Damn."

Laughing, Mama-Mama said, "You can say that again. I've wanted to share that with you for a long time, but I had to keep to what we started so many years ago. The only reason I am telling you this now is so you will have full knowledge of what's yours just in case something happens to me. That's a whole bunch of money in them accounts and you need to know what comes along with all of that money."

"How much money, Mama-Mama?"

She smiled at her son and said, "Over five hundred million the last time I checked. He has some investments set up and it makes more and more every year. You know I don't know all that mumbo jumbo stuff, but the people from across the water sends me stuff every few months. I check the balance at the bottom of it and as long as it's more than the last time I feel everything is fine. I put all of it in my chest that I keep under my bed. You can go get everything and go over it yourself and have it dealt with by Sacha. Now that this burden is lifted I feel relieved," Mama-Mama said and yawned.

Seeing that she was getting tired Taz told her, "Go on and get you some rest, Mama-Mama; we'll talk about this some more when you come home."

"Okay, Taz. We do have more to discuss. You have an uncle in prison finishing up a real long sentence. He's going to want a good portion of that there money. Won made sure that he has been taken care of while he was in jail. But Percy Hunter won't be satisfied with that when he comes home. He may be a future problem for you, boy. Won told me you would do the right thing by your family no matter what and he would leave it to you to handle. Won and Percy never got along, but he always made sure his brother was taken care of. So when the time comes you do what you feel is right."

*Great, just what I need: more fucking problems,* Taz said to himself. To his mother he said, "Don't you worry about none of that stuff. I can handle it. Now get some sleep and we'll come back this evening to check on you." Taz bent forward and gave his mother a kiss on her forehead and cheek. He smiled as she closed her eyes, sighed, and drifted to sleep.

# Chapter Eighteen

"I knew it! It didn't make sense to me and for the life of me I could never quite put my finger on it, but I knew it!" screamed Sacha after Taz told her and the crew about all of the money Won had left him. "That sixty million dollars he left you and Neema just didn't add up. I mean Won loved you too much. Those numbers never sat right with me. You were already worth two hundred million dollars. How could it be possible that he left you less than what you already had and he was the man who helped you guys get all of that money? He had to have more than that somewhere. It all makes perfect sense to me now."

"Yeah, you're right, li'l mama. It's more to this shit though."

"What?"

Taz smiled at everyone sitting in his den and said, "Won is, was, my daddy."

"What?" everyone inside of the room said in unison.

"Oh, my God! That means that Uncle Won wasn't my uncle. He was my real grandfather. Wow," said Tazneema.

"Damn, and to think we were almost to the point of taking him out," said Wild Bill.

"Shit, that means that Junior is your cousin, dog," said Snuffy.

"Junior? Who the fuck is Junior?" asked Taz.

"Remember the nigga I told you who did that fool Pitt?"

"Yeah, your mans from your way."

"He's Won's nephew."

"Is that right? Would you by chance know where his father is?"

"Yeah, Junior's old man is in the feds finishing a monster stretch. If my memory is correct he should be touching down soon."

"I think Junior and I need to meet. After everything is everything and I got Mama-Mama situated you need to bring him down here so we can chop it up."

"Done."

"So, now that you are damn near a billionaire how does that affect our current situation?" asked Bob.

"Yeah, dog, this shit is wild. We have to look at this entire scenario we're now caught up in real close like. Does the moves change or are we still going to be about the business with the arms dealing thing?' asked Wild Bill.

"Nothing has changed. I'm still the head of the Network and we will continue to progress and move forward as planned. We have to make sure that security remains tight for everyone. I mean everyone. That goes for the others on the council who are loyal to me. I don't want anyone slipping and I mean take nothing for granted. I will be informing the other council members of what I expect because I got a feeling in my gut that that sneaky-ass Saint Tramon is going to make a move sooner or later."

"She is a slick one, but I don't see her trying anything for real. She's more mouth to me than anything else," said Tari.

Shaking his head no, Taz said, "When it comes to security it's not always about what you see, it's about what you don't see that matters most. It's a must we remain safe at all times. I refuse to lose anyone of you or anyone loyal to me. Never underestimate anyone."

Tari gave him a nod of understanding.

"If this is how you feel then why not take it to the bitch and get her out of the way, dog? Fuck this defensive shit. Let's play offense and make our move first," said Red.

"I'm feeling that, but we have a lot to lose if we move on emotion and get too aggressive. Why meet our enemy sword to sword where their strength lies? It will better serve us if we can find a way to force them to show their sides where they are weakest and then strike the hardest and deadliest blow. It's all about the end game, my nigga. And believe me when it ends we will be the last ones standing."

Wild Bill started laughing and said, "Real fucking spill!"

"Umm, excuse me, Daddy, but I think I've heard way too much. I'm about to go home and get some rest, then I'll see y'all back at the hospital later on," Tazneema said as she stood and left the room without waiting for a response from anyone inside of the room.

Taz shook his head from side to side as he stepped to the bar and poured himself a glass of Courvoisier XO. After taking a sip of this drink he said, "Oops."

"Oops is an understatement, Taz, you keep doing that goofy shit," said Tari.

"Yeah, I know. Still tripping off this news Mama-Mama hit me with about Won being my daddy that I didn't pay attention."

"What's done is done, baby. Neema understands your life; she just doesn't want to be a part of the gangsta stuff. She'll be fine," said Sacha.

"Yeah, dog, you already know she's about her business so it's all good," Red said reminding Taz about his daughter and how she handled that situation with Cliff six years ago.

"Back to the business at hand. Snuffy, I need you and Charlene to get at Jay Bogard, Chinaman, Snack, and G.R. Make sure that they all understand that I want them to remain on high alert and keep shit tight with their security twenty-four/seven."

"Done."

"I'm going to get at Akim as well as Mr. Suarez to check and see if there's been anything added to the mix. I really want to hear if that bitch-ass nigga Malcolm Brown has been with any more of that treason shit."

"I think you should be more concerned about Danny Orumutto. He is the tricky one in this mix, dog," said Bob.

"You're right, my nigga. I'm all over it. When it's time we will be in the position to handle shit the right way."

"What if we're wrong and no aggressive moves are made against us?" asked Tari.

Taz shrugged and said, "Then everything will be everything and we all continue to eat and make a whole bunch of money. Everyone will be happy and that will be that. We're staying ready so we won't have to get ready and there is absolutely nothing wrong with that."

"I agree," said Sacha. "Now, what are we going to do with all of this money!"

Everyone started laughing.

"Since my daddy left me such a large chunk of change it's only right that we splurge on a little something-something. I'm buying a private jet. Using Akim's company jet has spoiled me. No more of that commercial shit for us."

"Dog, that's, what, every bit of twenty million used and God only knows what brand new," said Wild Bill.

Taz shrugged and said, "You didn't hear that amount that Won left me? Twenty milly ain't nothing. So get on top of that for me, li'l mama. Find us the best deal you can for a used G5."

"You do know that the maintenance as well as the pay for the pilots will be added to this right?"

"I'm good with it. I'll have Neema start interviewing for some pilots. I want this taken care of in the next month or so. We won't be doing any traveling too soon anyway while we're here during Mama-Mama's recovery. By the time she's back up and doing her thang full steam we should have everything situated."

"This splurge move is for the crew correct?" asked Tari with a smile on her face.

"What you got on that mind of yours, Tee?"

Tari looked at Sacha, smiled, and winked. "Since you got a toy for the crew us girls want something to splurge on as well. Why not surprise us?"

"Why not. You, Sacha, Gwen, and Charlene come up with something and we'll get it together. Now let's dead this for now. I need to get at Akim and Mr. Suarez; that is, unless we have anything else to bring to the table at this time?"

Everyone inside of the room agreed that all bases had been touched then one by one they left Taz's home. Sacha went upstairs to check on the twins who were just waking up from their nap. She heard Taz downstairs laughing loud so she went to go see what was so funny followed closely by her sons. When she entered the den she heard Taz talking to someone on the phone while holding his stomach trying to control his laughter.

"Come on, Mack, you got to be kidding me."

"I'm telling you, Taz, your fucking dogs have gone berserk. They're snapping at everyone who tries to get them inside of their kennels. They're going fucking nuts. We're running late as it is so if we don't get them inside of their kennels we won't make the flight to get you your damn Dobermans," Mack said clearly frustrated.

Taz calmed himself down and said, "All right go outside where the dogs are and stand right by their kennels."

"What, you think you can tell them to get inside of their kennels over the damn phone and they will obey? Come on, Taz, this shit is fucking irritating as it is."

"Do what I told you to do, Mack. Hurry up. You're running late remember."

Taz was smiling at Li'l Keno, Li'l Bo-Pete, and Sacha as they stood and watched him. When Mack came back on the line he said, "All right we're all outside in front of the truck and I'm telling you, Taz, both Precious and Heaven are growling looking like they want to attack us. I don't want to put your dogs down man so this shit better work."

"I already told you what would happen if you touched my dogs, Mack. Now put me on your speaker on your phone and open their kennels."

Mack pressed the intercom button on his cell phone and said, "All right, Taz, you're on speaker and it's turned all the way up."

"Hold it out toward the dogs so they can hear my voice."

Mack did as he was told and said, "Okay, ready."

"Precious, Heaven, get into your kennels now! Come and protect me!"

There was a brief pause and then Mack said, "I'll be a muthafucka! They went straight to their kennels and sat down. This shit is too fucking weird for real!" Mack said totally astonished by what he witnessed.

"Whatever, fool. I paid plenty of money to get my babies trained like that. Now hurry your ass up and get them on that flight. What time does their flight arrive out here anyway?"

"Midnight your time."

"Make sure you put something for them to eat inside of their kennels so they will be calm during the flight."

"I got you. We're on our way now. I'll shoot you a text once they are on the plane."

"Right," Taz said as he ended the call.

"You and your babies, all of y'all are just too dang spoiled. Really, Taz, a G5?" asked Sacha as she sat down next to her husband.

The twins sat on the other side of their father and started fighting for position on Taz's lap. After securing each one on each of his knees Taz told his wife, "It's not all about being spoiled, li'l mama, the company needs this. It makes things more convenient for us all for real. Now I know it's a little extreme, but for real it's more business than pleasure with this move."

She smiled and said, "But there will be some pleasurable times as well."

"You damn skippy. Gots to put you in the mile high club, li'l mama."

She smacked him on his arm and said, "Since when did you become a member of the mile high club, Mr. Taz?"

"Yeah, Daddy, when did you be in the mile club?" asked Li'l Keno.

Laughing, Taz said, "All y'all crazy! Let's get something to eat before we go see your g-mama. I'm hungry."

"Me too!" the twins said in unison.

"What about the calls you need to make?"

"I got a text from Akim and Mr. Suarez and they're both busy and will be getting at me later. So we might as well get something to eat and then chill until it's time for us to go check on Mama-Mama."

"What have you decided on dealing with her once she is released from the hospital?"

As they went into the kitchen Taz said, "She will have two choices and that will be to come and stay here, which I think she will go for, because the second option is staying with Neema and Lyla at Keno's place."

"You know Neema isn't going to want that. What if Mama-Mama chooses her house?"

"I doubt it. She would rather be here with her g-babies instead of fussing at Neema and Lyla all day. Her staying here will make things easier all the way around. When she is back on her feet in say a month or two then we'll let her go back to her house, but there will be round-the-clock help there. I've decided to hire a nurse or maid/nurse to move in with Mama-Mama."

"Of your choosing of course."

He smiled. "Of course."

"I hope this goes well with Mama-Mama," Sacha said as she opened the refrigerator and began to look for something to make her family for dinner.

Taz sat at the island with the boys next to him and said, "Me too, li'l mama, me too."

# Chapter Nineteen

Akim Novikov and Alexander Sokolov were seated in Akim's study having an afternoon drink of their favorite vodka when Akim received a long distance call from America. When he saw Mr. Suarez's face on his phone he had a bad feeling he was about to receive some bad news. And his feeling was absolutely correct.

"I'm sorry to disturb you, Señor Novikov, but I have received some serious information that has confirmed what we have thought all along about our oriental business associate," Mr. Suarez said seriously.

"Are you saying that he is planning to make aggressive actions toward our young colleague?"

"Sí. Very aggressive from what I have learned from Malcolm Brown."

"This is not good. Not only will it cause an all-out war, it will negatively affect all of the business we're putting together."

"Sí. Malcolm also informed me that Señorita Tramon is the key contact with our oriental friend."

"That's not much of a surprise now is it?"

"I guess not. What is a surprise is that she would deal with a man who could bring their entire organization into such turmoil. She is being one-sided on this matter for selfish reasons all because of her dislike of Señor Taz."

"This is true. My primary concern is Taz's well-being. By being his allies in this situation it is up to us to ensure he remains safe at all times."

"*Sí.* I was going to call him after our conversation and warn him of what's going on."

"No. that wouldn't be the best course of action at this time. If you did that he would react aggressively and then things would get ugly faster than we want them to."

"Are you sure?"

"I'm positive. One would think that Taz is too experienced to allow his emotions to run roughshod and dictate his course of action. Though Won taught him better than that he would lose it when he heard that aggressive moves toward his demise had been set in motion. He would without a doubt begin an all-out assault on everyone he deemed an enemy and that would definitely cause harm to all of our plans."

"What do you suggest we do, Señor?"

"Protect our young comrade. I'll have Alex send some of our people to Oklahoma City to give an added force to what Taz has in place already security-wise. The men we'll send will be the best from my country at what they do. A squad of our Spetsnaz from our special forces units should suffice. That way Taz will have an extra security blanket around him."

"Do you think he'll accept this kind of assistance without an explanation?"

"I know for a fact he wouldn't. That is precisely why I'm not going to inform him of our people being there. They will watch him from afar but close enough to be there in case they are needed. Again, they are the best at what they do. Taz will be protected totally."

"That sounds like an excellent plan. Next, I feel I should have a conversation with our oriental friend. Your thoughts?"

"Definitely. Better you than I. I for one would gladly like to fly some of our Spetsnaz there to remove this wart from our skin. Please relay that to him during your conversation. Though our business is our business it's best that he understands that the Network not being involved with drugs doesn't break him. He should look at the bigger picture of this situation."

"*Sí*. Again, I apologize for this call, but as you have seen it was of importance. I will be in contact with you again soon, Señor."

"Always a pleasure, Señor Suarez. Take care," Akim said as he hung up the phone. He turned and faced his comrade and watched as Alex made the call to arrange for a light squad of Russia's military special forces Spetsnaz to start preparing for a flight and lengthy stay in Oklahoma City in America.

Alex finished his call and said, "Ten men should suffice?"

"Yes. I want the best we have to offer, top pay, and everything they need to make sure they don't fail us."

Alex smiled and said, "You know they do not know what the word fail means, comrade."

Akim returned his smile to his comrade, sipped some vodka, and said, "Yes, that is true."


In Miami after hanging up with Akim, Mr. Suarez called Danny Orumutto to have a much needed conversation. Danny Orumutto was fuming the entire time he listened to Mr. Suarez talk. By the time the one-sided phone conversation ended he was so hot he was ready to order every hit man he knew to go out to Oklahoma City to murder Taz and his crew as well as his entire family. But he knew better than that. He knew that he had to calm down, think, and regain his composure. He took a few deep breaths and began to think about what had just been said to him on the phone. After ten minutes he snapped his fingers and grabbed his phone and called Saint Tramon. When she answered the phone Danny wasted no time and got straight to the point.

"Whomever you're sharing information with about our business concerning Taz has been running their mouth. Either they are on the payroll of Mr. Suarez or plain talking too damn much, and this shit has to stop. I just received a call and was told in so many words that if I don't step back from the Network's business I will be dealt with. One, I don't like that shit at all. I want to get stupid with this shit for real. But for business reasons I can't make a move. So you need to tighten shit up or all of this has to come to a halt. At least for a little while. I can give a fuck what Suarez or those fucking Russians think, my business will not suffer because Taz wants to deal arms instead of drugs."

"You may trust conversing like this on phones, Danny, but I don't. So I suggest you tone down your conversation. With that said, I don't understand what you're saying about whom I have been discussing our plan with. My circle is small and I highly doubt anyone would send any warnings to anyone concerning Taz's well-being," Saint Tramon said.

"If you say so. But can you tell me how in the fuck Suarez would know what he knows about our business together without someone informing him from your end?

Because I know for a fucking fact no one on my side of this shit has said anything to that fat fucking Cuban fuck."

"How can you be so sure about that, Danny?"

"I'm fucking sure because no one knows about this shit on my end but me! So tighten your fucking leaks or all of this is dead and your ass will be stuck up under that bitch Taz's thumb longer than originally planned!" Danny hung up the phone feeling better but still highly upset.

Saint Tramon stared at the phone in her hand and shook her head from side to side as she sat back and thought about what she had just been told. Someone was running their mouth, but why? What sense did it make to betray her when everyone she had spoken to about Taz's demise was all for it? That didn't make any sense, unless one of those she trusted was not really on her side. This thought made her frown as she grabbed her phone and called each one of her so-called allies and told each something different under the premise of being extremely critical to the demise of Taz. She then called Danny Orumutto back and told him that when she found out who had betrayed her she would have the situation taken care of.

"Good. Then we'll proceed on getting rid of that fucking country muthafucka Taz."

"Agreed."

# Chapter Twenty

Two months of Mama-Mama made Taz feel as if he was about to lose his mind. He loved his mother more than life itself, but her living with him could not continue as far as he was concerned. There could only be one boss in his home and that was not the case with Mama-Mama being there. Taz and Sacha decided that the twins would be home schooled and went about trying to find a suitable teacher who could come over to the house for a few hours a day during the week. Mama-Mama was against that totally and felt if the twins were to be home schooled then she would be the person to do it. Taz was okay with that. He figured it would give his mother something to do as well as being able to avoid letting a stranger inside of his home around his sons.

The next issue that drove Sacha nuts was how Mama-Mama had to dominate everything in the kitchen. Though Sacha wasn't as good a cook as Mama-Mama, she was no slouch and the twins liked her cooking, but they loved their g-mama's food and that slightly irked Sacha. She felt as if she was being run out of her own kitchen by Mama-Mama. She knew that Mama-Mama meant no harm, but it was still maddening to her.

What tipped the scale was when Taz stayed out late with the crew drinking and hanging out in Bricktown clubbing. As soon as he came home Mama-Mama was sitting in his living room with his Dobermans asleep by her feet. She went off on him about how a responsible father shouldn't be staying out so late like he had done too often for her tastes since she'd been staying there. Right then and there Taz made up his mind that it was time for his mother to go back to her home.

He sighed and sat down next to Mama-Mama and smiled. "You do know that I know what you're doing right?"

"What are you talking about, boy?"

Shaking his head from side to side with a finger raised he said, "Stop it. I'm not Neema, Mama-Mama. You can't trick me to get you back home. All you got to do is tell me that you're ready and then we'll make it happen. You trying to drive me to the loony bin by all this fussing ain't gon' work, old woman."

Mama-Mama smiled at her only child but remained silent knowing that he had her pegged.

"I've decided that we're going to stay out this way until at least the end of the summer so that should be long enough to make sure you're okay before we all head back west. So, if you're ready to go back home then we'll make it happen this week. But you're going to have to do right, Mama-Mama."

"What you mean do right, Taz? I'm eating right and taking my medicine as the doctor told me to. What you think it'll change when I get back to my house?"

He gave his mother a stern look she knew all too well.

She sighed and said, "Okay, okay, I will make sure I eat right all the time and take all of my meds like I'm supposed to."

"I know you will 'cause we're going to hire a live-in nurse to come and stay with you, Mama-Mama."

Shaking her head no she said, "No way. Ain't no woman gon' come in my house and boss me around, Taz Good. I don't know what you thinking, but I have been grown for quite a long time now and I am capable of taking care of myself and I don't need your permission to do so either."

"Look, you stubborn woman, I almost lost you, and that's not going to happen again if I can help it. If you don't want a nurse to live with you, then you need to find one of your friends from your church or something who would be willing to come and stay with you and help you around the house. It's either that or a private nurse. My mind is made up, Mama-Mama. This is how it's going to be, so you might as well accept it and figure out which way you want it. Now, I'm going to bed, and when I get up, I hope you've made your decision on how it will be. I love you," he said as he gave his mother a kiss on her cheek, stood, and went upstairs toward his bedroom. He was smiling when he heard his mother mumbling some choice curse words about her only child.

It was a little after midnight in California when Danny Orumutto received a call from Mr. Suarez. After speaking on the phone for twenty minutes with the Cuban drug lord, Danny was confused by what he had been told. Something was off base, and he needed to know what the hell Saint Tramon was up to. He called her even though he knew that it was past two a.m. in New Orleans. When she answered the phone she said, "This had better be an extreme emergency, Mr. Orumutto."

"Yeah, yeah, whatever. I just got a call from Mr. Suarez, and he was quite pleased that I've decided to back away from the Network's affairs. So whatever you did seems to have him in left field, which is a good thing, I think. Can you enlighten me with what it is exactly that you've done, Saint Tramon?"

Hearing these words from Danny snapped Saint Tramon out of her drowsiness from being woken up so late at night. She realized who it was who had betrayed her now, and she was starting a slow boil as she told Danny. "I made a few calls to my people and told them each a different story to see if I could weed out the leak."

"And?"

"And from what you just told me I now know that it's Malcolm Brown who is that person who has been giving Mr. Suarez information about our business."

"How are you going to handle that?"

"First, we are going to proceed as planned and make the necessary moves against Taz and his merry crew. Malcolm Brown will be dealt with accordingly for his betrayal. That's enough talk on this phone. I told you I don't care to have these types of conversation over the phone.

Good night, Mr. Orumutto," she said and hung up the phone totally frustrated. She quickly dialed her personal assistant, Damon without caring whatsoever that it was so late at night. When he answered the phone without any greeting she said, "First thing in the morning I need you to get at Ninth Ward Twine. I have something for him to take care of ASAP."

By the tone in his boss's voice Damon knew better than to ask what this was about, but he knew that Ninth Ward Twine was not to be messed with and would want some specifics. "What shall I tell him, ma'am? You know he will want some details about this summons."

She sighed and said, "Tell him to be at my house no later than noon and that he will be well compensated for his time, hell, tell him five thousand more than his usual fee. Understand?"

"Yes, ma'am. Is there anything else?"

Saint Tramon loved loyalty; she loved how Damon was the ultimate example of being loyal to her. She smiled and said, "No, Damon. I'm sorry for disturbing you like this."

Laughing, he said, "No, you not, ma'am. Thank you for saying that anyway. I know if you called me this late, or should I say early, it had to be a matter of extreme importance."

Shaking her head from side to side because he knew her so well, she nodded into the receiver as if he could see her and said, "You're correct. Get some rest. We've got a long day ahead of us in the morning."

"Yes, ma'am," Damon said and hung up the phone.

Sighing loudly Saint Tramon set her phone back on the nightstand then stuck her hands under the comforter and started fondling the genitals of her most recent boy toy who was sleeping soundly next to her. When she felt his manhood start to stir she smiled and said, "I do love the young and virile." She then slid under the comforter and began to give her boy toy some early morning head because pleasing him would all but guarantee him waking and pleasing her totally.

The next morning when Taz woke up he was surprised to hear laughing downstairs in the living room. After going to the bathroom and getting himself together he went downstairs to see Mama-Mama with the twins sitting on her lap, Sacha, and Mama-Mama's friend Mrs. Leslie. Obviously from their laughter Mama-Mama was in one of her clowning moods. When she saw her son she pointed at him and said, "There he is, y'all, the only man in the world who would put his sick Mama-Mama out of his house."

They all started laughing.

Taz shook his head and said, "You know you need to quit that, Mama-Mama." He waved to Mrs. Leslie and said, "Hello, Mrs. Leslie, how are you doing?"

"Fine, Taz, just fine. Your mother invited me over here this morning to discuss me moving in with her. Since I lost my husband last year I've been bored and kind of lonely so I feel this may be something that could work out fine for all of us. Especially since you've given your mother notice that she has to get out," she teased.

After giving his wife a kiss and his sons some dap he smiled and said, "I don't know what this old woman has told you, Mrs. Leslie, but she has obviously been putting it on real thick like this morning. I would really appreciate it. If you need financial help, please don't hesitate to ask."

"Oh no, Taz, I'm fine. Like I said this will help me as well. Your mother and I will be just fine. I'm rather excited about it actually."

"Good. That's settled then. Taz, you get them boys over here and have them start hauling my stuff back home. I'm outta here! I want to be in my own bed before the afternoon gets in good. Ya hear me?" said Mama-Mama.

"Yes, boss of me," Taz said and smiled.

"Oh and you do know I expect you to have my g-babies at my house every morning Monday through Friday no later than nine a.m. sharp for their home schooling."

"Nine a.m. is fine, Mama-Mama, I'm sure Sacha won't have a problem with that," Taz said with a smile on his face as he turned and tried to make a quick exit to the kitchen to avoid his wife's curses.

When he returned with a glass of juice in his hand Sacha told him, "Since you're being slick this morning, mister, I thought it would be a good idea to tell your mother about the private jet you are in the process of purchasing."

Taz groaned and watched the frown form on his mother's face. "A private plane? Taz Good, are you out of your damn mind? What you need a private plane for?"

"It's a luxury I want and can afford, Mama-Mama, please chill out."

Shaking her head from side to side she said, "Look at you, already finding a way to waste some of that money your daddy left your tail. That's just sad."

"Mama-Mama, you have to understand something: I have my own money and I could buy this jet with that and still be good. This has nothing to do with what Won left me. It's something I want and I feel will be a convenience. Especially when stuff like emergencies happen. So calm down. It's all good."

"Humph. How much is this plane going to cost, boy?"

Before Taz could answer her Sacha smiled and answered for him. "Well, we were looking at a used one, but your son here changed his mind and decided that he wanted a brand new one. So we're looking at every bit of forty-two million for the jet, another one to two hundred thousand a year for the storage hangars here as well as Burbank in California. Another two hundred thousand a year for both pilots; that's not counting the flight attendants who by the way have been chosen by Neema. So your son has decided on spending a nice piece of his inheritance."

Taz rolled his eyes at his wife and with a defiant look on his face told his mother, "It's my money and I can do what I want with it. I want a private jet that's what I will get. Period, end of it. Now, let's go, li'l mama. We got some business to take care of and your legal expertise is needed. Mama-Mama, I'll have Bob, Red, and Wild Bill come over and pack your stuff and help you get situated back at home. Mrs. Leslie, if you need any help in moving your stuff let me know and I will have it arranged as well."

"That won't be a problem, Taz. I'll have my nephew and some of his friends help me move what I'm bringing to your mom's house. Everything will be just fine."

"Okay. And please, if there is anything you need as far as money is concerned don't you hesitate to ask. I am so grateful to you for doing this."

"I'm fine there too, Taz. Like I said this is helping me just as much as it's helping you and your mother."

"Thank you so much, Mrs. Leslie, you're a true blessing," Taz said as he stepped to her and gave her a hug and a kiss on her cheek.

After giving his mother and sons some love Taz and Sacha left to go to the office for their weekly meeting with the crew and Tazneema. During the drive to the office Taz told Sacha, "You do know that was some serious hating you did back at the house, li'l mama. What was up with that?"

Laughing, Sacha hit him back with, "Hating? Like how you slick side locked me in on bringing the twins to Mama-Mama every morning for school way out in Spencer? No way, mister, you got that because you called yourself getting one over on me. You know damn well I won't want to be getting up every damn morning driving way out to the country."

"Touché."

"You better believe it!" They both started laughing.

# Chapter Twenty-one

Saint Tramon was sitting behind a large cherry oak desk reading a *Forbes* magazine when Damon entered her office followed by a light brown-skinned man who looked like he could break a person's neck with very little effort. At six foot four, 255 pounds, Ninth Ward Twine was one serious-looking dude. His calm demeanor was surprising to those who knew him; because of his profession one would think he was loud and overly aggressive. That was far from the truth. Ninth Ward Twine was the most calm, laidback killer that Saint Tramon ever came in contact with. Throughout her years of dealing with killers she knew some of the most ruthless. By far Ninth Ward Twine was the best and the most lethal, a cold-blooded killer who handled his business like no other. He could be up close and personal and torture a person or he could kill from a distance with a sniper's accuracy. Guns, hand to hand, knife, or whatever preference, Ninth Ward Twine could come through as long as you could afford his fee.

After he was seated, he smiled at Saint Tramon because he knew without a doubt a good payday was coming his way. She could definitely afford his fee.

"Ya boy here tells me I am going to get an additional five for this job. What's the catch, Saint Tramon?" asked Ninth Ward Twine.

"Time. I want and need this handled within the next forty-eight hours."

"Where?"

"Chicago."

"Any specifics with this one?"

"I would love for you to torture the disloyal bastard, but like I said time is of importance, so however you choose to handle it is fine with me," she said as she passed a large manila envelope across her desk to him.

Ninth Ward Twine opened the envelope and took a look at its contents and smiled. "I'll give you confirmation of the kill within twenty-four hours."

Saint Tramon returned his smile and gave him a nod of her head and watched as the hired killer stood and left her office followed by Damon. *Good riddance, Malcolm Brown, may you burn in hell with your stupid-ass uncle,* she said to herself as she sat back in her seat and began to map out her next move. The decision of who would become the new leader of the Network had to be made since she was about to lose her first choice. She had to think hard and decide if she wanted to take over the top spot.

Taz was smiling as he listened to Tazneema speak on all of the money they were going to be spending on his jet. When she finished he said, "I appreciate your concern, Neema, but as far as I'm concerned it's a done deal. So get everything finalized for me. With that out of the way how are things coming along with your project?"

"Fine. I found the building I want and I was waiting for your approval before I went ahead and moved on it."

"I told you you have the green light on this totally. There's no need to wait for me on any of this. Make it happen."

His daughter smiled and said, "I'm on it."

"Good. I want this place up and running by the summer, can you make that happen, Neema?"

"I'm aiming for the Fourth of July."

"I like that. Is there anything else we need to discuss?"

"As far as Good Investments Inc. is concerned everything is fine."

"Not everything. What are we going to do about the move back west?" asked Wild Bill.

"We're going to put that on hold for a couple of months, Bill. Let's see how things pan out with that chink for a minute. If things remain calm then we'll proceed as planned. Cool?" asked Taz.

"Yeah, I'm good with that. You know this fool Red here has been acting real funny style lately, like I don't know his ass or something."

"Whatever. Your girl has you stone gone, dog. I ain't mad at you though. I want you to be happy always, dog, remember that."

Red placed an open palm across his heart. "Love."

"Oh, that's so fucking sentimental. You two niggas are killing me," Bob said and started laughing.

Red and Wild Bill both gave Bob the finger.

Taz turned toward Tazneema and said, "Excuse me, Neema, but we need to discuss some more business and I am not trying to make the mistake I've been making with you and that lately."

"Thank you. Okay, guys, I'll talk to y'all later. I'm about to go help Mama-Mama pack. When are you guys coming over to take her stuff out to her house?"

"Give us a couple of hours and we'll be there," answered Red.

"Please be on time; you know how she is."

"We will."

"See y'all later," Neema said and left the office.

As soon as the door closed Taz said, "Okay, let's get to this business. Everything has been put in place. Seven shipments of weapons have arrived."

"Where?" asked Bob.

"Two in Texas. Snuffy is handling them as we speak. Two in Oakland. I've already spoken to Piper Dixon and she has secured everything and assured me that everything is good."

"I don't trust that woman," said Tari.

"She's not my biggest fan, but when it comes to business I am somewhat confident she will handle shit," said Taz.

"Her first fuck-up and she gets it right?" asked Wild Bill.

"You better say it," Taz replied with a smile. "Two more shipments arrived in the ATL. Snack assured me he has everything in order and that he has already arranged some serious sales for some of the heavier artillery throughout his contacts in the South. He smells the green and he's all over it."

"I bet, that fat nigga is serious when it comes to that paper," said Bob.

"That's six shipments, baby. Where's the last one?" asked Sacha.

"In a warehouse out in Yukon. After we're done here me and you are going to go out and check everything out then get with Akim and let him know that everything is good on our end. He's arranging some meetings for me with some of his connects so we can get rid of this stuff within the week."

Rubbing his hands together Wild Bill said, "I know you're going to keep some of the good stuff for us right, dog? We have to have the heavy shit just in case we have to take it to that chink fucker."

"Calm down, killer. After I've checked everything out I'm going to let Bob handle getting what we need for ourselves and secure them. When we get the G5 we'll fly everything west. I'm giving it two more months out here. As long as Mama-Mama is good we can then head back west."

Red decided that now was the time to let everyone know what Taz already knew. "Don't make any plans for the evening because I want y'all to join me and Paquita for dinner tonight at my place." He went into his pocket and pulled out a black velvet ring box and set it on the conference table and continued. "I want y'all there when I ask her to be my bride."

Sacha and Tari both teared up at the sincerity in his voice. Bob and Taz smiled.

Wild Bill frowned and screamed, "I knew it! I told your ass! I know when something is heavy on your mind, fool!" He smiled and then added, "It's about fucking time, Red. I know how you feel about her and I'm happy for you, my nigga." He stood and gave his homeboy a tight hug. "I wish you nothing but the best."

Laughing, Red said, "You might want to hold up on all that love, dog. I got some more to say."

Wild Bill's frown returned as he sat back down so he could listen to what else Red had to tell them.

"Paquita just ain't feeling the West thing. No matter how hard I press her on this she refuses to budge."

"What you saying, dog?" asked Wild Bill.

To make things easier on Red, Taz intervened. "What he's saying is he's not coming back to the West with us. He's going to stay out this way and take care of things on this end. We need muscle here anyway. Plus, I'm going to need someone else to be here for Mama-Mama and Neema just in case some shit pops off. Tari will be coming back with us and staying with you at the Winners Circle. This move fits us all and makes the most sense."

Wild Bill sighed and looked back at Red and asked, "What about the strip club, dog?"

Hearing how down Wild Bill sounded crushed Red, but he knew that his homeboy would be all right. He smiled and said, "You act like I'm not going to be a part of our business no more just because I'm staying back here. Li'l nigga, you tripping. We still gon' make our dreams come true, dog. Shit, with Taz buying this G5 I can hop a flight out there whenever we need to handle business together. In between time you will be the man and can handle shit. Don't tell me Wild Bill can't handle shit without his big homey on his bumper at all times," teased Red.

"Now your ass know that ain't shit. I gots this," Wild Bill said with his chest stuck out. "Damn, I may need to find me a fucking wife. All my niggas are tying the knot on me. I might have to follow suit and slow my ass down, too."

Laughing and in unison Tari and Sacha screamed, "Noooo!" That caused everyone in the room to start laughing.

"All right calm down so we can close this off real quick," Taz said steering the conversation back to the business. "Akim has told me that every state that the Network controls will receive a shipment of weapons within the next month so things are going to get real good real quick. This shit is about to make our pockets extra fat. Security will remain a top priority so I am going to need to be on point at all times with every one of the council members. I know I keep repeating this, but I want it understood. No slipping. Crew has to remain tight and if any of you sees or hears something that you feel is slightly important I need you to speak on it. We got to keep this shit tight all the way around. I am not trying to lose on this move."

Each member of the crew gave him a nod in under-standing.

"Not that I know much about these weapons, but what all are we dealing with here?" asked Sacha.

"Guns-wise, everything from nine millimeters, .45s, .380s, to the larger stuff like M110 7.62 by .51 millimeter sniper rifles, 7.62 millimeter mini guns, and M23 chain guns. The heavier stuff will be MK19 grenade launchers, grenades as well as several different types of rocket launchers and RPGs."

"Uh, okay."

Laughing, Taz shrugged and said, "You asked, li'l mama."

"In simple terms, girl, some heavy military *Rambo* gun type shit," said Tari.

"Exactly. All right, that's about it, y'all go on and get with Mama-Mama for me while me and Sacha roll out to Yukon and check on things that way. I'll hook up with y'all later when we get together for Red's engagement dinner."

"Taz, I don't have anything to do so if you don't mind I want to roll with you and Sacha?" asked Tari.

"I don't have a problem with that, Tee. Come on let's get it." As they all filed out of the office Taz got the chills. Goose bumps came all over his arms. Something wasn't right. He had a funny feeling that something was off. He shook the thought off as they left the office.

# Chapter Twenty-two

Taz, Sacha, and Tari were pulling out of the parking lot of the warehouse where the weapons were stored in the city of Yukon when Tari noticed a black Ford Focus parked across the street from the warehouse pull from the curb a few minutes after they passed by it. Alarm bells started to ring in Tari's head as she casually pulled out her lipstick from her purse and opened her compact as if she was applying some lipstick to her lips. Actually she was using the small mirror from her compact to check behind them from the back seat of Taz's Bentley without being obvious about it.

The Ford was staying well behind them so she hoped her instincts were off though she was pretty sure they were on point. Just as she was about to tell Taz and Sacha of her concern Taz turned the car onto the highway and she watched as the Ford drove right past the highway entrance. She sighed in relief and put her compact back inside of her purse happy that she hadn't said anything to Taz. She had been tripping. Maybe it was because she'd just seen enough weapons that could damn near suit a small war. That could be it. Yeah, that was it. She was spooked a little bit she thought as she sat back in her seat and relaxed.

Twenty-five minutes later when Taz was exiting Highway 40 Tari noticed another Ford Focus behind them, but this time it was a dark blue sedan. *Coincidence? Nah, fuck that, I don't believe in those,* she said to herself and then told Taz, "I think we have a roving tail on our bumper, Taz."

When we first left the warehouse I saw a black Ford Focus ease from the curb a minute or so after we passed it. I watched the car from the mirror on my compact, but when we got onto the highway they bypassed the highway entrance so I figured I was tripping. But as you just got off the highway I noticed another Ford Focus a few car lengths behind us. This time it's a dark blue one instead of black."

"I see it. Let's take them for a ride to make sure we're not tripping before we handle they ass," Taz said as he made a right turn and headed toward downtown as if he was going back to the office. Tari pulled her compact back out and was checking their rear as she was sure Taz was doing as well.

"Do you see anything, Tari?" asked Sacha sounding nervous.

"Yep. The blue Focus is no longer behind us."

"But the black one back there is huh?" asked Taz.

"Yep. A roving tail just like I thought. They're good, Taz. What are you going to do?"

"Take them on a ride for a little bit and try to confirm who they are first. If they're the peoples then we are going to have to get that shit out of that warehouse like fucking fast."

"And if they're not the authorities?" asked Sacha.

"Then we're going to set a trap for they ass and kill them. Before they die we're going to find out who put them on us and the shit will get really real," Taz said in a deadly tone.

"I was afraid you'd say something to that effect."

"The blue Focus is back and the black one is passing us

now."

"Yeah, I see it, Tee," Taz said as he pulled out his phone and made a call. When the line was answered he said, "May I speak with Detective Bean please?" While he waited for the police officer to come onto the line both Sacha and Tari were staring at him as if he'd lost his mind.

"This is Detective Bean, how may I help you?"

"What up, Detective, how you be?" asked Taz.

"Taz? I heard you were back in town. How's your mom?"

"Good. If you heard I was back why haven't you given me a call?"

"Been real busy dealing with all of this murder stuff going on out here lately. I'm telling you the drug scene with the PCP has turned these young kids in the city into monsters."

"That's sad, real fucking sad. Check it out though, I need a fave real quick."

Laughing, Detective Bean said, "Oh, I figured that much just as soon as I recognized your voice. You're just like Won. He never called me unless my services were needed. What's up?"

"I think I've picked some sort of tail and I need to know who they are. Can you run their tags for me real quick?"

After picking up a pen and scrap piece of paper the detective said, "Give me the tag."

"There's two of them. DJJ 116 and DNJ 088, both Oklahoma tags."

"That's DJJ 116 and DNJ 088?"

"Yeah."

"Give me a few minutes and call me back," the detective said and hung up the phone.

When Taz set his phone back on his lap Sacha asked, "When did you get the tag numbers to both cars, baby?"

Taz smiled and answered, "When Tee put us up on the tail I locked the blue Focus tag in my mind and I got the black one just before they made their pass. I couldn't get a good look at them though. The windows are tinted, but they look like white boys."

"Not good," said Tari from the back seat.

"Definitely not good. Fuck! We do not need any activity from the law. This will change shit dramatically."

"How in the hell did they get onto the warehouse is the question?"

"I don't know, but I got to get at Akim after we find out exactly who these people are and tell him we got to make some changes like fucking fast!" Taz turned onto Broadway and headed toward Bricktown. Once he was in the trendy area of the city called Bricktown he decided to stop at the Spaghetti Warehouse, an Italian restaurant he liked. He smiled at the ladies and asked, "Y'all hungry? Might as well get something to eat while we plan our next move. It might just be our last meal as free people. We might be in a cell in the county jail by dinnertime."

"That is really not funny, Taz," said Tari.

"I am so not hungry right now," Sacha said sounding even more worried.

Slapping her thick thighs and laughing Tari said, "You know me, I'm always hungry!" They all shared some nervous laughter as they got out of the car and entered the restaurant.

After they were seated and ordered a few appetizers Taz pulled out his phone and called Detective Bean back. When the detective came on the line he wasted no time. "The two tags came back as rentals from Hertz, Taz. I figured you'd want more on this so I gave Hertz a call and found out that the two cars were rented yesterday for a month."

"Thanks, Detective. Let me handle this shit and I'll get at you in a day or so and we can have lunch."

"Look, I don't need any more murders added to an already high murder rate for the city, Taz. Why don't you let me pick these guys up and run them through the wringer? I may be able to help you out."

"Nah, I'm good. I just wanted to make sure it wasn't the law on my bumper. I gots this, Detective. And trust, you won't have to worry about no crime scene. Later," he said as he hung up the phone. He sipped some of the Merlot he ordered with his lasagna and meatballs and then said, "Sacha, call Bob and tell him I said to get the crew rolling toward the country, Arcadia to be exact. We're about to take these clowns out the way and handle shit."

"How can you be sure they're not some kind of law enforcement, Taz? We could be making things worse by moving this way, baby."

Shaking his head no, he said, "Nah, li'l mama, no type of law would rent a car for a month. Whoever these fools are they on some other shit."

"You may be right, Taz, but the question remains how in the hell did they get into that warehouse where the weapons are being stored?" asked Tari.

"We'll get all the answers we need when we snatch these fools, Tee. You are strapped right?"

"You better say it. I don't leave home without my heat."

Taz smiled as he waited for Sacha to finish her conversation with Bob. When she hung up she sighed and said, "They were just getting to the house to help Mama-Mama move. They're rolling now and said they will be at the house in Arcadia within the next twenty minutes and will be waiting for instructions."

Taz checked his watch and said, "Okay, eat up, ladies, because after we're finished our meals we're about to have some fun."

"Yeah, some fun. Great," Sacha said as she scooped a forkful of her Ossobuco and dipped it into some creamy garlic sauce.

Taz saw the concern on his wife's face and said, "You don't have to ride with us on this, li'l mama. You can call Gwen and have her come and get you from here. There's no need for you to be a part of this, baby."

"Honestly, I think that would be best, Sacha. You're not fit for this part of the business," added Tari.

Knowing that they were both right Sacha just couldn't do it. She knew she would be worried sick if she didn't see this out with Taz. She sighed and said, "I know you two are right, but I want to be there. I want to see who these bastards are. Y'all hurry up and eat so we can do this."

Taz gave Tari a look. She shrugged in return and said, "You heard your wife, Taz, hurry up and eat. I do have one question though."

"What's up, Tee?"

"Who the hell is this Detective Bean you called?"

Taz smiled and said, "A teammate Won turned me on to years ago. Actually, he's Won's cousin so that makes him my second cousin. I have to remember to let him know about Won being my daddy when we do lunch."

"Should have known Won had to have some say in you calling a damn police officer for some assistance. Only Won can do shit like that."

Smiling, Taz said, "Not only Won, Tee. It's now all of Taz!" They shared a laugh as each dug into their meals.

Thirty minutes later Taz was back on the highway and noticed the black Ford Focus was back on their tail. He was about ten minutes from Arcadia and knew exactly where he was going to spring his trap on the men who were following them. He picked up his phone and called Bob. "Dog, I need y'all to get to Arcadia Lake and post up. I want Red and Wild Bill posted in the parking lot. Once I'm close to the entrance of the park I want you to roll out and leave them and bypass me. I need you to spot the other tail for me and then get on their bumper. If one of the Fords don't come into the park then we'll take them hard on the street since it's basically secluded at this time of the day."

"Got it, we're rolling now," said Bob.

"We need these fools breathing so make sure you keep the wild one calm, Bob."

"Dog, you know it's been a real long time since we've had some action like this. Wild Bill is smiling so damn hard right now that I don't think we'll be able to calm him if it gets thick. He's practically foaming at the mouth."

"I figured as much. That's why I want him in the park. If we have to move we'll move with him in a backup role instead of primary."

"Good thinking. Out!"

"Yeah, out!" Taz said and set his phone back on his lap.

Shaking her head, Tari said, "Wild Bill's ass is ready to get crazy, huh?"

"Yep. Here we go," Taz said as he turned onto the street that led toward Arcadia Lake. He checked his rearview and saw that the blue Focus was now following them from a safe distance. He called Bob back and told him, "Move out now, you and Red. The blue Focus is on my bumper about four car lengths back. Once you pass him bust a U-turn and get on his bumper. Tell Red to keep it rolling another mile or so and he should spot that black Focus with tinted windows. They began roving on me off and on every few miles so he should be able to spot them fairly easy. When he gets on their bumper tell him I said to stay on them until we make our move at the lake."

"Gotcha!"

Taz hung up the phone and stared at his wife and smiled. "Calm down, li'l mama, everything is going to be all good. We're about to have some fun," he said laughing.

She shook her head from side to side and repeated what she said at the restaurant. "Yeah, some fun. Great."

Taz smiled as he watched Bob in his black SUV pass by him followed by Red in his black Tahoe. He checked the rearview while keeping his speed slower than the normal limit because he wanted the blue Focus to close some ground on him while Bob made a quick U-turn and got behind the Ford. When he saw Bob make the U-turn he hit his brakes suddenly and brought the Bentley to a screeching halt. The driver of the Ford realized too late that he was now boxed in with Bob right behind him almost bumper to bumper. Before the driver was able to say or do anything Taz and Tari jumped out of the Bentley with their guns drawn and aimed directly at the men inside of the Ford Focus.

"Shut the car off and get out with your hands held where we can see them or die!" screamed Taz. He kept his gun aimed at the driver of the Focus while Tari kept hers aimed at the man on the passenger's side of the car. Bob hopped out of his SUV with his gun aimed at the Ford as well and covered their rear.

"Red, hit me. The black Ford is on its way with him on their bumper so you better secure this situation now, dog."

"Done."

Taz watched as the driver of the blue Focus slowly opened the door and raised his hands to show he was unarmed.
The passenger did the same on Tari's side; neither of their
guns wavered as they were both ready to fire if any sudden
movements were made by the men getting out of the car.
Once they were standing on the side of the car Taz stepped
to the driver and spun him toward the car and began a
quick pat search. Tari did the same to the passenger.

When they were satisfied that they weren't armed Taz
called out to Bob, "Come hold me down here, dog."

Bob came to his side with his gun trained on the driver
of the car while Taz turned and started walking down
the street toward the black Ford Focus that was headed
directly toward him. He raised his gun and aimed it at the
oncoming car. The Ford screeched to a halt.

Taz smiled when he saw Red come up fast behind the
Ford and stop. Red was out of his truck immediately with
his gun aimed at the driver's side of the car. Taz held up his
hand signaling for Red not to shoot. He then signaled to
the driver with his gun to get out of the car. Seeing that
they had been ambushed the two men inside of the black
Ford complied as their partners had in the blue Focus.
Red and Taz quickly went to each man and searched
them then marched them toward Red's truck. Once they
were in the back seat with Taz sitting next to them Red
drove up the street where Tari and Bob had their captives.
Bob and Tari quickly put the men into the back seat
of Bob's SUV just as Taz and Red had their captives.

All of this took less than three minutes and Sacha was
so relieved that no blood had been shed thus far. Wild Bill
pulled in front of the Bentley and jumped out of his truck
with his gun by his side as he saw that everything was
under control.

Taz stuck his head out of the window and yelled to Wild Bill and Sacha, "Let's roll! Follow us to the house!"

Sacha slid over to the driver's side of the Bentley and started the car as Wild Bill turned and got back inside of his truck and followed Bob's SUV to their small rental house in Arcadia. Sacha sighed but knew that even though things didn't get ugly they sure were about to and that scared her to death. She knew what Taz could do when he was angry. Right now Taz being angry was a true understatement. He was pissed off with a capital P. "God help us," she prayed loudly as she followed Wild Bill and the small caravan to the house.

# Chapter Twenty-three

No words were said until Taz and the crew had marched their four captives inside of the small two bedroom home Bob owned in Arcadia. After they had each man tied and secure in chairs brought to the living room Taz spoke. "Okay, you fucks, this is how it's going to go. You are going to tell us who you work for and why they have you following me. If you try to be tough this shit will get real painful. So you might as well make this easy for yourselves."

Each of the men kept blank expressions on their faces as if they hadn't heard a word Taz said to them. Tari sensed that they were highly trained from their physiques and military bearing. Suddenly something snapped inside of her head and she screamed in fluid Russian, a language that no one in the crew knew she spoke fluently.

"You disrespectful pigs! What, you don't think we don't know already that Akim sent you! You are about to die!" The stone-faced look on two of the men broke for a split second and Tari knew her suspicions had been correct. These men were Russians and that could only mean one thing: they were sent by Akim. Now the question remained. What the hell was going on?

Taz stared at Tari for a few seconds and then asked her, "Care to share with us what the hell you're doing here, Tee?"

"These men are Akim's men. They're Russians, Taz."

"How in the hell did you figure that one out, Tee?" asked Wild Bill.

She shrugged and said, "Look at them: beefy necks, boxy-like bodies in good shape with severe acne like most Russians who are a part of their military. Good as they were tailing us I'd bet they're part of the Spetsnaz."

"The what?" asked Red.

"The Spetsnaz," answered Taz. "That's Russia's form of special forces in their military. Like our Navy Seals or Delta Forces in the U.S. This is really fucked up. These fools were following us on orders from Akim. That makes no fucking sense. Akim is my mans."

"Is he?" asked Bob.

"This shit stinks," said Red.

"You're not lying, dog. It's a mean gangsta twist going around this bitch right about now," said Wild Bill.

"These fools are military so they are trained to take a whole lot of pain and honestly I don't have time for that shit. I know you speak English or Akim wouldn't have sent you out here. So this is what I'm going to do. I'm going to ask you one more time what the fuck is going on or I'm going to call Akim myself and let him know that we have his four-man team and that you have failed him. How do you think he will take that?" asked Taz.

Each of the captives still kept the stone-faced looks on their faces and remained silent.

Taz shrugged and said, "Okay, since that's how it is that's how it will be." Taz checked his watch and said, "It's a little after five now so that makes it what, a little after two in the morning in Russia? Yeah, that's it. You better hope Akim is at the club enjoying his favorite vodka and not at home in bed with one of those gorgeous females he likes to share his bed with 'cause he's going to be mad as fuck at you guys." Taz then pulled out his phone and put it on speaker as he dialed Akim's international number in Russia. When Akim answered the phone he sounded as if he was wide awake when Taz said, "We got a problem, Akim, and only you can fix this shit."

Hearing the anger in Taz's voice confused Akim. "Taz, what is this problem, comrade?"

"I have four men tied up in front of me who I think are actually four Russian men. They have the military bearing about themselves that makes me think of your special forces guys out that way, you know those Spetsnaz you always bragging to me about. Care to help me out here, Akim?"

Akim sighed loudly and shook his head from side to side as if Taz could see him and said, "I assume these men have refused to speak to you?"

"Correct."

"Then how do you know they are in fact Spetsnaz, Taz?"

"Kill the game, Akim, I have no time for this shit. The only reason they're still breathing right now is because I think they're your men, so are they or aren't they?"

"Yes, they are my men, Taz. I am glad you haven't harmed them. I'm on speaker?"

"Yeah."

"Commandant Ivanov, I give you permission to speak to my friend Taz. Identify yourself as well as your mission," ordered Akim.

Taz turned and faced the four men and waited.

When Akim didn't hear anyone speak he sighed and gave his cell phone to Alex. Alex then snapped loudly into the receiver. "This is Alexander Sokolov. Commandant Ivanov, Lieutenant Morozov, Sergeant Lebedev, and

Major Popov, I order you to speak to my comrade Taz and divulge your entire mission as it was given to you. You have greatly disappointed me, only because I have truly underestimated my friend's security measures so there is neither shame nor blame in this. You are to remain on your assignment until notified different. Am I understood?"

There was still silence from the four men.

Alex screamed again, this time in Russian, "I said, am I understood!"

Each of the men gave a glance at one another and in unison screamed, "*Da!*"

Alex gave the phone back to Akim. "Taz, after my team explains to you their mission you will understand the purpose for all of this. If you have any more questions they will have to wait until we are face to face. Know that you are not only a friend, you are my partner, and I have to take every safety precaution possible when it comes to our business ventures."

Taz sighed and said, "Akim, man, you almost got your men dead. I'll give you a holla after they put me up on everything."

Laughing, Akim said, "Thank you for not deading them. You are good, Mr. Good, very good."

"The best. Later, Akim," Taz said as he ended the call. He then turned toward Bob and said, "Take Red and Tari and go get their car before their shit get towed." He then went and untied each of the four Russians. After they were released each began rubbing their wrists. Taz smiled, shrugged, and said, "I won't apologize for doing what I felt had to be done. You guys slipped and I had to do what I had to do. Now, talk to me. What the hell is going on for Akim to send y'all out here to watch my back?"

The obvious leader of the group smiled and said, "I am Commandant Ivanov and these are my men. Lieutenant Morozov, Sergeant Lebedev, and Major Popov. We were tasked with the assignment of flying out here to be extra protection for you and your crew as well as your family."

"Protection? From who?" asked Sacha.

"From your enemies was all we were told."

"When did you get here?"

"We arrived yesterday and we are to remain until ordered to return back to Mother Russia."

Taz shook his head and said, "That fucking Akim. He has to cover every single base. What, he thought I couldn't protect myself so he sends help?"

Ivanov shrugged and said, "I only follow orders, sir."

"Taz. Call me Taz."

The Russian gave a nod. "Taz it is."

"If Akim felt the need to fly these men out here to protect us, baby, that means he expects for things to get crazy," said Sacha.

"Those are the same thoughts I'm having, li'l mama. Fuck."


Ninth Ward Twine arrived at Chicago's O'Hare Airport a little after ten a.m. He quickly went and rented a car and made his way to the suite he reserved at the Hilton downtown. He was on the clock and had to make sure that everything was in place so he would be able to handle Malcolm Brown and make his flight back home later on that night. Thanks to Saint Tramon's contacts he would be able to make the hit on Malcolm Brown relatively easily. It amazed him how those who had become rich through criminal activities seemed to lack with their security measures when they were on their home turf. One would think that would be where you made sure your security was the tightest. Suckers and fools never made it long term in this life when they made mistakes like this. Malcolm Brown was about to realize that this mistake was a fatal one.

Ninth Ward Twine grabbed his cell and called Saint Tramon's assistant to let him know that he made it to his suite and he was waiting for the equipment he requested to be delivered upon his arrival. After Damon assured him that everything was in place he took his clothes off and went to the bathroom to take a shower. He needed to get fresh and rested before he made his move on Malcolm Brown and ended his life.

His plan was simple. Drive out to the suburban area called Highland Park about fifteen minutes outside of the city and sit and wait for Malcolm Brown to arrive at his favorite lover's home. Malcolm Brown was just like his deceased uncle. He loved pussy and the company of a beautiful woman. Though he wasn't as stupid as his uncle had been; he felt he chose his lovers carefully by making sure they were not a threat to his well-being in any way. Even so, his love for the beautiful women of the world would play an intricate role in his demise.

Ninth Ward Twine would patiently wait down the street from Malcolm Brown's lover's home for Malcolm to arrive. From what Saint Tramon's contacts had informed him Malcolm Brown would be inside of the home no longer than two hours, which made everything very simple for Ninth Ward Twine. He would wait patiently until Malcolm Brown arrived. Once he was inside of the home he would then creep and get inside of Malcolm Brown's Audi S8 and slip a small but lethal device made of C-4 explosive under the driver's seat. He would then return to

his vehicle and wait for Malcolm Brown to return to his
Audi. He would then follow him out of the quiet suburban
neighborhood at a safe distance.

Just before Malcolm Brown made it to the expressway
entrance Ninth Ward Twine would then pull out his remote
detonator and boom! The life of Malcolm Brown, council
member of the infamous Network, would end. By the
time the fire department, police, and paramedics medical
people arrived on the scene Ninth Ward Twine would be
back in his hotel suite packing and getting ready to return
to O'Hare Airport for his flight back to New Orleans.
Mission complete.


By the time Tari, Red, and Bob returned Taz had let
the Russians know that they would no longer be needed
in Oklahoma City to protect him, the crew, or his family.
He met some resistance from Commandant Ivanov but
assured the Russian that after he finished speaking with
Akim he would receive his orders to return to Russia.

After thanking each of the Russians for their good intentions he told them they could leave and walked them outside to their vehicles. After they were gone he went back
inside of the house and sat down in one of the now vacant
chairs and told everyone, "Shit is obviously as dangerous as I expected so now we have to make sure we keep
things even tighter than we thought. Watch your six at all
times and never form a habit when you're moving around.
Keep all your moves different. We got lucky to spot those
Russians for real." He looked at Tari and nodded her way.
"Good work, Tee. I was slipping and that cannot happen.
What if those Russians would have been some of Danny
Orumutto's people or Saint Tramon's? I slipped and it

could have cost me my life. That is not the way we are going to go out."

"I'm feeling that, Taz, as I'm sure everyone is as well. But what has me fucked up right now is why would Akim feel the need to send his people out here to watch our back? He knows something that he's not telling you, dog, and that's not cool at all. If he's your mans he should keep it all the way real and get at you with everything," Bob said seriously.

Taz pulled out his phone and said, "That's why I'm calling this fool now." When Akim came on the line Taz said, "You do know you have a lot of explaining to do right, Akim?"

"Yes. I was just sitting here with Alex waiting for your call because I knew you would not want to wait for a face to face. I don't want to go into any specifics at this time; please bear with me. You know already about Malcolm Brown and where his loyalty lies. Our friend in Miami received some information that things may get hectic for you and your crew out there in Oklahoma City. So I decided to add some protection without your knowledge of it with the thought that this would be to our advantage. Now that things have been put in motion totally we cannot take anything or anyone for granted. All of the shipments have arrived and our business has already started to make an extreme profit. I'm not only protecting you, your family, and crew, but our business as well. I apologize if you feel deceived. That was not my intention at all."

"Why didn't you get at me and let me know what was what?"

"That should have been my best decision, but I felt this way without you knowing of my men we would have an ace up our sleeves so to speak."

"That makes sense," said Sacha.

"Another reason was because I didn't want you to become infuriated when you learned that a possible attack was in the works against you and the crew. I was afraid you'd want to go on the offense and do something without thinking it through thoroughly."

"You were right. I am now thinking about making my move on that chink muthafucka as well as Saint Tramon. I will not sit out here and wait to be attacked, Akim. But you were wrong; I don't get down without thinking every-thing through first. So while I let this marinate and go over things with my people I need you to give Commandant Ivanov and his men the order to return to Russia. We're good out this way and will continue to be good. I appre-ciate the added security, but they aren't needed for real. If Danny or Saint Tramon make any kind of move against us we will be ready to handle whatever they bring, trust that."

"I understand, Taz."

"I gave you and Mr. Suarez my word I wouldn't put our business moves in jeopardy and I never break my word, Akim, but I will not feel as if I'm being hunted; that's not my way. I'm the hunter, feel me?"

"Yes, comrade, I feel you."

"I'll give you a call tomorrow after I've thought this through some more."

"All I ask of you is to think this through with a rational mindset. There will be the time when we will make the necessary moves against those who we deem our enemy in all of this. I will do as you requested and remove my men from your home state within twenty-four hours, comrade. I'll be waiting to hear from you," Akim said as he hung up the phone and smiled at Alex.

Without saying a word to his longtime friend Akim dialed a number on his cell and waited while the phone rang. When Commandant Ivanov answered Akim told him in rapid Russian, "You did very well, Commandant. Now, I need for you to make sure everything is in place before you and your team return home."

"Everything is in order, Akim. The other team has settled in and is prepared to surveil Taz and his crew as well as his wife, daughter, and mother. While we were playing out this ruse you planned they were busy setting everything in motion. Taz really thinks he's that good because they were able to spot us; that is funny because if we didn't want them to see us they would never have known we were around."

"I know this. You know how Americans are. They have to be the best at everything they do. They continue to underestimate and that's one of their weaknesses. Taz is a good man though and a good friend. That is why I am making sure he remains above ground. Come home, comrades. You and your team will have a grand welcoming home party as well as being compensated for a job well done."'

Commandant Ivanov smiled into the receiver of his cell and simply said, "*Da!*"

# Chapter Twenty-four

Taz was spending the morning entertaining his mother and Mrs. Leslie. Actually they were the ones who were entertaining him with their jokes. Mama-Mama was busy cracking jokes about Reverend Collins and how he had been trying to get his mack on with her. Taz was in stitches as he listened to the women clown the poor preacher.

"I'm telling you, boy, that man think 'cause he's driving a brand new Cadillac he is the man!" Mama-Mama laughed.

"I mean really, the only reason he's driving that new car is because of the church. We chose to start the fund that saved the money to get him a new car because that old bucket he used to drive was barely getting his tail to service on time! Let alone trying to be able to move around the city to go visit our church members who aren't able to make it to church. Now he's some Billy Dee Williams wannabe pretty boy type. He better stick to serving the Word of the Lord!"

Laughing loudly, Mama-Mama said, "I know that's right, Mrs. Leslie, because he sure ain't going to have a chance to serve me anything else!"

Shaking his head from side to side Taz said, "You are too cold, Mama-Mama." He checked his watch and said, "Okay, since you two seem to have everything in order here I've got to get going. If you need anything make sure you get at me, Mama-Mama, me or anyone of the crew. Cool?"

"Cool, dude. Don't worry about me, boy, we're just fine."

Before he could speak again his cell rang. "Excuse me, y'all, this is a business call," Taz said as he stepped into the kitchen with his phone to his ear. "What's good, Snuffy?"

"I just got a call from Chinaman. He told me Malcolm Brown got blown to bits last night leaving one of his broads' houses."

"Blown to bits?"

"Literally. They blew his ass up with a bomb or some shit in his car."

"Damn. Okay, what about the business that was out on his end?"

"I've already gotten at Jay Bogard and he is having his people in the D get out to the Chi as well as Indiana so they can take care of everything. From what I've heard from Snack, Malcolm had already made the moves and everything was in place. I'll know more when Jay Bogard gets with me, Malcolm's second in charge."

"Did Snack say anything about what happened to Malcolm Brown? You know like what's the word right now?"

"Right now everyone is like 'what the fuck?' No clue who did this shit, dog."

"All right, stay on it and let me know what's what."

"Will do."

"What's up with your end?"

"Everything is great. The amigos out of Laredo are about to get with us so we'll have one of the loads out the way by the end of the night. Man, you were right about this move. It's crazy easy and the money is stupid dumb."

"It looks like it's going to get crazier before it gets all the way good."

"Dog, that's how this life is. Stay safe."

"Always," Taz said as he hung up the phone and then called Sacha and told her what happened to Malcolm Brown.

"Great. Now every time I get into one of our vehicles I'll have this shit on my mind."

"Calm down, li'l mama, we are better than that and this shit has nothing to do with us. I'm sure whoever made this move against Malcolm was on some other shit. Most likely the man of one of the many females he was messing with, or some shit."

"I know you don't believe that, Taz. What normal man has access to blowing up a man's car? Especially a man like Malcolm Brown. He was respected as well as feared all around his city. There's more to this and you need to look into this deeper before you automatically assume any different."

"Makes sense. All right, I'm on my way home. Call the crew and have them meet me there. Love you, li'l mama."

"Love you too."

Taz came back into the living room and Mama-Mama could tell something was heavy on his mind. She stood and motioned for Taz to join her in her bedroom. "Excuse me, Mrs. Leslie. I need to speak to my boy in private."

"No problem, I'll get something started for lunch," Mrs. Leslie said as she went into the kitchen.

Once they were inside of the bedroom Mama-Mama asked Taz, "Is everything all right? You look like death has knocked on your door, boy."

Amazed at how well his mother knew his looks and moods he said, "Yeah, a so-called friend of mine was murdered last night in Chicago."

"So-called? What kind of friend can be labeled like that?"

"Long story, Mama-Mama. The thing is things are getting out of hand and I need to make some firm decisions soon."

"I know when it comes to these decisions you will make the right ones. You must do what you have to do in your business to make sure things remain intact."

"Yeah, but it seems as if it's more than just business. It's getting personal and before I let anyone of my people get hurt I'll do what I have to do."

Nodding her head in understanding, Mama-Mama said, "Always hope for the best, Taz. Remember, it's easy to hope for the best as long as you're prepared for the worst. Your father was the best at that; he made sure that he was always thinking ahead of everyone else around him."

"That's exactly what I've been trying to do but every time I think I got a proper hold on a certain situation something else pops up unexpectedly and causes me more confusion. It's crazy and in a way I just want to fall all the way back and leave this life alone and raise my sons with Sacha and live happy with my family."

"Why don't you do that then?"

"I took this responsibility six years ago because it's what Won wanted me to do. I can't shy away from it just because things have gotten a little heated on me. Especially now that I know he was my father. I can't let him down, Mama-Mama."

She smiled lovingly at her son and said, "Boy, if you ain't your daddy's son. There is nothing in this world that I could say to change your mind because I know you won't listen anyway. Won wanted you to have the power he chased his entire life. You have it, son, so do what needs to be done."

"I will. This power he left me is like a heady drug: only the strong can resist its pull. I'm not addicted to power but at the same time it makes me feel different at times. I know I have to flex my muscle and when I do I ask myself am I doing the right thing. But I know I have to use it to further our purpose. We got to win at all costs so I can't and will not relinquish this power for nothing in this world."

Mama smiled and said, "You just make sure you don't let nothing happen to you or I'll have to step up and show my gangsta side and you know Mama-Mama don't play!" They started laughing and gave one another a hug. "Everything is going to work out fine. You're a leader, Taz Good. Lead like you're supposed to. Lead like your father expects you to. It's in your blood to lead, boy."

Taz smiled at his mother and gave her a nod in understanding. There was no need for any more words; he knew he had to handle his business. He gave Mama-Mama another hug and kissed her on the cheek. "You take it easy out here, Mama-Mama, and remember to call any one of us if you need anything or feel like talking."

"I will. You just make sure Sacha brings my g-babies on time for their home schooling."

Taz smiled at that and said, "Well that kinda got me in trouble so it may be me bringing them over here."

"I don't care who brings them. You just make sure they get here, ya hear me, boy?"

"Yes, Mama-Mama," he said as he stood and left the house. Business needed to be addressed. Shit had just gotten more hectic.


When Mr. Suarez received the call that Malcolm Brown had been murdered in Chicago the first name that came to his mind was Taz. Would Taz break his word and move on Malcolm Brown? After thinking about that for a few minutes he couldn't shake how he was feeling so he picked up the phone and called Akim in Russia. After bringing the Russian up to speed on what happened to Malcolm Brown he asked him, "Do you think our young friend in Oklahoma City had something to do with this, Señor?"

Akim thought about that question for a few seconds and answered honestly. "Taz would not break his word. The only way he would go against what he promised was if he felt a direct threat from the man. Malcolm was under your control so Taz wouldn't move on him. If he felt threatened he would have moved on Saint Tramon or Danny Orumutto first."

Shaking his head in agreement into the receiver of the phone Mr. Suarez said, "Sí, this makes sense. Now we've lost some of our advantage with this situation, how do you think we should precede, Señor?'

"Very cautiously, Mr. Suarez, very cautiously. I think our friend Malcolm Brown's murder was a message of sorts."

"From who?"

"Who else? Saint Tramon. This has her devious hand-prints all over it. I don't know why. She must have deemed Malcolm Brown a threat or no longer useful and had him disposed of, knowing that this will cause the proper amount of confusion within the Network."

"But why?"

"That, my friend, is the million dollar question. The answer will come soon though, that I'm positive of. Let me go now. I need to speak with our friend in Oklahoma City. I will give you a call later this evening, Señor Suarez," Akim said as he ended the call. He then called Taz. When Taz didn't answer his phone he hung up and sat back at his desk. *What the hell is going on over there in America?* he asked himself as he poured himself a shot of vodka.


By the time Taz made it to his home every member of the crew was already inside of his den waiting for him. He stepped straight to the bar and poured himself a shot of XO and downed it before speaking. Sacha checked her watch and saw that it was way too early in the morning for him to be drinking. That told her one thing: Taz was pissed. *Not good, not good at all,* she thought as she waited for him to speak.

"What's wrong, dog? You look pissed off," said Bob.

"I'm tired of the games. I'm to the point where we need to just say fuck it and smash Saint Tramon and Danny Orumutto and get this shit over with so we can move forward with our business. I'm not used to this laidback shit we've been on. I've tried this because Akim and Mr. Suarez feel it would be best for our business."

"What's good for business could be bad for all of us," Tari said wisely.

"My thought exactly, Tee."

"Go with your first mind, dog; don't second-guess your instincts," said Red.

Taz nodded and said, "I'm about to get back at Akim after that conversation; then we'll decide what's what. Either way I feel it's time to become more aggressive with this shit."

"I think I can speak for us all on this, Taz. We're with whatever you're with, my nigga," said Wild Bill.

Every member of the crew plus Sacha shook their head in agreement with Wild Bill's statement.

Taz pulled out his phone and called Akim. As soon as Akim answered Taz wasted no time with greetings. "I'm tired of the games being played, Akim. I'm ready to take the offense on this and bring all of this shit to an end. Saint Tramon and Danny Orumutto have pushed me to my point."

"What? Calm down, Taz. What makes you think Saint Tramon and Danny Orumutto have done anything?"

"Come on, Akim, who else would blow Malcolm Brown to pieces?"

"What good would it do for them to have had that done to him, Taz? That's the question you need to ask. Honestly, I was calling you to ask if you had made this move against Malcolm Brown."

"You fucking with me right?"

"Answer the question, Taz."

"I find it best to ignore wild accusations, Akim, especially when you know damn well I am a man of my word. If I would have moved on Malcolm Brown you would have known it because I would have told you."

Akim sighed and said, "I wanted to hear you speak those words, Taz. I don't think you did this and I must agree with you that Saint Tramon and Danny Orumutto are the most obvious suspects. But why? Why take Malcolm Brown out?"

"Somehow he overplayed his hand or pissed them off; who knows and for real who gives a fuck? Saint Tramon is lying in the cut trying to play me. Before I let the snake bitch strike I'm going to make my move. I'm tired of this soft shit, Akim. I'm not trying to ruin our business because it looks like it will be a success just as you predicted, but what good am I to this good business if I'm no longer breathing?"

"What are you saying, Taz?"

"I'm saying I'm going to give them one last time to come at me and make me feel shit is good. If they don't come correct and make me feel as if it's all good then it's time for them to go. I already have to find a replacement for Malcolm Brown on the council; finding one for Saint Tramon wouldn't be a problem at all."

"Are you going to have a meeting with them to discuss these concerns of yours?"

"I'm going to get in contact with Danny and set some-thing up. I'm sure I'll see Saint Tramon at Malcolm Brown's funeral and we'll talk afterward. Then I'll make my decision."

"Understood. I support you on whichever way you choose to go with this, Taz. I too am tired of these games. Let's address it together, comrade, and move our business forward as planned."

Taz had a smile on his face and so did every member of the crew sitting inside of the den. The only person who wasn't smiling was Sacha. *Oh, shit, it's about to get crazy now for sure,* she said to herself as she stared at the man she loved more than anything in this world.

# Chapter Twenty-five

Tazneema was smiling brightly as she hung up the phone and quickly called her father. When Taz answered the phone she said, "I just got off the phone with the company attorney and everything is ready for you to sign off for the purchase of your G5, Taz."

"That's cool, Neema; send me whatever needs to be signed by fax and I'll handle it."

"Okay. You do need to know that along with the over fifty million we're spending it's going to cost at least a million more yearly for maintenance and operating costs as well as paying for the pilots and flight attendants."

"The money made from the interest on my money that Won left me should cover all yearly costs so we're good there, Neema. Let's close this deal. I want my plane ready as soon as possible."

"Actually, everything is already, Taz. Your Gulfstream 5 will be delivered to Will Rogers World Airport by this time tomorrow afternoon."

"Good. Did you make sure everything was as I requested?"

"Yep. Everything has been confirmed. You will have your office, a bed, TVs, Wi-Fi, state-of-the-art avionics, a full bar, seating for fourteen; all we need to do now is hire your pilots and flight attendants."

"Cool. Looks like you've handled everything, Neema, good job. Fax me the papers so I can sign off on everything, then get me some pilots and flight attendants hired ASAP. I plan on taking a few trips soon."

"I'm on it. Check the fax machine in a few minutes," she said and hung up the phone.

After Taz hung up the phone Sacha was frowning at him. He stared at her and asked, "What's wrong with you, li'l mama?"

"I still can't believe you're spending all of this money on a damn private jet."

"You need to get over that and think about all of the up sides that come along with having our very own private jet."

"What up sides, Mr. Freaky? Joining the mile high club?"

Laughing, he said, "Exactly! Seriously, we can move at a faster clip when need be, you can be able to bounce back and forth to Cali and the City for your many philanthropic endeavors, and when I need to go out of the country we will be able to save a lot of time. To me the money is well spent."

"If you say so. It's just hard to believe you've actually spent all of this money."

"Believe it, because here comes the fax now with the papers for me to sign," he said as he stepped to the fax machine and grabbed the papers that Tazneema faxed him. After reading everything that was sent he quickly signed the papers and faxed them back to his daughter. When he was finished he smiled at his wife and said, "Done deal, li'l mama. Your husband now has his own G5."

"You and your damn toys, Taz Good," she said with a smile on her face.

He was about to respond but was interrupted by his phone ringing. He frowned when he saw that it was Saint Tramon's number in New Orleans. He answered the phone by putting it on speaker so Sacha could hear the conversation. "Hello, Saint Tramon."

"Good afternoon, Taz. How are you doing?"

"Good, and you?"

"Alive, alive and well."

"Yeah, well that's better than old Malcolm Brown."

"True. Actually, that's the reason for this call. I think it's of great importance that we hold our quarterly council meeting earlier with this sudden tragedy occurring."

"I was thinking about that but since our next meeting will be next month I don't see why it can't hold off until then."

"With certain decisions needing to be made for the replacement of Malcolm on the council that should be reason enough to have the meeting sooner I think, Taz."

"There's no rush to find a replacement, Saint Tramon. That is unless you have someone in mind to replace Malcolm already?"

"Actually, I do."

*It figures,* Taz said to himself. But to Saint Tramon he asked, "And who may I ask is this person?"

"It makes perfect sense to let Malcolm Brown's second in command of his business affairs be elected to the council."

"From what I've heard Ed Polly has been handling things quite well since this went down. But we will have to bring this to everyone on the council's attention before we make a vote."

"I know this; that's why I am asking for our meeting to be stepped up."

"Again as long as the business has not been hindered I don't see the need to up the date of our quarterly meeting. You will be contacted when and where the next meeting will take place next month. But since you are so interested in having a sit-down with the council I thought maybe we can get together and have a sit down of our own. You and I only, Saint Tramon."

"Concerning?"

"I think you already know."

"If I knew I wouldn't have asked, Taz," she said with obvious attitude and irritation in her tone.

The dislike between the two was palpable. Taz gave a sarcastic laugh and said, "It's time for the game to stop, Saint Tramon. I will not speak on this while on this phone. When we see each other at Malcolm Brown's funeral Saturday we will finish this discussion. That is if you're attending the funeral service?"

"Of course I am attending the service; Malcolm was a longtime friend of mine."

*Some friend. You have your friends blown the fuck up, hate to see what you'd do to me,* he said to himself. "Okay then, we will have a chat then. Afterward hopefully things can be clear as to how things are going to be from now on."

"I must say you have piqued my interest with this conversation, Taz. To my knowledge everything has already been made quite clear. Things have progressed positively as you predicted they would. Everyone on the council has contributed to the new order of business and the profits have been great. That's why I'm so intrigued by this conversation."

*This bitch thinks she can play mind games with every-one. Stupid.* "True, everything has progressed as I knew they would. The business is doing well and everyone is eating good. Real good. What we need to discuss is the future. I'll see you at the funeral, Saint Tramon," he said and hung up the phone tired of the weak mental games she was playing.

"Ugh! She really thinks she can manipulate you. I really can't stand that woman, baby."

"She is a trip, li'l mama. After this meeting either she will accept what I have to say or she will die. I'm tired of her games and it's time to show her who I really am."

"Normally I would try to talk you out of handling things violently but this woman is dangerous, baby. I hate to say this but Saint Tramon is evil and she needs to be dealt with."

"I've killed for many different reasons: revenge, out of anger, and to protect me and mines. I know for a fact the bloodlust for revenge is the most destructive. Keno and Bo-Pete's deaths showed me that I'm capable of committing cold-blooded murder without a care who's in front of my gun. If I decide to take care of Saint Tramon it's going to be me who takes her out. I will not order a hit and stand back and wait for the confirmation of the kill. If she has to die she dies by my gun."

Bob and Gwen had just finished another of their extremely intense sex sessions and they were both winded as they lay wrapped in one another's arms. After catching his breath Bob slid from his wife's embrace and went to the bathroom to relieve himself. While he was in the bathroom he received a couple of back-to-back text messages. Gwen reached out and grabbed his phone off of the nightstand to see if it was someone important. She stared at the text and read it aloud. "'Stop playing games, Bob, and call me.'" She checked the next text and read it. "'You're pushing me, Bob. Not good.'"

Gwen had a frown on her face when Bob came back into the bedroom and saw her holding his phone. Before he could speak she asked him, "Who is this texting you these kind of messages, Bob?" She tossed him the phone so he could see the texts for himself.

After reading the texts he glanced at her nervously and said, "It's business, baby. Nothing for you to be worried about. What were you doing checking my phone?"

With raised eyebrows and much attitude Gwen said, "No, the fuck you didn't just get at me like I'm some weak bitch. I'm your wife, nigga! I'll check your fucking phone whenever the fuck I feel like it! Now! Who! The! Fuck! Was! That! Texting! You! Bob!" she screamed.

"You need to calm the fuck down. Like I said it was business. Business only, Gwen."

"Business my ass! That was a bitch! Nobody gets at you like that and it's just business. Nigga, you think I'm stupid or something? Don't you fucking dare stand there and insult me, Bob. I don't deserve that shit!"

Shaking his head from side to side he said, "You're absolutely fucking right. You don't deserve that shit. You are my wife! I love you more than I love my life itself! You are not only my wife you are the mother of my kids. You mean the world to me and there is no fucking way I would ever risk losing you by fucking with some bitch. I got all the money I need in this world. I have a perfect family. There is no way I would ever do anything to lose you. Never! I would never do anything to come close to disrespecting you, Gwen. You should know that shit. When I say its business that's exactly what the fuck it is: business!"

Feeling thoroughly checked and ashamed Gwen started to apologize to her husband but her female intuition got the best of her and she had to follow what her gut was telling her. Something wasn't right. "I love you and I trust you, Bob, I really do. But something about how those texts sound has made me feel fucked up. Your words are touching and all that but right now I need more than words, baby. Prove to me that those texts were business related, Bob."

Bob looked down nervously then looked back up at her and said, "Your lack of trust is fucked up, Gwen, and that's the true fucking insult." He then stepped to the bed and sat down next to her and pulled the text back up on his phone and then dialed the number the text was sent from. He showed Gwen what he did and pressed the send button to connect the call. When the phone started ringing he pressed the speaker button before the line was answered.

A male answered the phone. "Damn, Bob, why the fuck you not returning my texts, man? We have some serious business to discuss."

Staring directly at his wife Bob took the phone off speaker and said, "I was taking care of something with my wife, Robert. It only takes one time for you to text me, white boy; you're not my bitch so stop acting like it. I'll get at you in a couple of hours," Bob said and hung up the phone.

After setting his phone back onto the nightstand Bob stood and said, "I'm about to take a shower now. As you've just heard I have some business that I need to take care of." He turned toward the bathroom, stopped, and turned back around and faced Gwen and added, "Oh, and don't you ever fucking check my phone again, Gwen. If you gon' act like a fucking kid you don't have that fucking right. My wife should know me better than that."

Feeling totally wrong and extremely stupid Gwen couldn't find the right words to even try to apologize for insulting her husband. She just dropped her head in shame as he turned and went back inside of the bathroom just as his phone started buzzing with another incoming text. She stared at it, frowned, and then threw herself back on her pillow wanting to smother herself with it for being so stupid. *Fuck!*

# Chapter Twenty-six

After interviewing over twelve different pilots and over twenty flight attendants Tazneema finally came to the decision who she was going to hire as the pilot and copilot and the two flight attendants for the company's G5. She sighed with relief as she grabbed her phone and called Taz as she left the office to go have some lunch. When Taz answered the phone she told him, "I'm on my way to the Outback in Edmond; care to have lunch with me and Lyla, Taz?"

He had just finished a strenuous workout with the crew and a big, thick, juicy steak sounded perfect. "Sure, babygirl. I was just about to take a shower and get dressed so I'll meet you there in about forty minutes, cool?"

"That's fine. I've made my decision on the hires for the G5 and wanted to let you go over their credentials during lunch."

"Did you pick the flight attendants, too?"

"Yes, I did, Daddy."

Laughing, he asked, "Are they cute?"

"Ugh! I swear between you and Uncle Wild Bill! He called me every twenty minutes reminding me to make sure they were cute."

"Well, are they?" Taz asked and laughed again.

"You're a happily married man."

"But I am still a man, Neema. And if I'm going to be traveling for long periods of time in my private jet I want to be looking at some cute flight attendants. So, again, are they cute?"

"Ugh! I have their pictures with me in their files; you'll see for yourself when you get to the restaurant. Bye!"

Taz was laughing as he hung up the phone.

By the time Tazneema's and Lyla's appetizers arrived Taz was entering the restaurant casually dressed in a pair of black slacks, crisp white dress shirt, and some brand new Air Force Ones on his feet. Lyla smiled appreciatively at Taz and told Tazneema, "I swear you have one super sexy fine daddy, girl. If he would only give a white girl like me a chance to steal him from Sacha his sexy ass would be forever in the wonderful world of sexual bliss."

Shaking her head Tazneema said, "Trust, if there was going to be a white woman in Taz's life it wouldn't be you, besty. It would be Tari."

"Damn shame." They both laughed as Taz made it to their table and sat down.

"Good afternoon, ladies. You're both looking good this day."

"Thank you, Taz. I was just telling your daughter here how I wish I could steal you from Sacha. What you think my chances are?" Lyla asked flirtatiously.

Laughing, Taz said, "I must commend you for your determination, Lyla. You been on me since you were a little freshman in college. I wouldn't bet any money on that happening though, babygirl. I look at you as my daughter too."

"Damn! Damn! Damn!" They all laughed.

"Order you some food, Daddy, so we can go over this stuff and I can see if you like who I chose to pilot you around the world, as well as take care of your needs while you're up in the air," Neema said as she gave Taz a menu.

After Taz gave his order to the waiter he sat back in his seat and went over the files Tazneema gave him. He had a smile on his face while going over the flight attendant's file. After a few minutes he set the files down and said, "We're good to go here, Neema. The pilots' creds are impressive and so are the flight attendants'."

"Plus they're cute," she said with a smirk.

"Very cute. Young, but not too young, and experienced enough to maintain their professionalism. I think they will work just fine. What did you offer as far as pay?"

"I haven't brought that up to them. I wanted to check with you first on that."

Taz shrugged and said, "As long as they agree to remain on call and know that they will be bounced back and forth from here out to California I'm willing to give them a healthy salary as well as top-of-the-line benefits. Set up a package for health insurance as well as a good retirement deal for them. Salary-wise let's give the flight attendants thirty-five thousand a year and fifty thousand for the pilots. How does that sound?"

"Generous? Shit, if I knew you were paying thirty-five thousand to be your flight attendant on call I would have hired some help for my boutique and do that shit for y'all. That's crazy easy money right there!" said Lyla.

"I want my flight team well paid and ready at all times so paying a little extra is fine with me. We can afford it."

"True. I'm sure they'll accept these terms so I'll give them each a call when I return to the office."

Taz stared at his daughter for a few minutes while she nibbled on her salad and asked, "What you been up to, Neema, besides work I mean? Are you having any fun?"

Pointing toward Lyla, Tazneema said, "There is no way I wouldn't not be able to have any fun living with a party animal like this white girl here. She makes it a point to get me to go out with her at least every other weekend or have drinks twice a week down in Bricktown. I'm good, Daddy."

"Yeah, she's good, Taz, and that's the freaking problem, she's too damn good! She refuses to give any guy a chance to get remotely close to her. She doesn't trust her judgment of men anymore and for that she is causing her coochie to get cobwebs!"

Taz was sipping some water when Lyla made that statement and he had to quickly cover his mouth with his hand before he spit a mouthful of water all over them. After wiping his mouth and hands Taz set his napkin down and said, "You don't mince your words, Lyla, I respect that. But you are crazy you do know this right?"

Lyla smirked at him and said, "Nah, Taz, I'm not crazy, I'm serious. I love my besty and I want her to enjoy her life and not live like some old dried-up maid. She is young, college educated, financially secure, and damn hot and gorgeous. There's no way in the world she should be living monk-like out here. And all because of a bad decision made when she was in her teens."

Taz nodded in agreement with Lyla and stared silently at his daughter waiting for her to say something in her defense.

Tazneema sighed and said, "I wish it was as easy as you make it seem, Lyla."

"It is! Girl, you got to forget the past. What don't kill you only makes you stronger, Neema."

"This is true, baby girl. God knows I am not a real fan of you being with any man for real, but that's the father in me. I have to agree with Lyla: you got to move on with your life. I always want you to remain cautious. You know how I am about security for my family. But that doesn't mean I don't want you to meet someone and be happy. That stuff that happened with that fool Cliff is ancient history. Time to move on with your life, Neema."

Tazneema stared at her father for a moment and in a small voice that touched him deep within his heart she said, "I'm scared, Daddy. I don't ever want to feel that pain I felt with Cliff. I don't ever want to feel betrayed like that ever again. Honestly, I'd rather be by myself than go through that again."

At that moment Taz wished he could bring Cliff back alive so he could kill him a thousand times for the pain he caused his oldest child. He reached across the table and took hold of his daughter's hand and gave it a squeeze and in a stern but loving tone said, "Listen to me, Tazneema Good. No man can ever steal your joy. No man can stop you from being the sweet, gorgeous, strong black woman you have become. What happened with you and Cliff was one of your life lessons that you had to learn from. You are not a weak woman by any means; that's not in your pedigree. You're a Good and there is nothing weak about us. This is the last time we will speak on this subject. Live your life and enjoy what you got. If you need some time off to go fly somewhere and chill to get your mind right then let me know and you and Lyla can take a flight somewhere on our new G5. Do whatever it is you need to do; it's time to get back on that horse and date and live your life. You hear me, Neema?"

She smiled at her father and said, "Yes, Daddy, I hear you. Thank you." She smiled at her besty and told her, "Though you have told me all of this repeatedly, thank you too, besty."

"You know this girl right here got your back, besty," Lyla said and smiled at her best friend. Their food arrived and they all enjoyed a pleasant lunch together.


On the other side of town Sacha and Gwen were having lunch but instead of dining at a steakhouse they were sitting inside of McDonald's eating chicken McNuggets and fries while watching their kids as they played in the small playground in the front of the fast food restaurant. Gwen sighed heavily as she nibbled on some fries and said, "I screwed up big time, mommy. All these years together Bob has never given me a reason to even try to think he was screwing around on me. And what do I do, I go left on him the other night 'cause he received some back-to-back text messages that seemed out of line to me."

"Wait, first off what were you doing checking Bob's phone and looking at his texts in the first place?"

"It wasn't even like that. We had just finished having another one of our super sex sessions and I was lying on the bed getting my wind back. Bob went to use the bathroom, and his cell started buzzing and beeping signaling he had some texts. So I reached over to check them for him while he was using the bathroom, not trying to be snooping or anything like that. I trust Bob one hundred percent. But when I read the texts the shit sounded kinda fishy to me."

"What did they say?"

"One said, 'Stop playing games, Bob, and call me.' And the other said, 'You're pushing me, Bob, not good.'"

"And you took from that what, Bob was cheating on you?"

"Come on, mommy, you have to admit that sounds kinda off right?"

"It depends. What did Bob say when you asked him about the texts?"

"He said it was business related and for me not to be tripping. But he looked nervous for a few seconds and that threw my bullshit detector into high gear."

Sacha rolled her eyes at her best friend and said, "Oh, my God, mommy, what did you say?"

"I went semi-ballistic because he actually asked me why was I checking his damn phone. I told him I'll check his phone whenever I wanted to and demanded he told me who was sending him those texts."

"Did you accuse him of anything, mommy?"

With an ashamed look on her face Gwen shook her head yes and said, "When he said again that it was just business I told him it wasn't business and that it was a bitch texting him."

"Not good."

"Don't I know it. He grabbed the phone, sat down next to me, and dialed the number the text came from and put the phone on speaker."

"What happened next?"

"When the phone was answered a man said, 'Damn, Bob, why the fuck you ain't returning my texts?' And something about them having some serious business to discuss. Bob then checked him and told him not to be texting him like he was his bitch."

"So right then and there you felt like shit."

"What an understatement, mommy. I felt less than a piece of shit. What made me feel even worse is before Bob made the call to show me it was in fact business related he swore how much he loved me and the kids and would never put what we have together in jeopardy by cheating on me."

"After hearing that you still accused him of doing something foul?"

"Basically, yeah. Like I said my bullshit detector was off the charts and I wasn't trying to hear none of that shit he was talking. Then he goes and makes that call and made me feel lower than dirt. He hasn't said a word about it since but he's been icy toward me to the point where I don't know what to do or say to him. I've apologized and he shrugged it off like it was nothing. I fucked up, mommy."

"Yeah, you fucked up big time. Bob loves you though and he will get over it. He's making a point at your expense so you will know not to ever question his love or loyalty for you. Right now with all the stuff they got going on with the Network business he's not trying to have to deal with some weak issues like that, especially when he knows he hasn't done anything wrong."

"I know huh? Damn, mommy, I love that man more than I love life itself. I never thought I'd be able to love a man again after losing my family. Bob came into my life and has blessed me with a happiness I never thought I could ever have. And what do I do, accuse him of cheating on me. Ugh!"

Laughing, Sacha said, "You turn that man on like crazy so you will have to resort to what he likes best. Sex. Put it on him and make up for your wrongs. I'm sure after another one of you guys' super freaky sex sessions he'll forgive you and all will be good again."

"I wish it was that easy. He's only been icy toward me since then he's been staying gone late at night and coming in well after I've went to bed."

"He's that salty at you? Damn, that's not good. Love isn't only sex but sex with you two is one of the key components to your relationship. If he's ducking the sex with you that means he's really bothered by your actions."

"Exactly and that scares the hell out of me, mommy. I love that man and there's nothing in this world I wouldn't do for him. What if I've pushed my man away from me?"

Shaking her head no, Sacha said, "No way. Men can be stubborn creatures just like we can when we're in the right. He's teaching you a lesson, mommy. I'm sure of it. That and he's probably in fact handling business. Don't you think for a second that he doesn't love you and is even thinking of leaving you and those kids; y'all are his universe. So be patient and take your punishment like a big girl. Everything is going to be all right."

Gwen smiled at her friend and said, "I sure hope you're right, mommy, because not only am I stressed out about all this, I'm horny as I don't know what for my man! Ugh!" They both started laughing as their kids came running inside of the restaurant winded and ready for something sweet to eat.

# Chapter Twenty-seven

Taz and the crew arrived at Will Rogers World Airport at eight p.m. sharp. After passing through the security clearances they met the flight attendants Tazneema hired and each male member of the crew was pleasantly pleased with the way the flight attendants looked. Tari shook her head because she knew without a doubt Wild Bill would be all over their flight attendants every time they went on a trip on Taz's G5. *These girls better have some real tough skin,* she thought as she followed the flight attendants as they led them to a hangar where the G5 was being prepped for their flight to Chicago. When they made it to the hangar they watched in awe as the brand new G5 was being towed out of the hangar. Taz smiled proudly at his jet and couldn't help but stick out his chest a little.

"Damn, dog, that's a beast of a plane right there," said Bob as he admired the private jet.

"You better say it," Taz said and laughed as the flight attendants led them toward the plane. Once they were on board the flight attendants formally introduced themselves.

"My name is Angela Womack but I would appreciate it if you all called me Angie."

"And my name is Kamden Johnson, and you can call me Kam. We're here to make sure whenever we fly that you all are comfortable for the duration of each flight. If there is anything we can do for you please don't hesitate to call on us."

Wild Bill smiled and said, "Please believe me, we won't hesitate one bit, darling."

Taz shook his head at the attractive flight attendants and said, "I'm sure we all will get along quite fine. I'm already impressed with your professionalism, ladies. My name is Taz Good. These are my friends as well as close business associates. Sometimes they may be flying without me and I expect for them to be treated the same as if I was with them. I don't have any doubts otherwise; I just wanted to be clear on that." The women each gave a nod in understanding.

The pilots came into the cabin from the cockpit and shook hands with Taz and introduced themselves.

"I'm Karl Horne," said the captain who was a tall man standing around six foot five with a slender build. Taz could tell he was fit and in some pretty good shape. With a light brown complexion complemented by some light brown eyes the captain was a handsome man. Taz liked him immediately.

"And I'm Keith Leverette. I'm your copilot." Keith was a smaller man but looked equally fit as Captain Horne. He had the same slim build and his dark brown skin was smooth as milk chocolate.

"It's a pleasure to meet the both of you. I'm sure we will get along fine together being that I expect to be doing quite a bit of traveling. I am comfortable with the selection my daughter made by hiring you all. And by the way my associates here are staring at you all, I'm sure they are just as satisfied as I am."

"You better say it," Tari said and smiled at the handsome pilots. *Shit, Wild Bill may not be the only one on the prowl when we're in the air,* Tari said to herself.

Everyone started laughing.

Angie, light skinned with a model's slim figure, smiled at Taz and said, "Well, we might as well get everyone situated while the captain and Keith finish doing their preflight check. We have a little over thirty minutes before we will be cleared to depart."

"I'll notify everyone over the PA system when we're ready to leave," said Captain Horne.

"That's fine," Taz said as he watched as the pilots returned to the cockpit.

Kamden, who had brown skin with a body that could stop traffic because of her thickness, smiled at Wild Bill and asked, "Is there anything I can get for you, sir?"

"Bill, Wild Bill, darling. And no, I'm good right now."

"Okay, Wild Bill. I hope I'll get the chance to learn why you're called Wild Bill," she said with a smile that made Wild Bill's heart skip a beat.

"Oh you will, Kam; believe me you will."

"Stop that, you two!" teased Tari.

While the flight attendants fussed around the plane getting the crew drinks or snacks the crew was still in awe of Taz's brand new toy. They were impressed with everything from the expensive leather seats to the several flat-screen televisions located on each side of the plane. Taz didn't miss a thing with this purchase; top of the line entirely.

After everyone was comfortable Angie and Kam went and checked on the pilots. Taz took this moment to tell the crew, "Look, when we get out to the Chi I want to play this real tight. Ed Polly is going to provide security for us but I have a feeling we need to be on point ourselves so I had Jay Bogard arrange for our vehicles to be fully stocked. Once we land at O'Hare Airport we will have our own weapons."

"That's what's up," said Bob.

"What, you think someone might try some shit while we're paying our respects to the dead, my nigga?" asked Red.

Taz shrugged and said, "Who knows? I just want to be prepared for whatever."

"I feel you on that, dog, but don't be all paranoid on us. They know better than to try us. If they miss they know they can kiss their ass bye bye," Wild Bill said arrogantly.

Tari shook her head and said, "You're really tripping, Bill. Who is they? We don't know who to look out for for real, so Taz is right. We have to be prepared for anything at any given time and don't you forget that shit."

Knowing she was right with what she said Wild Bill nodded his head and said, "You're right, Tee, my bad."

"I may be paranoid, my nigga, and rightfully so. Shit is getting thick and will only get thicker before everything is all said and done. Paranoia is not to be ignored. Only a fool in our lifestyle would do some shit like that. The key to dealing with being paranoid is to not let it cripple you. Address it directly and aggressively at all times. That way we will remain on point and then hold an advantage over whomever we have the drama with. We basically know that it's either Danny Orumutto or Saint Tramon trying to plot against us so we will be prepared as if it's both of them together. I have a gut feeling that they are trying to orchestrate a mean demo on us sooner or later and I intend on being prepared for it whenever they make their move. Won taught me to always think in strategic terms, like being on the battlefield in war. Flanks must always be protected. Your center must be anchored with reinforcements."

"In other words, dog, it's like we've always said: stay ready and stay strong," said Red.

"Exactly," said Taz.


Captain Horne announced over the PA that they had been cleared to depart and the G5 started to move slowly out onto the runway for its first flight. Taz made himself comfortable and sipped his drink as the plane began to gradually pick up speed. Once they were airborne he smiled and said, "Yeah, nothing like flying in your own shit."

"You're so full of it, nigga," said Bob and everyone started laughing.

Once they reached their cruising altitude of 51,000 feet Captain Horne's voice came back over the PA system informing everyone that they would be flying for a little under two hours and if they wanted to use their cell phones or Wi-Fi connections for laptops it was okay to do so.

Taz pulled out his cell and called Sacha to let her know that they were in the air and that he would give her a call in the morning before they left for the funeral service. After hanging up with her he checked some e-mails and texts. He saw that Snuffy had texted him so he called him to see what was going on.

When Snuffy answered the phone he said, "All is good, dog; just wanted to let you know that me and Charlene are on our way to the airport now and we'll be on time tomorrow."

"That's cool. Anything else?"

"Yeah, Chill Will has handled the business in Dallas with the Tango Blass Mexicans. Those young fools are planning on making some noise so it looks like they will be some steady customers."

"Good."

"Remember you told me you wanted to hook up with Junior?"

"Yeah, what's up with him?"

"He's been getting at me talking about when can that sit-down take place. I told him you're his cousin and he wants to holla."

"Shit has been so hectic I haven't had a chance to even think about that. I'll fly down your way after we get back from the Chi and we can get together."

"That's what's up. I'll let him know. See you in the morning," Snuffy said and hung up the phone.

Taz sat back in his seat and thought about how smoothly things were going with the arms dealing and smiled. He felt comfortable that leaving the drugs alone was one of the best decisions he'd ever made. Right at that moment his cell rang and he saw that it was Danny Orumutto's number in California. He rose up and said, "Say, y'all, this is that chink fool Danny. I want y'all to pay attention." He then pressed the speaker button on his cell and said, "What's good, Danny?"

"Nothing much big time. Word is you copped that new Gulfstream and I wanted to congratulate you on doing big thangs."

"That's right. I'm sure it's more to this call than you giving me props on buying a jet. So, again, what's up, Danny?"

"Damn, Taz, what's with all the hostility in your tone? I thought we were good."

"We are good. I just don't have time for the bullshit and I feel like you're playing with me and that is insulting to me and my time."

"I never play, Taz, you know that. But check this out, I would like to do some business with you along the lines of your new business venture. When can we get together and make something like that happen?"

"If you want to seriously make some moves you can get at Saint Tramon; she has permission to make moves for you. That way you can be relaxed and comfortable while conducting the business."

Laughing, Danny asked, "Why would I be relaxed and comfortable in the company of that old cougar?"

"You're playing games and feeding me weak shit again, Danny. Please stop fucking insulting my intelligence."

Danny's laughter stopped and a sinister tone came into his voice when he said, "Watch ya mouth. Watch your words when you talk to me, Taz. You are a boss in your own right and so am I. I demand respect at all times."

"You know what, Danny? I have always respected you and your get down. That is until you started playing these games. I don't respect that and I honestly no longer respect you. I got at you like a boss is supposed to do. I gave you the utmost respect and told you about my moves and even offered discounted prices for my moves in the future. What did that respect get me, Mr. Orumutto?" Taz asked sarcastically. Before Danny could answer he continued. "Nothing. Nothing but a fucking headache. But it's cool 'cause I'm used to dealing with headaches. So let's save the bullshit. You want to do some business then by all means let's make it happen. I turn down no dollars. Get at Saint Tramon and she will make it happen. If you got something else on your mind then let's do that too. I'm tired of the weak shit because that's not how I rock. You got something on your chest then speak it and let's deal with it however we need to deal with it."

"Ahh, I like that gangsta shit."

"Me too. I love it."

"Believe me, you have no desire whatsoever to be the subject of the barbarity I'm capable of dispensing."

"Why is that, because of the rumor of you killing your father and uncles? Am I supposed to fear the myth of Danny Orumutto?"

"You're supposed to fear the chaos I can create in your perfect world, Taz."

"Now that's funny."

"Out of chaos comes opportunity, especially to those who are ruthless enough and bold enough to not give a fuck about the consequences and repercussions."

"I'm done with the verbal sparring. It's in the open how I feel about the weak shit, so make your next move your best move," Taz said and hung up the phone.

"What the fuck was that?" asked Tari.

Bob smiled and answered for Taz. "That was Taz making the first power move on our behalf."

"That's right. The games stop and the real shit begins now," added Wild Bill.

"About fucking time. I'm sick of all this waiting shit anyway. Let's take it to that chink and bring this shit to an end," said Red.

"Is that what that was, Taz, you ready to take Danny to war?"

"I'm ready to send Danny Orumutto straight to hell, Tee. I had to let my position be known so he would know that it's on. He's strong but only because of his position. Now that he knows I fully expect him to make a move he loses some of his strength because he has to worry about what I'm going to do. He doesn't know if I'm ready to play offense or if I'm going to sit and wait for him to make a move against me."

"And that does what for us?"

Bob answered for Taz again. "That puts us in the driver's seat, Tee. Taz just put us in a tactical position to win. We have the high ground now and can either wait for Danny to make his move and be totally secure and prepared to defend ourselves. Or we can take it to his ass and give him all we got and bring this shit to a close."

Tari stared at Taz for a few seconds and asked, "Which is it then, Taz, which way are we going to move?"

"I'll be able to answer that question by the time we return from Malcolm Brown's service tomorrow evening. Either way it's time to address all issues. I have a few moves in my head marinating right now y'all so bear with me; trust it's all good. The first thing I want to discuss though is Ed Polly."

"What's up with him?"

"Saint Tramon has suggested that he take Malcolm's place on the council."

Laughing, Bob said, "Yeah, I bet she did! She knows that he will be totally loyal to her if she gets him approved on the council."

"That's what I was thinking. But at the same time it would be a logical choice because Ed was the second in command of all of Malcolm Brown's moves in the Chi, Indiana, Milwaukee, and Minnesota."

"True. But you want and need more loyalty to you on the council, Taz. That would neutralize Saint Tramon and her allies on the council who are against you," said Tari.

"Yeah, dog, don't give that broad a chance to put another enemy in line against you on that damn council," said Red.

"Yeah, that makes no fucking sense, dog," said Wild Bill.

Nodding his head in agreement, Taz said, "Okay, I'm feeling y'all but the question remains, who do we get to replace Malcolm Brown?"

Tari smiled and said, "Give it some time. I'm sure we can think of something."

Taz smiled at her and asked, "What do you got going on in that blond head of yours, Tee?"

"I may be blond, baby, but there is nothing blond about my brain. It's time to remain ahead of the enemies, Taz, and I think I've come up with a way to push everything in our favor."

Taz stared at her as well as the rest of the crew waiting for her to continue.

"I think you should stall on making the announcement of the replacement for Malcolm Brown. At least for a little bit. Let Ed continue to run things out there and let Saint Tramon feel that Ed Polly will be the likely replacement."

"For how long?"

"Long enough for me to approach Damon and give him an offer that he would be a fool to turn down."

"Damon!" the entire crew yelled in unison.

Tari smiled and said, "Yes, Damon."

"Damon as in Saint Tramon's personal assistant Damon?" asked Taz.

"Mm-hmm. I got a feeling he would love to be appointed to the council of the Network and be pulled out from under Saint Tramon's thumb. And if things go as it looks, he will most likely be in charge of a lot more soil than just Chicago, Indiana, Milwaukee, and Minnesota."

"What makes you think he can be trusted if we approach him with this proposition of yours, Tee?" asked Bob.

She shrugged and said, "It's a hunch. My gut tells me we can make this move and then we will have the real upper hand over her ass. We will have an inside line on every move she makes. So when she gets too cute we'll slam her ass down before she can make any moves she intends to make against us. After that we reward Damon for his services for being the ultimate Benedict Arnold."

"Damn, you using your head for real, Tee," said Taz.

"I'm with it. That shit can work," said Wild Bill.

"I agree," said Bob.

"Me too," added Red.

Using the perfect blend of strategic vision along with his street smarts made Taz realize that Tari's idea was the best way to ensure his enemies' demise. Taz was ready to bring them down hard and this seemed like the best way to make it happen. "You're on point all the way here, Tee. Let's make it happen," Taz said and smiled at the crew. *Let the games begin!*

# Chapter Twenty-eight

Malcolm Brown's funeral was fairly small attendance-wise. One would have thought he would have had a bigger turnout for his funeral since he had been looked upon as one of Chicago's elite in both the legal and the illegal businesses he had been involved in. Even though he was considered a ladies' man he didn't have any children and never married, so even the family turnout was minimal. A few local businessmen along with several representatives of the biggest gangs in the Chicago area were there as was the entire council of the Network. They came to pay their last respects to the fallen member of the Network.

Outside of the church after the funeral was over Taz stood with his crew tightly around him. Ed Polly did a good job with his security and that showed Taz that he was on point and capable of making wise decisions. Taz thought that he might just agree to let Ed become a member of the council. He decided right then that an impromptu meeting of the council was in order. He motioned for Ed to come to him. He then whispered his plans in Tari's ear giving her instructions. After he was finished she stepped over to Bob and relayed what Taz told her.

When Ed was in front of Taz he asked, "Is everything all right, Taz?"

"Yeah, Ed, everything is cool, under the circumstances. You did your boss a good service here. Everything was well put together."

"Thanks, Taz. I still can't believe this happened. What's even more crazy is after eight days there's still no word on the streets who did this to Malcolm. Makes me think this was a professional hit all the way."

Taz nodded but didn't speak for a few seconds and then said, "I think we need to have a sit-down, Ed, and I need you to set it up for me."

"No problem, Taz, all you have to do is tell me when and where."

"ASAP, like within a couple of hours at my suite at the Waldorf Astoria. I want you to get with the council members over there and inform them of this meeting and let them know that I expect all of them to be at my suite so we can have this quick get-together. If they ask why let them know I said there's certain issues that I need to address and leave it at that. Can you handle that for me, Ed?"

"I'm all over it, Taz. Am I to join you guys for this meeting?" Ed asked hopefully.

"Since a part of this meeting will concern whether or not you're going to be appointed to the council I think you should be there, so yeah, I want you to join us, Ed. Let me tell you something: I know you've been loyal to Malcolm Brown for over a decade and I have heard nothing but honorable things about you and how you get down. Since this tragedy Jay Bogard has assured me you've been nothing less than stellar in all areas and that has gained you favor with the council. Malcolm Brown and I were not on the same side of things when it came to the business of the Network. He challenged me on every single move I ever made. I'm sure you know this. What I want to know is, if I give the final stamp of approval on your appointment to the council where will your loyalties lie? Will you follow your predecessor and be against me or will you align your loyalty with me?" Taz stared at him with that faintly mocking smile on his face and waited patiently for his answer.

Ed Polly had waited years for an opportunity like this and now that it had presented itself there was no way he was going to blow it. He returned Taz's stare for a moment and spoke honestly. "Taz, I'm my own man, always have been and always will be. Malcolm and I went back to when we were both heavy in the streets. When he asked me to become his right-hand man I jumped on the opportunity because I knew he was plugged with the Network from his uncle. He had the aspirations of some day being the top dog of the Network; that's why I feel he was always on the opposite side of things with you so much. He respected you and, honestly, he feared you, Taz. He saw something ferocious in you that made him uneasy. I have watched from the sidelines and saw how you made all the right moves as far as the business is concerned and it is proven from this latest move you made that you are one hell of a leader. I would have no problem at all being one hundred percent loyal to you if given the opportunity to become a member of the Network's council. To show my loyalty is real. I have already been approached by Saint Tramon; she all but guaranteed me that I would become a council member as long as I was true to her, Chill Will, and Piper Dixon."

Taz laughed and said, "I figured that; that's how she rocks. The thing is I am the one with the final say, always. My word counts the most. It's not that I need another council member on my side because my say is final regardless. As I stated you have received stellar reports and I feel you're worthy. By hearing you are willing to be loyal to me as well as the Network I am going to stamp you. If you ever disappoint me, Ed, I'll know that you played me on this day; then I'll know your word ain't shit."

"I don't play games, Taz; my word is my word. I stand on it at all times."

"That's right. Set this meeting up for me so we can get this out of the way and I can be out of here by this evening.'

"I'm on it." Ed shook hands with Taz and stepped quickly to Saint Tramon who was busy holding conversations with Chill Will, Piper Dixon, and Chinaman, and let them know about the meeting that Taz wanted to have at his hotel suite at the Waldorf Astoria. Taz watched as Bob spoke quietly to Snack and Jay Bogard. Tari had already spoken to G.R. and Snuffy so everyone knew that there was going to be a meeting. Boy, were they all about to be surprised, Taz thought as he stepped toward the limousine Ed arranged for his transportation while in Chicago.


Two hours after leaving Malcolm Brown's funeral service Taz and the crew minus Tari were all inside of Taz's suite along with every member of the council of the Network. With drink in hand Taz stood and stared at everyone to get their attention. Once everyone was silent he began. "Thank you for joining me for this impromptu meeting of sorts. I originally wanted to save this for next month for our quarterly meeting but I decided that now would be a good time to put certain things in order before then. We have a lot to discuss but for now I want to address a few issues that I feel should be brought to your attention. The first order of business is replacing Malcolm Brown on the council. Does any of you have an issue with Ed Polly here becoming Malcolm Brown's replacement? If so please speak now."

The room remained silent.

"It's agreed then: Ed Polly will be the new council member of the Network and take full control of the Network's responsibilities in Chicago, Milwaukee, and Minnesota." Taz turned and faced Ed Polly and raised his drink in the air for a toast. "Welcome aboard, Ed. Cheers!"

Everyone inside of the suite who had a drink in their hand followed Taz and said, "Cheers!"

"The more formal rituals that need to be done will be taken care of next month at our quarterly meeting. You have the reins now, Ed, don't disappoint us."

"I won't, Taz. Thank you and the rest of the council for making me a member of this organization. I am grateful."

Taz gave a nod and then continued, "Now, to other matters of importance. The murder of Malcolm Brown needs to be addressed."

"Yes, it does. We need to find out who ordered that hit and deal with him pronto. This shit cannot go without being addressed properly or we'll look weak as fuck," said Chill Will with serious emotion in his voice.

Taz was staring directly at Saint Tramon when he said, "I agree, Chill Will. When we find out who the person or persons are who had this done they will be dealt with." Without taking his eyes from Saint Tramon he continued. "As you know before I made the moves to put our arms dealing officially in place I went and had meetings with Jorge Santa Cruz of Colombia, Mr. Suarez of Miami, and Danny Orumutto in California. Two of the three men agreed to do business with us with the arms dealing and accepted that we were pulling out of the drug distribution business. Danny Orumutto was the only man who was disgruntled with my decision."

"Are you saying that Danny Orumutto had Malcolm Brown killed, Taz?" asked Piper Dixon.

Without removing his eyes from Saint Tramon, he answered, "What I'm saying is that in my meeting with Mr. Suarez I learned that Malcolm Brown was a traitor to us and had committed treason against the Network. He had been giving information of the Network's business dealing to the Cuban drug lord for years."

"Come on, Taz, you can't slander Malcolm's name now that he is no longer here to defend himself. Let the man rest in peace will ya?" said Chill Will.

Before Taz could respond Ed Polly stood and asked Taz, "If I may speak?"

Taz shook his head yes, granting Ed's request.

"What Taz has said is true. I have been Malcolm's right hand for years and I knew that he was divulging certain information to Mr. Suarez in Miami. What I cannot tell you is why. He never revealed that to me. He did say that sooner or later his time to run the Network would come and that's all he cared about."

"Thank you, Ed," Taz said. "It's simple: Malcolm Brown was a traitor to all of us. He wanted so badly to get the top spot that he betrayed the oath we all took as members of the Network. What's done is done. It's not like we can punish him for his wrongs against us. But, I want to take this time to let each of you know that the punishment for treason within the Network is death. A very painful death. I will not tolerate being belittled by our peers because someone within our very own ranks has chosen for selfish reasons to betray us. I know I may not be well liked by some of you here and that's fine. I told each of you when we first met six years ago that I'm not here to be liked but I am here to be respected. I want the Network to remain a powerful organization as well as a force to be reckoned with for many years in every aspect so that our peers will know that we're not to be challenged in any way, shape, or form. How can we be respected as well as feared if we have shit like what Malcolm Brown did continuing? We can't," Taz said answering his own question.

"The weak shit has to stop and I mean stop now. As you can see by the moves being made in the last month we have made more money in thirty days of arms dealing than we would have made in six months of distributing drugs. I've spoken to Akim and have been assured that it's only going to get better. So as long as everyone continues to do their part this will only gain us more and more money."

Though he was on the record as not being a Taz fan Chill Will spoke honestly. "I understand everything you have said and I agree with you on all accounts, Taz. Malcolm Brown broke the oath and if he was alive I'd kill the bastard myself for his crimes against us. We may not agree on things but we all have the same common goal and that's to handle the Network's business to the best of our ability. I was not with the drug dealing business being shut down at all, but I have to admit that the moves being made with the guns and shit is looking like one hell of an idea. I have one question and that is do you feel anyone else on this council has betrayed the Network in any way?"

Taz stared at Saint Tramon, smiled, and said, "If I did, that business would be handled by me personally. On my flight here I received a call from Danny Orumutto and it ended with me telling him to make his next move be his best move. I feel he had something to do with Malcolm Brown's murder but I have no proof to answer your question from earlier, Piper."

"Understood," she replied.

"I do have a lot of suspicions and I am in the process of checking into them as we speak. By this time next month I should have the answers I'm looking for and then everything will be addressed accordingly."

Saint Tramon smiled at Taz and said, "I for one cannot wait to find out your findings on all of this business. It seems very intriguing, and at the same time sad because this organization was built on loyalty and for that loyalty to be tainted is wrong, totally wrong."

Taz stared at her with laughter in his eyes and said, "I couldn't agree with you more, Saint Tramon."

"Was there something humorous in what I just said, Taz?"

Taz was tired of the games. It was not time to reveal his hand, but he felt he could give just a little bit. "What I find amusing is you and your nonchalance to the matters at hand. You either think you're super intelligent or I'm an absolute idiot. Either way the games are about to come to an end. I have my suspicions about you on several issues and if any of them become factual your days as being a part of the Network will come to an abrupt end."

"Threats are a waste of time, young man. Especially silly threats without any facts behind them."

"Because I haven't spoken on my suspicions doesn't mean I don't have the facts to support them. I don't have the facts needed to bring to the table against you. But I will tell you what my gut is telling me. You're in bed with Danny Orumutto. You want to continue the drug business and either become the top dog of the Network or place someone in charge who you will be able to have influence over."

Laughing, Saint Tramon said, "You are out of your mind and I should be insulted by this but it's so absurd that I can't be offended by any of it. I'm making just as much as everyone else on your arms dealing business. I spoke on behalf of the changes in the last meeting and this is how you repay me for my loyalty? Everyone inside of this room knows I am not a fan of yours but for you to form these types of conspiracy theories against me because of some of my past grievances against you, Taz, is flat out wrong."

"Noted. Trust and believe if I am proved wrong I will give you my most sincere apology in front of every man and woman here today. But if my suspicions or as you said, conspiracy theories, are proven correct then it's like I said: your days will be over with the Network."

Piper cleared her throat and said, "I have a question, Taz: why didn't you expose Malcolm Brown to us when you first found out about his treason?"

Taz stared at Saint Tramon as he spoke. "For a couple of reasons. One, because I wanted him to continue to feed information to Mr. Suarez in hopes that he would be able to tell me via Mr. Suarez some plots being planned against me. What better way to do that than to keep my knowledge of his treason to myself for the time being? I don't expose my hand totally until I'm ready to make a point or a very strong move. And, second, I was waiting so I could bring everything to an end all at once. This infighting is a waste of time and will only serve to cost us time and money. I don't have time for any losses so it's time to tighten everything up and move forward one way or the other."

"By telling Danny Orumutto to make his next move his best move you've basically called him out for a war. War is never good for business," Chinaman said seriously.

"I agree. Before I let that man get in the way of our money I will do what needs to be done. Trust me if a war is what he wants I'll give him that and some and my word it won't last long at all."

"Don't we have a say-so in this decision, Taz? Or is this all about how you rocking now?" asked Snack.

"Yeah, my brother, it seems as of lately you have been making all of the decisions and we have little or no input in anything," said G.R. "It's on record how I get down. I support you fully. At the same time we need to be on the same accord on all facets of this business. A war involves us all as well as our well-being. You must consult with us before making strong moves like that, Taz."

Not wanting to offend any of his supporters on the council Taz gave a nod to G.R. and said, "I apologize for my brashness but I let him get under my skin because no man can challenge me without me stepping to the plate and face that challenge head-on. You're right, G.R., and that will not happen again. My word. This business isn't about me and what I want. It's about all of us and the better good of the Network for the long run. I apologize to every member in this room for my over aggressiveness of late. But I must stand on what I have said about treason being committed against me or the Network. Cross either and you die."

While Taz was busy with his impromptu meeting with the council Tari was downstairs at the bar having a drink with Damon, Saint Tramon's personal assistant. Taz had been right on the money when he told Tari that odds would be high that Damon would be downstairs waiting for Saint Tramon to finish up with the meeting since she rarely went anywhere without Damon being close by.

Tari, looking good as always, knew she would be able to work Damon as soon as she stepped into the restaurant and headed toward the bar. His eyes bulged as he watched as she approached him. She was an intoxicating combination of simple and stunning at the same time with her long blond hair hanging freely past her shoulders and her sparkling blue eyes complementing her Amazon-like features perfectly. This is going to be too easy. She was ready to work him whichever way she had to but for some reason her gut told her that the direct approach would be best. If she had to get extra with it and use what God blessed her with she would. Shit, it had been a real long time since she had some anyway, she thought as she sat down at the bar next to Damon and smiled.

"Mind if I join you?"

"Sure, especially since I don't have a clue as to how long I'll be here. Do you have any idea what that meeting is for?"

Shaking her head no, Tari said, "Just as clueless as you are, buddy. Damon right?"

"Yeah. Tari?"

"Yep. So tell me, Damon, what are you drinking there? Looks pretty good."

"Just a margarita with Patrón. Have one?"

"Sure."

Damon waved the bartender over and pointed toward his drink and held up a finger signaling for another drink and then turned on his stool and asked, "Would you be offended if I asked were you single?"

Laughing, Tari answered, "Not at all."

Smiling, he asked, "Are you?"

"Yes."

"Mmm."

"What does mmm mean?"

"Means I'm interested in getting to know you better. What are the chances of that happening?"

She smiled sweetly at him and said, "You got a six-ty-forty shot."

"I like those kinds of odds; at least they're in my favor."

"Well, let's see what you can do to impress me to raise those odds even higher in your favor," Tari flirted as she accepted the drink from the bartender and raised it in a toast with Damon. After they clinked glasses and each sipped their drinks Tari asked him, "So, tell me, how long have you been working for Saint Tramon?"

# Chapter Twenty-nine

In Oklahoma City Lyla was at home busy getting herself organized. Even though it had been almost three months now she had finally gotten all of her stuff moved into her new home with Tazneema. Now that she was situated she felt like Keno's home was really theirs and that felt good.

She saw a few small boxes that she'd forgotten to take and put up in the attic, so she grabbed them and headed to the attic. When she was inside of the attic she saw that she was going to have to do some rearranging in order to make some space for her stuff. She grabbed a couple of bigger boxes she had put there earlier and started to move them aside to make the space needed. After she had the space she needed she noticed a small DVD player plugged into a socket that she hadn't noticed when she brought her stuff up there before. Curious, she hit the eject button and watched as a DVD slid out of the DVD player.

*Now why would a DVD player be hooked up here in the attic?* she asked herself. She quickly grabbed the DVD out of the player, grabbed the boxes and arranged everything how she wanted. She left the attic so she could go see what was on the DVD she retrieved from the player. After taking a shower and getting herself fresh, Lyla sat in front of the TV in her bedroom. She inserted the DVD she found in the attic into her DVD player. She grabbed the remote, sat back on her bed and got ready to turn on the TV when her cell phone started to ring. She set the remote down and answered the phone.

After a steamy ten-minute conversation with a guy she had met at a club a few weeks back she got off the phone smiling and fanning herself with her right hand. She ran to her closet so she could pick something cute to wear on her dinner date. Her mind was so totally on choosing the perfect outfit and getting dressed that she forgot all about the DVD she was about to watch. She was more focused on the cute guy Kirk and hoping he would be worth her time. *I wonder if he's packing a big tool in them jeans,* she thought as she reached and grabbed a pretty pastel dress by Zuhair Murad and some Jimmy Choo heels she felt would complement her dress perfectly. The dress showed just enough leg and cleavage for her taste. *Yes, tonight is going to be a good night,* she said to herself and smiled.



Once everyone was on board of Taz's G5 and the captain told them that they were cleared for takeoff Taz asked Tari how things went with her and Damon.

"He's with it."

"Huh?" asked Wild Bill.

"Damn, Tee, what you do to that fool?" asked Red.

"Wait! I'm not sure we need to hear those details; you're like a sister to us!" joked Bob.

Frowning, Taz said, "I know you didn't go there with that fool, Tari."

"Calm down, you jerks. You are some of the dirtiest men I have ever met in my life! Ugh! If I would have had to fuck him to get that information and to get him on the team then I would have. It would have been strictly business, and I am with this business all the way. I'm all in just like y'all."

Each male member of the crew placed their right palm flat against their chest and gave her a nod of respect.

She continued. "But none of that was necessary. As I walked up to him something inside of me told me that I could get at him directly and he would be with it. Call it female intuition if you want, but I was right. After a few strawberry margaritas with Patrón we got to flirting back and forth, having a good time. I asked him was he happy working for Saint Tramon and he was like yes and no. He loves the money but he doesn't see himself doing this job for her for the rest of his life. That gave me the opening I was looking for and I got at him with the real. I asked him straight up how would he like a position on the council of the Network."

"What did that fool say?" asked Wild Bill.

"At first he just stared at me like I was stupid. Then he grinned and asked me was I playing with him. I told him what you said and that you were a man of your word. As long as he did what he was supposed to do then he would not only be appointed to the council, he would inherit all of Saint Tramon's territory. No one else could run it as good as he could since he knew all of the ins and outs by being Saint Tramon's longtime personal assistant. He sat there stunned and ran everything I told him through his head for a few minutes and then said he was with it."

Taz sat there for a moment and processed what Tari just told them and then said, "There's always a 'but.' What was his 'but,' Tee?"

She smiled and said, "Actually he has two 'buts.' The first is that he will not have to physically hurt Saint Tramon or anyone. I assured him that when it was time for any violence if there would be any he wouldn't be asked to participate physically. He was needed primarily for internal only."

"Very good, Tee, real damn good," said Bob.

"And the last 'but'?" asked Taz.

Laughing, she said, "He wants the opportunity to get with me. He figures if he's about to up his status to boss level he needs a gorgeous woman by his side." She shrugged and said, "His words not mine."

"Your answer to that was?" Taz asked with raised eyebrows.

Tari winked and answered, "That's between Damon and myself, big boy." Changing the subject she asked, "Now that we got him in our pocket what's your next move, Taz?"

Taz smiled and said, "My next move is my best move. We're about to bring closure to all of this nonsense. First I want you to get at Damon and get some confirmation on a few things for me. Is Saint Tramon linked up with Danny Orumutto? Did she have Malcolm Brown hit and why? What are her plans? Get me that info and then when we have the council meeting next month everything will be taken care of."

"Where are we having the meeting this time? I hope somewhere like Cabo or Jamaica. I'm trying to see some island life for a long week," said Wild Bill.

Shaking his head no, Taz said, "Sorry, my nigga, this is a simple one; we're playing this close to home this time."

"How close?" asked Red.

"The closest. We're having the next quarterly meeting here in the city. I'm going to reserve suites for the entire council at the Skirvin and we will have the meeting in a suite of our own. So once everything is everything we will be able to make our move and address the council with the facts necessary to terminate Saint Tramon's ass."

"The end game huh?" asked Bob.

Taz looked at each crew member and gave a nod of his head yes and said, "Exactly."

By the time Saint Tramon made it back to her hotel suite she was still fuming from Taz's direct threats to her. She couldn't believe that that young bastard had the audacity to come at her as if she was some petty underling from the streets. She was a respected leader in her own right and would be damned if she let that so-called leader get the best of her. She knew that she had to move fast because odds were he would get the information needed to move against her. *The fool, he actually gave me the time I need to have his ass dealt with first. That's the difference between a leader and a woman who knows how to lead. I give no warnings. I make the most aggressive moves needed in order to win,* she said to herself as she grabbed her cell and sent a text to Damon summoning him to her suite. Five minutes later Damon was standing in front of Saint Tramon awaiting her instructions.

"I need you to get in contact with Ninth Ward Twine. Have him meet us at the house tomorrow evening."

"Am I to give him any specifics, ma'am?"

"Yes, tell him what I have lined up for him will make him a half a million dollars."

Damon raised his eyebrows and asked, "Who's worth paying a half of a million dollars to eliminate, if you don't mind me asking, ma'am?"

She stared a Damon for a few seconds and then gave him a one-word answer. "Taz."

It was well after two in the morning when Lyla made it back home. She was exhausted and all she wanted to do was crawl into her bed and get some sleep. She never intended to spend the entire evening with Kirk, especially when she knew she had to get up early for some deliveries that were due to arrive at the boutique at eight a.m. She went into the bathroom, removed her makeup, and smiled as she thought about how close she had come to giving in and letting Kirk have his way with her. She stood strong and resisted the temptation to have sex with him but chose to give him some mind-blowing head instead. He reciprocated the favor and it got really hot and heavy in there after her orgasm rocked her entire body. She didn't know where she found the resolve to make the decision to leave but she was glad she did it. *Give him something to look forward to. I'm sure he will be calling for another date real soon,* she thought as she went and sat on the bed.

She grabbed the remote control and turned on the TV and before going to bed decided to watch the DVD she found earlier in the attic. She pressed the play button on the remote and began to watch the DVD. She was confused because it looked as if she was watching the front of the house. Then her eyes grew wide when she saw Keno come into view and walk toward the front door. What she saw next made tears start falling from her eyes as she watched in horror as Sacha pulled a gun out of her purse and shot Keno in the back of his head. *Oh! My! God!*

# Chapter Thirty

Taz was lying down next to Sacha having some pillow talk after their lovemaking. He explained everything that went on in Chicago as well as what Tari accomplished with Damon. Sacha was amazed but not surprised because she knew Taz could outthink any of his peers when he was calm and thought things through. When he was angry he was prone to make mistakes because he would let his emotions get the best of him. That's really when she feared for him most, when he was emotional. The more calculated he was the more comfortable she felt everything would be okay. After hearing what he had just told her she knew that he was in total control and calculating his every step.

"When you are calm and thinking rationally you are better equipped to make the right decisions, baby. When you are caught up with emotions you tend to become more dangerous to yourself and everyone else around you. Looks like you're about to bring this to a close and things can get back to normal. We can go back home and get back to our daily routine."

"Yeah. But for real, I'm thinking about not going back west. Our home is here in the City. I like the Cali life and all but I'm an Oklahoma City man born and raised. What you think about us coming back, li'l mama?"

She smiled and gave him a kiss on the cheek. "Whatever you want is fine with me, baby. You know I go where my husband wants me to go."

"You know I love it when you roll with me without a fuss. Come here, let me give you some more of this thang for being such a good wife to me," he said as he pulled her into his arms. Just as their kiss went from tender to passionate they were interrupted by Taz's phone ringing. He pulled from Sacha and grabbed his phone because he knew it had to be important for someone to be calling him this late at night. He listened to Tari speak and sat up in the bed. When she finished he told her, "Okay, Tee, this is what I need you to do. Get confirmation on the things I asked on the plane."

"What, whether or not Saint Tramon had Malcolm hit?"

"Yeah. Also if she is linked with Danny Orumutto against me."

"Okay, I'll hit him right back now. But, Taz, did you hear what I just told you? Saint Tramon is going to order a hit on you and she's paying the assassin a half a million dollars. What are you going to do about that?"

Taz smiled into the receiver and said, "I'm not going to do nothing, Tee. Get me that info and get here with the rest of the crew around noon. We'll talk more then. Don't panic, snow bunny, everything is going to be all good. Out!"

She sighed into the receiver and said, "Yeah, out!"

Taz set his phone back onto the nightstand and grabbed his wife. "Looks like the silly broad is forcing my hand, li'l mama."

"Who, Saint Tramon?"

"Yep."

"Uh-oh, she's in big trouble now."

Taz smiled at his lovely wife, gave her a kiss, and said, "I couldn't have used better words. But right now the only one who's in bigger trouble is your fine ass. Bend over and gimme some of that Good good from the back, li'l mama."

"Ooooh, you know I like it when you give it to me like that, daddy," Sacha said as she turned and got onto her knees so her husband could give it to her just how he wanted to.


After Tari hung up with Taz she sent a text to Damon and told him she needed for him to confirm whether Saint Tramon was in cahoots with Danny Orumutto against Taz and if she had anything to do with what happened to Malcolm Brown in Chicago. His response to her text was for her to call him. She dialed his number wondering what she was about to be told. When Damon answered the phone he wasted no time with a greeting.

"Yes, to your questions. She has been hooked up with Danny Orumutto from the start of Taz's decisions to end the drug activity within the Network. She enjoys the profits she is seeing from the new adjustments Taz has made but she feels they should have never even thought about abandoning the former. She's a greedy woman, not only for the money but for the power as well. She hired the person responsible for the explosion in Chicago, too. That's the same person she is going to hire to take care of Taz. A problem arose though so all of that will have to wait because that particular person has informed me that he is out of commission for the next sixty days. He was in an accident and won't be available until he heals properly. She doesn't know this yet so I'm sure she's going to be extremely pissed off when I let her know."

"That's good, gives us time to make our counter move. You done good, babe. Keep it up and real soon you'll have all the power in the Bayou. You ready for that, sugar?"

Laughing, Damon said, "I've been ready for something like that my entire life. You know what else I'm ready for, sexy gorgeous?"

Tari smiled into the receiver because she had a feeling she knew what he was about to tell her. She played along and asked, "What's that, babe?"

"I'm ready to make that tall, sexy body of yours shake and tremble. I'm ready to have you all to myself so I can devour all of you."

"Mmmm, that sounds so sexy and turns me on, babe. But are you sure you can handle all of me? I'm a lot of gal." They both started laughing.

"This is true. I want every inch of you, sexy gorgeous. Honestly, I know you're not going to get at me like that, Tari, so don't tease a man of my intelligence. It's business and I respect that. I've done my homework and I know you are totally loyal to Taz. I respect that, too. You can't blame a man for trying though."

In a serious tone Tari told him the truth. "You're right, Damon; I am loyal to Taz and Taz only. But don't forget that Taz is a married man. I'm a grown woman who has needs and when I choose to have those needs met sexually Taz has nothing to do with that decision. Keep up the good work and you will be surprised what your rewards will be, other than being put in a position of power. Never say never, big boy." She hung up the phone with a smile on her face.

She then sent Taz a text telling him that everything was as he suspected and they would talk more in the morning. After that she set her phone down and wondered how all of this mess was going to play out. She sighed heavily, let her head fall back on her pillow and wished Won was there to deal with everything. She shook her head from side to side. *Won may not be here but Taz is and no matter what I will not lose faith in him,* she thought as she closed her eyes and tried to get some sleep.

Lyla couldn't sleep at all; she tossed and turned for the rest of the night. She was confused, scared, and frustrated. She didn't know what to do with the DVD she found in the attic. Should she tell Tazneema and give her the DVD? Or should she call the police and give it to them so they could arrest Sacha for the murder of Keno? Or should she tell Taz and let him deal with this crazy situation? She didn't know exactly what Taz was into but she'd been around the Good family long enough to know he was a boss and into something high powered on the not-so-legal side of things. She was no fool either; she would never do anything to upset Taz Good, so that meant not turning the DVD in to the police.

She sat at the island in the kitchen eating some oatmeal thinking about how no one ever heard from Cliff ever again and shuddered at that thought. Cross Taz and you disappeared forever. *What if I give Taz the DVD and Sacha disappears forever; would I be able to live with the fact that I assisted in something foul happening to her? Would Taz be so cold as to harm his wife and the mother of his sons? Oh,*

*God, help me,* she prayed silently as she stared into her bowl of oatmeal and swirled the spoon around inside of the bowl.

Tazneema came inside of the kitchen and went straight to the fridge and grabbed a bottle of orange juice. After taking a swig she sighed and said, "Ahhh, good juice. What's up, white girl, why you up this early in the morning?"

"Got some deliveries arriving at the boutique so I have to start my day way earlier than normal. What about you?"

"I have to go out to Bricktown and meet with the carpenters so we can get the ball rolling for the restaurant."

"Cool."

"Real cool, I'm so excited. I finally got all of the permits situated thanks to Taz's connections so everything is a go. We should be open by mid-July. Later on this week I'm going to start interviewing for the cooks and other staff. So I'm going to have my hands full for sure, but it's going to be fun, too."

Laughing, Lyla told her best friend, "Only Tazneema Good can find constant work fun. I wish I enjoyed my work as much as you do."

"Stop it. You know you love owning your boutique and all of the challenges that come along with it."

"True, I love what I do but that doesn't mean it's fun. I'd rather be doing something fun for real. Like you know, flying to an island and having hot sex with a stud on the beach."

"Sex. Sex. Sex. You always have to have sex on the brain. You are too crazy, white girl."

"Maybe I am." Changing the subject Lyla asked, "Can I ask you a question without sounding as if I'm prying in your personal business?"

Laughing, Neema said, "Now when was the last time you asked to pry in my personal business? That's too damn funny. Ask away."

"Whatever happened to Cliff? I know you said something to the effect like he would never come around you again but that was so vague. Where did he go?"

Tazneema stared at her friend for a few seconds and then answered her honestly. "I don't know where he went and I don't care. I do know that he will never bother me or come around me again."

"'Cause Taz made sure of that?"

After taking another swig from her bottle of orange juice Neema had a frown on her face when she asked Lyla, "What has you on this Cliff stuff? What's wrong, girl?"

Knowing that she wouldn't be able to hide anything from Neema she took a deep breath and said, "Remember when I overheard that phone conversation Cliff had when he was in the bathroom of our apartment?"

"Yeah, thanks to you I found out what a lying bastard he was."

"Was? Don't you mean is?"

Neema rolled her eyes and sat down at the island next to Lyla and said, "Talk to me, Lyla. Something is obviously bothering you. You look real funny and you're scaring me, white girl."

"I have tried to forget about Cliff and leave all of that in the past because I felt that if I said anything about him I would upset you or Taz and that's the last thing I would ever want to do. But I can't help but wonder what happened to him. I know Taz is heavy into some things; what things I don't know and you know I don't want to know. Your dad is not to be messed with, that I do know."

"You are like really confusing me here. What does Taz being into some heavy stuff have to do with you Lyla? Has someone said something to you about Taz? Has someone tried to threaten you? If so tell me so I can tell Taz and he will take care of it. Don't be afraid. Taz loves you girl and he would never let anything happen to you."

Shaking her head furiously, Lyla said, "No, nothing like that has happened, Neema, honest."

"Something has happened and you need to tell me, Lyla. Now."

"I can't tell you, Neema, because putting what I found into words seems like the most difficult thing in the world for me to do. I can show you. Come on," she said as she led her best friend upstairs to her bedroom where the DVD she found in the attic was still inside of the DVD player in her bedroom.

# Chapter Thirty-one

Saint Tramon was highly upset when Damon informed her that Ninth Ward Twine was laid up hurt and therefore not available for the task she needed him to complete. There were plenty of other hired guns she could summons but she wanted the best to take care of Taz and in her eyes Ninth Ward Twine was the best. Frustrated and dejected she gave Damon a nod and said, "Okay, we wait. It's not like Taz will be able to find anything concrete against me so time isn't a major concern of mine."

"I thought you wanted to get this out of the way as soon as possible so you could move forward with your plans, ma'am," said Damon showing concern as only a loyal assistant would. At least that's how he hoped he was coming across to his employer.

"That was the plan but this accident with Twine has set me back. Still everything will work out in my favor because before the summer begins Taz will no longer be in my way. I need to figure out who we will appoint as our next leader. The Network needs a person who knows not only how to lead but to make the hard decisions. Decisions that will continue to push us forward for many decades to come."

"Why not yourself? You have the vision as well as the leadership skills. You would be perfect to lead the Network."

She smiled at Damon and said, "This may be true but that is something I've never wanted. I prefer to assist and remain in my current position. I can't really explain it but I just don't care to be the top person. Malcolm Brown was my first choice but since his obvious disappointments he had to be discarded. Stupid ass. Chill Will is too emotional. Any of the others are too Taz-like for me and I will definitely not support anyone who supported Taz."

"That leaves just one person."

"Yes, it does. A woman. Piper Dixon. But I wonder if she is really ready for something like becoming the leader of the Network. Not only that, but the first female leader of any organized criminal enterprise. Mmmm, interesting. This is something I have to think about." As she sat deep in thought about this her cell phone started ringing and snapped her from her thinking. She grabbed her phone and saw that it was Danny Orumutto.

She answered the phone by asking a question. "Can you please tell me when you're going to handle the situation with Taz in Oklahoma City? I feel it's way past time. In fact if my people would have been operational I would have put this in motion by now. Since that's out can you handle this shit please? Taz has been on my ass and actually feels he will soon have enough evidence against me to be able to present it to the council and move against me with their blessings."

"Calm down. That prick is not as tough as he thinks he is. His days are numbered. I have people in place right now waiting for the right opportunity to do what they do. Taz is not stupid by a long shot and I don't want to tip my hand by making a move without it being on target all the way. I miss, then the war begins and the losses will be heavy on both sides. That's not good for business because then the Russians, Cubans, and Colombians will be pissed and shit will get really thick."

"When you hit him they will still be pissed so what's going to stop them from acting a damn fool then?"

Danny smiled into the receiver and said, "Me. I'll agree to take Taz's spot with the arms dealing shit at a much lower percentage. Those greedy fools only care about the dollar and when they see they can keep everything going and save more money then it will be easy for them to forget the former leader of the Network."

"I like."

"I figured you would. Like I said, calm down and let me handle this. Taz told me to make my next move my best move and that's exactly what I intend on doing. When my people feel they have the best angle they will get at him hard and that will be that. The end of Taz."

"You make it sound so simple that I have no other choice but to trust you on this and see how it all turns out."

"That's all you need to do, Saint Tramon. Go get one of your young bucks and do whatever it is you cougars do!" Danny Orumutto said and hung up the phone laughing.

As soon as he ended the call he received a phone call from a longtime friend he hadn't heard from in quite some time. Danny smiled as he answered the call. "Well I'll be damned, the one and only Siggy Loko. What in the hell have you been up to, my man?"

"Same old same old, Danny boy, working and enjoying life as a free and legal man."

"That's what's up. So, how's the family and all your damn kids?"

"Great. All of them getting bigger and bigger every day trying their best to drive me crazy. Got to love them though."

"And your man Squid, what is his crazy ass up to?"

"He's good too. As a matter a fact he's sitting right across from me right now. He's the reason why I made this call. Word got to him from the street's grapevine that you're into some heavy shit and from what the streets are saying a war is slowly brewing with your organization and the Network. What's up with that, Danny?" Siggy asked with genuine concern in his voice.

"Nothing to it, Siggy. You know how it goes; sometimes beef can't be avoided."

"True. But real men can do real shit and make certain compromises for the better of their business. Ain't no weakness in compromise, Danny. I don't know that dude Taz, but from what I've heard he's a fair type of nigga. You on the other hand I do know, and I know you can be one stubborn asshole when you want to be. Everything can't always go your way, Danny."

"This is true. But I cannot let people dictate my moves either. Got to stand for something or fall for anything, Siggy, you know that."

"So, what, the word on the streets is real?"

Laughing, Danny said, "You know damn well the word on the streets is always amped up more than what it really is."

"Come on with that bullshit, Danny. This is me you're talking to. You can't sell that weak shit to Siggy, dog. What's the real, beef or what?"

Sighing loudly, Danny answered his friend honestly, "Yeah, it's beef. But I'm handling it and everything will be all good in a minute."

"One thing I know about beef is the beef don't stop until somebody dies, dog."

"Exactly."

"We go back, Danny, and you already know I got mad love for you and yours. Watch yourself."

"Always. You never know, I might need you to knock the dust off and come out of retirement and bring your gangsta side back out to help me make it through this power move. Can I count on you if I need to, Siggy Loko?'

"I told you when I first came home years ago that my days in that life were done. I have six kids and a wife to look after, dog; that wild Wild West shit is over with. After Tanisha's death I vowed to make sure I'm here for mines and there's nothing in this world that can make me go against that vow. I know you, Danny, and I know how that devious mind of yours rocks. You got to have it all your way and sometimes that's not a good look, dog. Sit back and look at this beef from every angle and I'm sure you will see a way out of this without having to rock with a war. It won't show weakness; it will show smarts."

"You asking me to duck shit and ducking any beef does show weakness, Siggy. There is nothing weak about me or the Orumutto organization. I did what I had to do to get this far and I will continue to do what I need to do to further my business."

"Actually, I did what needed to be done for you to continue to do what you needed to do for your business. Don't forget that fact, Danny."

Thinking about how Siggy, along with some serious Samoan Bloods and his right-hand man Squid, had murdered his father and uncles in self-defense years ago to put Danny in his current position of power as the head of the infamous Orumutto crime family made Danny smile. "How could I ever forget what you did for me, Siggy? You know better than that. Don't you forget that I too played a key part in saving your ass."

Siggy sighed and said, "Don't make me have to choose between helping you and risking losing my family, Danny. That shit ain't cool at all, dog."

Laughing, Danny said, "Same old emotional-ass Siggy Loko. Don't worry I'm good. Glad to know you still got my back though. I give you my word: I won't call unless I have absolutely no other choice. Cool?"

"Whatever."

"Give my love to the wife, the kids, and all your other baby mamas!" Danny said and hung up the phone laughing.

# Chapter Thirty-two

Taz and the crew met at his house for a workout down in his personal gym. After they were finished working out they each stripped down to their shorts and went for a swim in Taz's Olympic-sized swimming pool. Tari, clad in her sports bra and panties, brought a bunch of obscene remarks from the crew as she stepped into the pool. She politely gave each one of them the finger and began to swim her laps. Each member of the crew swam fifty laps in under twenty-five minutes. Taz stressed to them that they had to get themselves back into the best shape because they'd gotten somewhat lazy and now was a time to be fit and on point at all times. He knew that something was coming and he wanted to be prepared for whatever came their way. While relaxing in the shallow end of the pool Taz called for his beloved and well-trained Dobermans, Precious and Heaven, to come and join them in the pool for a swim. He wanted his dogs to be fit and prepared as well.

"Precious! Heaven! Come swim!" he commanded and smiled as he watched as his dogs without any hesitation whatsoever ran and jumped right into the pool and began swimming laps as they had just watched their master do.

"I don't care how long it's been every time I see those damn dogs do shit like that it amazes the hell out of me," said Bob.

"Real spill. Them dogs are getting old but they seem to be even stronger the older they become," said Wild Bill.

"That's because they've received the right amount of love and care along with the proper diet and exercise. They'll be with us longer than any other well-trained dogs that's for sure," said Tari.

"I want to be in defense mode all the way whenever we move about the city. We know Saint Tramon's move against me has been stalled but that doesn't mean that bitch chink Danny might not go with his move. I feel in my heart he knows if he moves on me he has to move on all of us 'cause he knows y'all will bring everything we have at his ass if he gets at me successfully. So remember we move in sets of twos or more. Take nothing for granted and make sure we stay in contact with each other so everyone will know where everyone is at all times. Understood?" asked Taz.

Each crew member shook their heads yes.

"When are we going on the offense, Taz? This shit is fucking with me, dog," said Wild Bill.

"I'm getting at Akim later on and I'm going to let him, along with Mr. Suarez and Jorge Santa Cruz, know that it's been confirmed about Saint Tramon and she is out of there. Once that happens I'm sending a monster hit team at Danny Orumutto to end his existence. This will not be a prolonged war. When we move we will move hard and end this shit."

Smiling, Red said, "When you say monster hit team at the chink I know you aren't talking about hiring guns to handle this business, dog."

Returning his longtime friend's smile Taz said, "You know better than that, Red."

"Yeah, fool, that monster hit team is us. Who else can get the job done better than this crew?" Bob said with a smile on his face.

"Oh, God, why did I have to walk in here at this time and hear this conversation?" Sacha said as she stepped to where Taz was leaning against the side of the pool.

"What's good, li'l mama?" asked Taz as he turned and looked up toward his wife.

"Nothing much. Just got back from the office from going over your little spending spree."

Taz groaned and said, "Come on, li'l mama, miss me with the trivial stuff. We got heavier stuff on the plate right now."

"I know. But you do know you owe us girls something real fly and we expect to collect, Mr. Taz. That's me, Tari, and Charlene!"

Laughing, Tari said, "That's right!"

"On the business side of things I made the reservations for the council meeting so everything is set for the Skirvin downtown. Nine of their best suites are reserved for the weekend after next for the meeting. I also reserved their largest conference room for the actual meeting to be held."

"That's cool. Have you sent texts to the council members informing them of this?"

"No. I was going to make sure you approved of everything before I sent out the texts."

"All right, go on and send those texts. Everything is good, li'l mama, thanks."

Noticing how short he was being with her told her that there was more dangerous talk to be discussed among the crew and even though she knew most of what was going on she really didn't care to hear what needed to be discussed. "Okay, after you guys finish do you want to ride out to Mama-Mama's with me to pick up the twins?"

"Yeah, that's cool. Give me about an hour and I'll be ready."

Sacha knelt and gave him a kiss on the top of his head and said, "Okay, baby. See y'all later."

As soon as Sacha left Bob said, "Are we going to hit Saint Tramon before or after the meeting, dog?"

"After. I want to see her face when we expose her to the council. Plus, I want to make a point to each member who opposes me on the council. Cross me or the council and death is the punishment."

"Who gets the privilege of doing that old cougar bitch?" asked Wild Bill.

Taz smiled and turned toward Tari who was playing with Precious and Heaven who had swam to the shallow end of the pool after swimming thirty laps. Tari looked at Taz and returned her smile. "My pleasure. Tell me when and how you want it done, Taz, and the old bitch is history," Tari said and continued playing with the Dobermans as if what he wanted done was no problem at all. Murder was nothing to any of the members of the crew. If they had to do it they did it; it was as simple as that. Nothing and no one would ever get in their way without getting dealt with accordingly.

Tazneema sat on Lyla's bed with a shocked expression on her face. She couldn't believe what she had just seen. She sat there numb as she let what she saw on the DVD register inside of her mind. Sacha murdered her uncle

Keno! *Why? Why?* was the question that kept running through her mind over and over. *Oh my God! How do I tell Taz this?* Her heart began to beat so fast that she began to take deep breaths to try and calm herself down. Lyla saw this and gently started rubbing Tazneema's back.

"Now you see why I was tripping out, Neema? This is the absolute worst thing I could have ever stumbled across. What are we going to do?"

"Play it again, Lyla." As Lyla replayed the DVD Neema watched in horror as her stepmother shot her uncle Keno in the back of his head twice in cold blood. The shock she had now was slowly turning into anger. The look of no remorse or fear on Sacha's face was starting to piss Neema off. But just as her anger was consuming her, her confusion took more of a grip on her mind. "Why? Why would Sacha do that to my uncle Keno?" Neema asked aloud.

"That's the same thing I was wondering. I mean this is like totally baffling, Neema. What scares me is what will Taz do when he finds out what Sacha did to your uncle? Do you think he will hurt his own wife? Doing whatever he did to Cliff is one thing, but could he be that cold and hurt the woman who shares his bed, the mother of his sons?"

Tazneema stared at her best friend for full minute before speaking and then shook her head for a moment as if deciding that what she was about to do was the right thing to tell her best friend. She took a deep breath and said, "What I'm about to tell you is to never be repeated. Lyla. Never. Promise me that you will take this to your grave with you."

"You know whatever you tell me in confidence will die with me, Neema. I promise I will never repeat what you're about to tell me."

"My daddy didn't do anything to Cliff. I did. I shot Cliff several times and took his life. All Taz did was dispose of Cliff's body. Where, I never asked, and to this very day I don't know nor do I care to know." Tazneema saw the shocked expression on Lyla's face and knew that she had to break it all down to her, so she went back six years and told her best friend everything that took place with her and Cliff and how she ended up taking his life at Mama-Mama's house in the country.

When she finished she didn't even realize that tears were sliding down her face. "See, that's why it's been so hard for me to move on and be with another man. I just don't trust my judgment when it comes to men. But shit, that's nothing. That problem of mines is so minute compared to the problem I have in front of me right now. Taz was so mad at me back when he felt I was going against the grain that he actually made me feel as if he would hurt me. And if he was capable of hurting me then there's not a doubt in my mind what he would do to Sacha when he sees that DVD."

"Then we can't let him see this, Neema. We either destroy it and keep this between us or we take it to the police and let them handle it the legal way."

Shaking her head furiously, Tazneema said, "There is no way we're even considering the police, Lyla, so dead that. We don't do that in my family that is for certain. It would be wrong to hold this from my father and my uncles; they deserve closure. We cannot let Sacha get away with what she did to my uncle Keno."

"So you are going to tell Taz?"

With her tears falling down her face faster than before she shook her head yes and said, "I don't have any other choice. I promised my daddy I'd never go against the grain ever again. I have to tell him. I have to give my daddy the news that will most likely break his heart. And the mere thought of that happening is tearing me apart right now. Damn."

# Chapter Thirty-three

Danny Orumutto was sitting inside of his office thinking about what his longtime friend had told him about war. War was never good for business and he knew a war with Taz could cost him more than he really cared to lose. But fuck that; there was nothing weak about him and sometimes war had to happen just to establish strength of position. To let the other players in the game know who had the strength as well as the courage to wage war on anyone they deemed necessary. Whether right or wrong it's about standing on one's principles. Taz was taking money out of his pockets and no one did that without being looked at. *Fuck Taz,* he said to himself as he sat back on his deck and smiled. Danny Orumutto didn't know if it was luck, fate, or a sign from the gods but just as he became comfortable with his decision to go to war with Taz he received a call from the man he had in place to kill Taz in Oklahoma City.

"Talk to me, Kal."

"I know you told me to take the best opportunity to get at Taz when he is with his crew but right now he is headed out toward the country, I think toward his mother's home, and we're on his ass at a safe distance. We can speed up and hit him now and be able to make a clean getaway since we're so way out of the city limits. Shall we move on him or wait until his crew is with him, Mr. Orumutto?"

"Who's with him now?"

"His wife."

Danny Orumutto sat back in his seat and thought about the decision before him for a moment and then said, "Fuck it, hit him. Hit his ass with all you got and make sure they both die, Kal. After that get shaded and wait for the next opportunity to hit his crew. That should be very soon. The sooner the better, Kal."

"Yes, sir."

"Kal."

"Sir?"

"You and Karlo are being well paid for this hit. Don't. Fucking. Miss."

"We won't, sir," Kal said and hung up the phone. He then gave a nod to his brother and said, "Speed up. We're green to get at his ass; they both die."

Karlo didn't say a word as he punched his right foot hard on the accelerator in pursuit of Taz and Sacha. He was so focused on catching up to Taz that neither he nor Kal paid any attention to the black Dodge Challenger that was following them.

Both of the highly trained Spetsnaz who were assigned to watch over Taz and his family realized at once that the dark gray SUV that was following Taz was now in pursuit. Without any hesitation Major Kuznetsov picked up his cell and called Akim in Russia to let him know that an assassination attempt was about to be made on their primary. When Akim answered the phone Major Kuznetsov spoke in rapid Russian giving his employer the details as he saw them.

"You're in place to stop this attempt, Major?" asked Akim.

"*Da.*"

"Are the other teams there to assist?"

"*Nyet.*"

"Get the support needed and do what needs to be done. Keep me informed," Akim said as he hung up the phone and quickly dialed Taz's cell. As soon as Taz answered the phone Akim started speaking to him extremely fast in Russian without realizing he was speaking to Taz in his native tongue until Taz screamed at him to calm down and speak English. "Shit, sorry, Taz. Listen to me and do not ask any questions, my friend. An attempt on your life is about to take place within the next few minutes. Check your rearview and you should see a dark gray SUV closing in on you."

Taz checked his rearview and saw that Akim was right and thought, *how the fuck did Akim know this shit?* To Akim he said, "Yeah, you right. I see them. What the fuck?"

"Remain calm and listen, my friend. Not too far behind the SUV is help for you. I still left two teams in place for just this type of situation. Major Kuznetsov and Lieutenant Kozlov are the team that's on point directly behind the SUV. Continue the route you are on; from what I have been told it's somewhat in a remote area and this will help assist my men by surprising these assassins who think they have the upper hand on you."

Checking his rearview and watching as the SUV slowly closed the gap between them Taz said, "Okay, I'm with that."

"You will have to do some excellent driving maneuvers, my friend, to keep them behind you a little longer and the rest will be handled."

"I got this, Akim. We'll talk later. I need to handle this shit. One thing I do need from you though."

"Speak."

"Tell your men to keep those bastards alive. I need them alive to make sure they were sent by Danny Orumutto."

"Understood, comrade, I'm making the call now," Akim said as he ended the call.

Sacha turned and faced her husband with fear all over her pretty features and asked, "What's going on, Taz?"

Taz shot a quick smiled at his wife and said, "Just about to have a little action, li'l mama. A hit team is behind us and they're about to try to make their move on us in a few minutes. But we're in the best position. Don't worry about a thang. We got the Russians on their bumper protecting our ass. Tighten up your seat belt, li'l mama; we about to turn it up a little bit," Taz said as he sped up. The powerful Bentley Azure lurched forward and easily pulled away from the SUV, which had gained ground on him. Taz was watching his rearview closely now and could vaguely see a black Dodge in back of the SUV; this brought a smile to his face. "Okay, suckers; here we go."

Since they were almost in the city of Spencer, which is considered the country, this would be the perfect spot for the assassins to make their move on Taz. Taz smiled because it was an even better spot for him and the Russians to twist this shit on they ass. Taz grabbed his phone and called Wild Bill and told him what was going on. "Get the crew and punch it out to Mama-Mama's, dog. This shit goes right then we're taking these muthafuckas and get some answers."

"We're on our way. Stay fucking safe, Taz!" screamed Wild Bill.

"You fucking right!" Taz said and hung up the phone. He then dialed his mother's number. When she answered the phone he tried his best to remain calm when he said, "Mama-Mama, I need a big favor from you okay?"

Knowing her son better than he thought she did Mama-Mama's trouble radar started going off like crazy when she asked, "What's wrong, Taz?"

With no time for a lie Taz quickly told her, "I need you and Mrs. Leslie to go over to the church for a little while. Or to Mrs. Leslie's house until I call you. Please don't ask me why, Mama-Mama; just do this for me, okay, and I'll explain everything within the hour."

Knowing that Taz would never ask this of her unless it was real important Mama-Mama wasted no time battling him on this. "Okay, we'll be out of here in the next five minutes, boy. But you will tell me everything that's going on, Taz Good," she said in a stern voice and hung up the phone. She then told Mrs. Leslie to grab the twins so they could go.

Taz was checking the rearview when he saw that the SUV was maybe twenty feet behind them and coming on strong. "Here we go, li'l mama!" Taz said as he slammed on the brakes hard, making the SUV swerve strongly to the other side of the street to avoid ramming into the back of Taz's Bentley. By the time the SUV stopped and the assassins were getting out of their vehicle the Dodge Challenger with the two Russian Spetsnaz agents inside pulled their car in front of Taz's car blocking and protecting Taz and Sacha from the assassins. Major Kuznetsov was the first out of the Dodge.

"Get down and stay down, comrade!" he screamed as he raised what looked like some kind of assault rifle and started firing fully automatic rounds at the assassins who were running toward them firing guns of their own. Not expecting to be fired upon by fully automatic weapons it caught them totally off-guard; each man was cut down immediately.

The gun battle was over before it ever really got started. The assassins never had a chance. The only reason why they were still alive was because Akim gave Major Kuznetsov a direct order not to kill them. Lieutenant Kozlov was by his comrade's side as they ran toward the assassins who were on the ground writhing in pain from their wounds to their legs and arms.

When Taz saw that they were good he got out of the car and ran toward the assassins as well. When he was standing in front of them he smiled and said, "Y'all fucked up. Y'all fucked up bad." He turned toward Major Kuznetsov and said, "No time for thanks; we need to move." They then scooped the assassins up and carried them toward their SUV.

Once they were inside Taz jumped in the driver's seat while the major kept his gun aimed at their captives. Sacha slid over to the driver's seat of the Bentley and quickly followed Taz as he drove toward Mama-Mama's house. Lieutenant Kozlov had a smile on his face as he followed Sacha because he knew they would be greatly rewarded by Akim for a job well done.

# Chapter Thirty-four

It had been well over forty-five minutes since he had heard from Kal and Karlo so Danny Orumutto was instantly worried. He sat back at his desk sipping a glass of wine as he stared at his phone trying to will it to ring with the news that Taz was no longer breathing. After fifteen minutes had passed he knew in his gut that something went terribly wrong. *Fuck!*

By the time Taz, Major Kuznetsov, and Lieutenant Kozlov had the assassins secured inside of the back room at Mama-Mama's house the rest of the crew arrived. Tari stepped straight to Taz and asked, "Are you okay?"

Taz was so angry that he could barely speak. He took a few deep breaths and said, "Yeah, I'm good, Tee. These punk-ass bitches tried to hit me with my li'l mama. They actually tried to kill me and my fucking wife!"

"Calm down, Taz. Please calm down, baby," Sacha said as she came to his side because she knew he was about to lose it totally.

Taz looked down at his gorgeous wife, the woman who gave him his two beautiful sons, and let a single tear drop. He quickly wiped his eye and regained his composure. "Take her home, Tee, and then get back out here as fast as you can."

The tone in his voice told Sacha not to say a word against his order to have her taken home. So she gave her man a kiss on the cheek and turned to follow Tari outside to her car.

Taz marched into the backroom where the assassins were tied up in some chairs facing each other bleeding profusely. Red, Wild Bill, and Bob stood next to the Russians and watched as their man handled their business. Each hoping that they would be the one to be able to put a bullet in the heads of the assassins.

"You already know you two are dead men so don't waste any of my time and I won't waste any time taking your life. It will be bang and it's over. If you try to be tough and protect the man I already know sent you then it's only going to cause you more pain. One question. Answer it and you die quickly. Lie to me or don't answer and you die slow. Real fucking slow. Who ordered this hit on me?"

Both assassins were in pain and both men knew that they were going to die. They knew that all they had working for them was the knowledge they possessed of who hired them to kill Taz. And each hoped that that knowledge could be used as a bargaining chip to save their lives. Kal spoke first. "Don't kill us, man. We were only doing a job. Don't kill us and we'll give you what you want as well as a whole lot more. We know things that you need to know, Taz. Let us make it and you get the upper hand on a lot of shit."

Feeling that his brother's play may just work Karlo quickly followed suit. "Yeah, Taz, we got all the inside information you need against your enemies. Let us make it and you will gain the advantage you need."

Taz stood there and stared at them as if he was really contemplating what they were saying for a few minutes and then said, "If you would have made a move on just me or my crew here I maybe could have given you the pass you are asking for. But you moved on me while my wife was with me. That shows me that you niggas don't deserve a pass."

Bob stepped up to Taz and winked. "Wait a minute, Taz. This may be the opportunity for us to not only find out who sent these fools but get an edge on whoever this is getting at us. We can't blow that chance, my nigga." Bob turned toward Kal and Karlo and asked, "What guarantee do we have that you will serve us the real about our enemies? You niggas could serve us some bullshit and then we would have to come and hunt y'all asses down. Tell me something to make me feel good about convincing my nigga here to give you fools a pass."

"Man, we got plenty of shit for you. We can prove whatever we tell you, too," said Karlo.

"But wouldn't we have to fly back to Cali to get that proof?"

"Yeah, but that's nothing; we know where everything is. Mr. Orumutto . . ." Kal caught himself but it was too late and he knew it. He had just killed himself along with his brother Karlo by slipping. Just like Bob figured one of them would.

Laughing, Bob said, "You two have to be some of the dumbest coward-ass niggas I have ever seen in my life. Thanks for saving us the time; we already knew that Danny Orumutto sent you dumb niggas and now you confirmed it."

Wild Bill gave a questioning look hoping he would give him the nod to murder their captives. Taz didn't disappoint his longtime friend. He gave Wild Bill as well as Red a slight nod of his head and turned and left the room followed by the Russians and Bob. Wild Bill and

Red each pulled out nine millimeter silenced pistols and shot both of the assassins twice in the head then turned and went and joined everyone else in the living room.

Taz pulled out his cell phone and made two calls; the first was to Akim in Russia. "Everything is everything, Akim. You know I should be pissed at you right?"

"Why, comrade, for adding extra security? I knew you would continue to be stubborn, that's why I made sure that you wouldn't be able to spot my men. They were good correct?"

Taz laughed as he stared at the two Russian Spetsnaz agents and said, "Yeah, they were all right."

"Did you get confirmation on who sent those men at you?"

"Yep."

"Danny Orumutto?"

"Yep."

"He dies?"

"Yep."

Taz hung up with Akim and called Bob to give him the run down.

"So what are we going to do with the bodies?" asked Bob.

"I can call my cousin who works for Temple & Sons and see if he can hook us up to use their crematory hookup and burn those bitch-ass niggas to ashes," said Red.

"Make the call and see if they can do us this service and make sure your cousin knows that he will be paid well for his time."

"I'm on it now."

"All right, let's get those fools wrapped up so I can call Mama-Mama so her and Mrs. Leslie can come back home." Taz's cell phone started ringing. He checked the caller ID and saw that it was Tazneema. "What up, Neema?" he asked when he answered the phone.

"We need to talk, Taz, you busy?"

"Very. Can this hold up for a couple of hours?"

It had been six years since the murder of her uncle Keno so she figured another couple of hours wouldn't hurt. Neema sighed and said, "That's fine. I'll check back with you later."

"Hey, what's this about, Neema? You sound funny. Talk to me, baby girl."

"Handle your business, Taz, we'll talk later," she said and hung up the phone and stared at Lyla.

"The quicker you do this the faster Taz will be able to deal with this mess, Neema."

"I know, white girl, I know. But what I don't know is how Taz is going to deal with this mess, and that right there scares the hell out of me. Fuck!"

# Chapter Thirty-five

Taz and Tari were at his house waiting for Bob, Red, and Wild Bill to return from getting rid of the assassins' bodies. Taz was on the phone talking to Mack in L.A. setting everything in motion for their trip back to the West Coast. Taz's mind was made up: they were flying out later in the evening and were going to move on Danny Orumutto within the next twenty-four hours. Taz was in no mood to discuss his decision. He felt that the longer he waited the more danger everyone would be in. It was time for Danny Orumutto to die.

After he finished his conversation with Mack he then called Captain Horne and informed him that his services along with the flight attendants' and his copilot were needed for a two-day trip to Los Angeles. He then told the captain the time frame he wanted for departure and Captain Horne assured him that everything would be arranged as he wanted and he would call him back when everything was in fact cleared.

Tari stared at Taz until he was finished with his call and then asked him, "Okay, you got Mack preparing for this shit on Danny Orumutto but how are we going to actually put this down, Taz? It's not like we have the element of surprise on our side here."

"Fuck the element of surprise, Tee. That bitch-ass chink tried to do me and my wife! I'm having Mack put men on that fool's house and sit on his every move until we arrive. Once we land we strap up and I send Mack and a team in to clear the way for us. We come in hard and handle our fucking business and that will be that."

Staring at Taz as if he'd lost his damn mind she said, "Taz Good, your ass has been watching way too much fucking television if you think we're going to be able to successfully run into that fool's well-guarded estate in the middle of the fucking city of Oxnard. Even if we did make it in and handle the business it's going to be hell to do this quietly enough to not draw attention and that will cause the police to join the party. What, we're going to shoot it out with them too? You need to come up with a better damn plan than that, mister, 'cause you trying to lead us straight into a fucking train wreck."

Knowing what she told him made perfect sense Taz went to his bar and poured himself a drink of XO. "Fuck, this chink has to die, Tee. We can't wait too long. If we do he'll make another move on us. I'm done with this passive shit; it's time to play offense and score the final touchdown and end this game."

She nodded her head in agreement and said, "I understand what you're saying, Taz, and you're right. But we have to make sure every move is thought out and not on no wild cowboy shit. We're not trying to lose anyone with this move and we're damn sure not trying to get caught! So you better come up with a detailed plan of attack other than running in there shooting up the entire fucking place."

"Actually that's a damn good plan if it's executed properly," Bob said as he entered the den followed by Red and Wild Bill. "We could hit that fool at his spot if we use the right amount of stealth and precision. Shit with all the weapons we got I'm sure we can blow that bitch up without making too much noise.'

"All right, let's come up with a sound plan to make it happen. We're flying out of here no later than eleven tonight," Taz said as he took a sip of his drink.

Tazneema sighed and checked her watch; it had been over three hours and she finally got up the nerve to call Taz back. When he answered the phone she took a deep breath and said, "Daddy, I need you to come to the house; we need to talk. Better yet I need to show you something and it's very important."

Taz checked the time and saw that it was close to six p.m. and he still hadn't told Sacha of his plans of flying to L.A. "All right, Neema. I'll be over there in like thirty minutes, cool?"

"That's fine just make sure that you come by yourself, Daddy."

That request seemed strange to Taz but he chose not to speak on it; instead he said, "All right, I'll see you in a little bit."

After she hung up the phone Neema sighed and told Lyla, "All right, white girl, he'll be here shortly so you need to scram. This is going to be one of the hardest things I've ever had to do and I know Taz is going to lose it. It's best that this happens in front of family only."

"Believe me I do understand. I'm sorry, Neema. I'm sorry I had to be the one who found that damn DVD."

"Everything happens for a reason. Everything in the dark comes to the light sooner or later, white girl. I just wished that those damn sayings wouldn't have come true in this case. Damn."


Sacha came home from Gwen's place with the twins just as Taz and the crew were leaving. After giving his sons a hug he told Sacha about their trip to Los Angeles to take care of some important business and she knew instantly what that important business would be. Murder. The murder of one Danny Orumutto to be exact. She sighed heavily but chose not to say one word about that. Instead she asked, "Since you're leaving later where are you going now? Can't we at least have dinner together before you leave?"

"Yes, we can. Go on and hook something up. I'm about to run over to Keno's, I mean Tazneema's, place real quick. She has something important she wants to talk to me about. I think she's found a male friend."

"What makes you think that?"

He shrugged and said, "She told me to make sure I came by myself, so that leads me to believe she wants to talk about something personal like that. I don't know, I could be wrong. Either way I'll be back within the hour so we can eat and chill before I meet the crew for our flight to the West."

"How many days will you be out there?"

"A couple tops."

"You want me to pack your bag for you while you're at Neema's?"

"Yeah, that's cool."

"Anything specific, baby?"

He stared at his wife and then said, "Yeah, li'l mama, all-black everything."

*Shit.*

When Taz pulled into the driveway of his best friend's home he instantly realized how much he missed Keno. He sighed as he got out of the car and walked toward the front door. Tazneema opened the door just as he was about to knock with a sad smile on her face. *What the hell is going on?* Taz thought as he followed her inside the house. After closing the door Taz asked his daughter, "What's wrong, Neema? You are starting to spook me."

Tazneema stopped in the hallway and pointed behind Taz up at a small vent and said, "I need you to stand on that chair and look at that vent up there for me, Daddy. After that I have something to show you." She stepped quickly into the dining room and brought back one of the dining room chairs and gave it to Taz.

Taz took the chair and set it against the wall, stepped on it, and looked closely inside of the vent. He saw a lens of some sort, like a video camera lens. He turned around and asked, "What, you decided to have some hidden cameras installed for security, Neema?"

She shook her head no and said, "Not me, Daddy. Uncle Keno did."

Taz's body went rigid as he stared at her while still standing on the chair. He slowly stepped down from the chair and followed his daughter into the living room. "What are you saying, Neema? Talk to me, baby girl."

Tazneema stepped to the coffee table and picked up the remote to the television mounted on the wall in front of her and pressed play for the DVD player to start. She remained silent as the DVD Lyla found in the attic came on and played for Taz.

Though there was no sound Taz looked on in horror as if he could hear every word being said between his wife and his best friend. His eyes grew wide as saucers when he saw Sacha pull out a small pistol which looked to him like a .380-caliber handgun, and shoot Keno three times: two in the back of his head and one in his neck. He flinched as if he could hear the gunshots. He stared at Sacha's lips as she said something as she stood over Keno's dead body.

Feeling totally numb, yet his mind was turning a million different things inside of his head, Taz stood and walked in front of the television and told his daughter, "Rewind it back real quick for me, Neema." After she did as he told her to he watched again as his wife murdered his best friend. This time he focused on her lips and tried to read her lips when she spoke over Keno's dead body. "'That was for my brothers, you bastard. I hope you burn in hell,'" he said, reading Sacha's lips from the video perfectly. "Well, I be a muthafucka. Fuck!"

"What are we going to do, Daddy? How do we fix this mess?" Tazneema asked as she stared at her father as he sat back down on the sofa with tears sliding down his face.

His body trembled with pain from watching the murder of Keno as well as from the anger that was slowly mounting toward the woman he loved more than anything in this world next to his mother and children. "I don't know, Neema. For the first time in my wretched and cursed life I don't have a fucking clue as to how I'm going to deal with this shit."

Tazneema went and sat down next to her father and said, "There's only one way you can deal with this, Daddy. Sacha went against the grain and you have always told me never go against the grain no matter what."

"I know. This is a decision that I cannot make alone though. The crew has to be in on this decision, baby girl."

"You pretty much know what they're going to want."

"Yep, I know, that's why this is so fucked up. Fuck!"

# Chapter Thirty-six

Each member of the crew received a text from Taz informing them that everything that they had discussed earlier as far as flying to Los Angeles was put on hold. Taz gave no reason for this decision and this confused each member of the crew. *What the hell is going on?* thought Bob as he called Red to see if he knew anything. After Red told him that he was just as lost about Taz shutting everything down for the time being Bob called Tari and Wild Bill and received the same results: zilch, nothing. Taz wasn't returning any of their texts nor was he answering his phone when they called him. That spooked the hell out of them and they each began to assume that something happened to Taz. Tari sent him a text and asked him to confirm that he was in good health. Taz read the text and realized that he had everyone going crazy with worry and hurried up and called Tari. When she answered the phone she was well beyond irate.

"What the fuck is wrong with you? You send us this weak-ass text telling us that everything is dead for now but you give no reason and then duck our texts and calls! You are really fucking tripping, Taz! This is way out of protocol and plain just fucked up! Talk to me!"

"If your ass stop screaming and listen for a minute I will."

Tari was fuming as she tried her best to slow up her heartbeat, which was beating like a sledgehammer. "Talk to me, Taz."

"Like I said in the text, everything is on hold for the time being. Something has come up and it takes priority over everything else."

"What, what the fuck is going on?"

"Tell everyone that I'm good and that I will hit y'all in the morning and everything will be clear then. Right now I need to take care of some shit solo. I'm good; trust me, Tee, please."

"No. I want to know where you're at right now, Taz."

"I'm with Neema."

"Let me speak to her."

Taz sighed heavily and said, "I don't have time for this shit." Then he passed his phone to Neema so she could speak with Tari.

"Hey, Tari. Taz is fine; we're just going through some personal stuff right now. Tell everyone he's fine and not to worry okay?"

After hearing Tazneema speak a slow calm came over Tari. "Okay, Neema. Thank you. Give the phone back to your father."

Taz accepted the phone from Neema and said, "Satisfied?"

"Fuck no! I still want to know what the hell is going on. But at least I got something to tell Bob, Red, and Wild Bill. You were about to make us get real stupid around this piece, mister."

"My bad. Look, let me go I'll get with you all in the morning."

"You do that shit."

"And, Tee."

"What?"

"Tell the crew that if Sacha calls or send any of y'all texts looking for me tell her I'm good."

"Huh? You're not talking to your wife now? Come on, Taz, what the fuck is going on here?"

"Just do as I said, Tee. Y'all will be put on everything in the morning; out!" he said and hung up the phone. He turned and stared at his daughter for a moment then stood and went into the den where Keno had a fully stocked bar. He grabbed a bottle of XO and came back into the living room. He sat down and popped the bottle of the liquor, took a large gulp straight from the bottle and frowned as the smooth liquor burned its way down his throat. He then grabbed the remote off of the coffee table and re-played the DVD of Sacha murdering his best friend again and started crying.

Shaking her head from side to side Tazneema said, "Don't. Don't do this to yourself, Daddy. All it's going to do is fuel your anger and you're going to do something you will regret. Try to calm yourself so you can think straight and do what's right."

"What's right, ha! What's right, Neema? What the hell is the right way to deal with a situation like this? Right in front of me is proof that the woman I am married to, the woman who gave birth to my two beautiful sons, the woman I love more than anything in this world next to my children and my mother is the woman who mur-dered my best friend in cold blood. Now I have to decide how to deal with this and believe me there is no way I can even begin to think about this while being sober." He took another gulp of the cognac and sighed.

"So, your answer to this is to sit here and get drunk?"

"Yep, that's the plan."

"What about tomorrow, what are you going to do then?"

"I'll tell you tomorrow." Taz's cell rang and he checked and saw that it was Sacha. He frowned and tossed his phone on the sofa next to him and drank some more liquor.

Watching her father get drunk frustrated Tazneema more and more but she knew there was nothing she could do to change his mind so she sat down next to him and laid her head on his shoulder and prayed that everything would work out okay. Her phone started ringing and when she saw that it was Sacha calling her now she knew better to answer. She set the phone on the coffee table and laid her head back on her father's shoulder and cried. *Damn.*

Sacha was going crazy with worry. Taz was not answering his phone and that was something he never did whenever she called him. Something was wrong; she knew it and she prayed that he was okay. After what happened earlier all she could think about was Taz being murdered and that thought scared her to death. She called Tari and asked her if she had heard from Taz. When Tari told her that Taz was good but didn't want to talk to any of them Sacha was totally confused.

"What's going on, Tari?"

"Honestly, Sacha, I don't have a damn clue. Taz told me that he would explain everything in the morning and for us not to call him anymore."

"That's it?"

"Yeah, pretty much."

"No fucking way! He needs to answer his damn phone!"

"He's not going to; he made that pretty clear, Sacha. Why don't you do your norm and get the twins ready for bed and maybe he will get at you. If not we'll find out in the morning what he's up to."

"Taz is out of his fucking mind for this; this is so crazy," Sacha said and sighed. "Thank God he's okay though."

"He's fine, that I am sure of. Relax we'll find out what's what in the morning."

"Relax. Humph, easier said than done, Tari. I guess I'll see you in the morning. Bye, girl," Sacha said as she hung up the phone furious at her husband. *One minute he's here talking about having dinner with me and the boys and the next he's gone MIA on me. Nah, Mr. Taz, your ass will have some explaining to do in the morning,* she said to herself as she went to feed the kids.

Taz woke up early the next morning on the sofa with Tazneema sound asleep on the floor right next to him. His head was pounding as he tried to get to his feet without stepping on his daughter. He quietly went to the bathroom and relieved himself. After he handled his business he checked the medicine cabinet and found a bottle of Aleve. He sighed as he popped the top and poured four of the pain pills in his hand, tossed them into his mouth and drank some water from the faucet to wash the pills down. He then went back into the living room and scooped Tazneema in his arms and carried her to her bedroom. When he laid her down on the bed he smiled and gave her a kiss on her cheek. "I love you, Tazneema Good."

"I love you too, Daddy. You okay?" she asked opening her eyes.

"Nope. I got a monster headache and I have to make some mean decisions in a little bit."

"What are you going to do?"

"Honestly, I don't have the slightest idea at this time. Go back to sleep I'll give you a call later. It's time for me to go have a talk with my wife," he said as he kissed her on her forehead and left the bedroom. He went back into the living room, and grabbed his phone and the bottle of XO that had maybe two inches left inside of it. He emptied the bottle with one gulp and set it on the coffee table. "Ahhh, here we go, Taz, here we go," he said aloud as he stepped to the DVD player, retrieved the incriminating DVD and left the house. It was time to go talk to his wife and see what she had to say for herself about the murder of his best friend. *Damn.*

# Chapter Thirty-seven

While driving toward his home Taz called each member of the crew and told them to meet him at his house. Though it was a little after seven in the morning each member was up and moving so they could hurry and get to Taz's place to see what the hell was going on. By the time Taz made it home the entire crew had already arrived. He sighed as he got out of his car and went into the house.

Sacha was standing at the top of the stairs when he entered. "Before you go into the den to discuss whatever business that needs to be discussed with the crew can you please come speak with me for a moment?"

Taz shook his head no and said, "Nah, Sacha. Throw something on; we got someplace to go."

"Where are we going?"

"Get dressed, Sacha," he said as he turned and went into the den. He entered the den and went straight to the bar; he needed another drink. After pouring himself a shot of XO he stared at the crew and said, "This has been the most fucked-up time I've ever experienced in my life. I know y'all are wondering what the fuck is wrong with me. I know I had y'all spooked and I apologize for that. I've been hit with the most fucked-up news I could ever have been told."

Sacha entered the den dressed in some jeans and an OU sweatshirt. Taz stopped speaking and stared at his wife for a moment before he continued. "Look, I need y'all to bear with me. I got to go somewhere with Sacha, and when I come back y'all will then know what is what." He then pulled out the DVD of Sacha murdering Keno on it and set it on top of the bar and said, "As soon as I leave I want y'all to watch this DVD. When I return we will discuss how we're going to proceed from this point on. Remember this: no matter what, majority rules. What you decide while I'm gone talking to my wife is how we will roll."

"Come on, Taz, what the fuck's going on, my nigga?" asked Wild Bill.

"Yeah, my nigga, you tripping the fuck out on us," said Red.

Bob and Tari stared at Taz and then at the DVD on top of the bar with a puzzled look on their faces.

"Trust me, y'all will know what the business is when you see what's on that DVD. I'll be back within the hour," Taz said as he walked out of the den followed by his wife.

Once they were inside of his car Taz sighed and told Sacha, "Please do me a favor and don't say a word to me while we're driving. You will have your time to speak, just not while I'm driving."

*What the hell? Something is wrong; something is terribly wrong,* Sacha said to herself as she stared at her husband. "How long will we be gone? The twins are going to wake up in a little bit."

"They'll be fine; my entire crew is at the house remember?" Taz said as he pulled out of the driveway. "No more talking, Sacha."

Fifteen minutes later when Taz pulled into Trice Cemetery and drove toward Keno's gravesite Sacha's heart began to beat faster and faster. *Does Taz know? How could he know? No, this is something else; he's stressing and wants to come to Keno's grave to talk to me. Oh my God, please don't let Taz know of my darkest secret. Please, Lord,* she prayed as she followed Taz toward Keno's final resting place.

When they were standing in front of Keno's grave Taz knelt and pulled some weeds away from the tombstone and gave it a kiss. "I love you, dog. I miss you. I know you're looking down on me shaking your head because you know my heart. You know me. No matter what, we crew, and I will always have your back, my nigga." He stood, turned, and faced his wife and said, "Now, tell me."

"Tell you what, Taz?" Sacha asked with her heart beating so fast she felt as if she was going to have a heart attack.

Taz reached behind himself and grabbed his nine millimeter pistol from the small of his back, cocked a live round into its chamber, and said, "Tell me why you killed Keno."

Back at Taz's house each member of the crew had tears sliding down their faces as they watched Keno being murdered by Sacha. Each member couldn't believe what they were looking at."

"Oh! My! God!" screamed Tari.

"This has to be the most fucked-up shit that could have ever happened to us," said Red.

"Now I see why Taz was tripped the fuck out," said Bob.

"That nigga wants us to actually vote on whether we should kill Sacha. Oh hell nah!" said Wild Bill.

"Why? Why would Sacha do that to Keno?" asked Tari.

"I guess that's what Taz is trying to find out right now. Did you see how he looked at Sacha? I've never seen him have that kind of look toward her," said Bob.

"Vote? Nigga, are you stupid? Keno was our nigga, crew. We all loved him like we all love one another. Never in a million years would he want us to hurt Sacha because of what she done to him. He knows that would hurt Taz and that's the one thing Keno would never have done. He could never hurt Taz; he loved him too much for that," Red said sincerely.

"I'm with you," said Bob.

Me too," added Tari.

Wild Bill sighed and said, "Damn. This has to be killing my nigga. Where do you think he took her?"

"If I had to guess I'd bet money he took her to the cemetery," said Tari.

"Should we go out there? He might want to do her; he may actually trip the fuck out if she says the wrong shit and hurt her," said Wild Bill.

Bob shook his head no and said, "Nah, he's getting the truth out of her. He wants to know just like we do, why? Then he's going to come back and want a decision from us."

"A decision from us, like we would do that to him. I love that nigga's loyalty but he has to be out of his fucking mind if he even thought for a fucking second we would ever hurt Sacha behind this," said Wild Bill.

"Yeah, but at the same time I see where his head is at. Gotta respect his gangsta. 'Cause if we did choose to take Sacha he would not hold it against us and would be behind that decision one hundred percent," said Red.

"That has to be the most gangsta shit I have ever seen in my life," said Bob.

"No, that's Taz being loyal to the crew no matter what. No one is above being done when it comes to crew. That's some real deep shit," Tari said and started crying as she felt all of the pain she knew Taz was feeling. *Fuck!*

"Don't you dare insult Keno's memory by standing there trying to lie right over his grave. The very grave that I already know you are responsible for putting him in. So again, tell me, Sacha. Tell me why you killed my dog, or I swear to God I'll kill you right now," Taz said in a tone that showed Sacha that he was serious. Dead serious.

Shaking her head no she said, "No matter what I tell you it won't change anything so why should I, Taz? I'm sure the crew is going to want me dead for what I done and I'm equally sure you won't go against them for me, so why should I say a thing?"

With tears sliding down his face he said, "Because I need to know why, Sacha. Because I need the closure to this most fucked-up situation. Because maybe, just maybe, I can understand why the woman I love more than anything in this world would do something like this to hurt me to my core." He stepped a little closer to her, gritted his teeth, and said, "No, fucking telling me!" He then did something he never in his life thought he would do and that was hit a woman. He slapped Sacha so hard that she twisted almost in a full 360-degree turn before falling to the ground. "You've always told me that I'm most dangerous when I'm in an emotional state of mind. So you can see now where my head is at, Sacha. Tell me before I lose my fucking mind and take your life right here right now."

Without moving she looked up at her husband and stared into his brown eyes, the same brown eyes that always had nothing but pure love in them for her. Now all they held was contempt and disgust and that hurt her more than the slap she just received from Taz. She began to cry silently as she continued staring at him. "He killed my twin brothers, Mitchell and Michael."

Taz stared at her. *Mitchell and Michael? Twin brothers?* "That's why you wanted the boys' middle names to be Mitchell and Michael because of your twin brothers who were killed by Keno?"

She nodded yes and continued. "My brothers were young hustlers in the city and were heavy into the drug scene. You and your crew added them to your hit list to rob when you were doing your jack-boy thing. They refused to give up their stuff to you guys so Keno chose to kill them. He killed them because they weren't cowards and would rather die than let something be taken from them."

"How? How in the fuck did you find all of this out, Sacha?"

She smiled sadly at Taz and said, "From Keno. He told us all the story at the house after Bo-Pete's funeral. He broke it down how Bo-Pete wanted to let my brothers live because he was once cool with them when you guys played football together at John Marshal. You said it yourself how Bo-Pete was so mad at Keno for killing them."

Taz thought back to that day in his den after Bo-Pete's funeral and remembered the conversation and everything became crystal clear to him. *Damn, this is some even more fucked-up shit,* he thought. "Why just Keno? What about the rest of us? I mean we were the crew; we all had a part in it for real."

She looked at him as if he was stupid. "Not in my eyes. I love you and there is no way in the world I would ever be able to cause you any physical pain. I'd die before I did that. As for the rest of the crew, I love them as well. I've grown to love them as my very own family. But I could never love nor forgive the man who took my big brothers from me. Never. It took me weeks to gain the courage to do what I did. After thinking about it I decided with what was going on with you guys and those Hoover Crips that could be a way for me to get my revenge without ever having to worry about you finding out."

Nodding he said, "That was some slick shit; we would have never found out neither. That is if Keno hadn't been smart enough to have security cameras installed inside of his home. Lyla found the DVD player that held the DVD of you murdering Keno and gave it to Neema. She in turn gave it to me."

"Great, now everyone in the family knows I'm a murderer. You might as well kill me now and get it over with, Taz."

"I love you, Sacha. You are my wife. I know I can use my power over the crew to get them to forgive you. But I can't do that. I have to let you face the crew and let them decide your fate. If they want you to die then you will die by my hand. I am not going to play no games with you or lie; I will kill you to avenge Keno's death. I cannot and will not let anyone else touch you; if it has to happen it will be done by me."

"If they decide not to harm me then what, Taz? What about us? Will we be able to make our marriage work after all of this?"

"To be honest, I haven't even given that any thought; the only thing that's been on my mind is what if they tell me they want you to die. This is a fucking living nightmare for me. A fucking nightmare," he said as he turned and started walking toward his car. Sacha got to her feet and quickly followed him.

Once they were inside of the car headed back to the house Taz's cell phone rang. He sighed when he saw that it was Mama-Mama's number. "What's up, Mama-Mama?" he asked when he answered the phone.

"No, Taz, this Mrs. Leslie."

"Oh, hi, Mrs. Leslie. Is everything all right?"

"I wish it was, Taz, I really wish it was. But I just went to go check on your mother because you know she's normally up before the rooster crows. She was still sound asleep when I went to check on her so I decided to start breakfast. I went back to get her up a little later and saw that she was gone. Mama-Mama has gone to be with our loving Heavenly Father. I'm so sorry, Taz," Mrs. Leslie said somberly.

Taz calmly pulled over to the side of the road and said, "Thank you, Mrs. Leslie. I'll be right over." He hung up the phone and stared straight ahead as he was in a trance.

"What's wrong, Taz? Is Mama-Mama okay?" Sacha asked with fear in her voice.

Taz started shaking his head from side to side violently then he screamed, "My! Mother! Is! Dead! Mama-Mama died in her sleep! God, no! God, fuck no! Why are you punishing me like this! Why! Will this nightmare ever fucking end!"

## *THE END*

*Preview of*

# Gangsta Twist 4:

*The End of a Nightmare*

# Chapter One

Bob couldn't believe how all of a sudden their lives could go from being content and living the way they wanted to all of the turmoil, confusion, and pain they were all now having to deal with. Sacha murdering Keno was the shock of all shockers to them all; then Mama-Mama dying in her sleep from a heart attack broke them all down in ways that none of the crew felt they would be able to bounce back from.

*Now on top of all of this shit here I am about to meet with a fucking FBI agent who has been hounding me for the last two months. What the fuck else can go wrong?* he asked himself. He pulled into the parking lot of a McDonald's on the corner of Twenty-third and Broadway, the designated spot the federal agent Warren Bornstein chose for the meeting. Bob tried his best to ignore the calls from this agent. His hand was forced after receiving a threatening text from the agent saying he would be forced to raid his home along with Taz and the rest of the members of the crew if they didn't meet. To say he was scared would be straight-up lying; he was fucking terrified! The FBI didn't get at you unless they had some serious shit on you and that alone was totally terrifying. Just the thought of being taken away from his family made Bob begin to tremble in fear. After taking a few breaths Bob got out of his car and went inside of the fast food restaurant to see what this FBI agent had to say.

As soon as he was seated Special Agent Bornstein, a small white man with bright red hair and freckles all over his nose, smiled at him and said, "It's about time we met, Bob. Thank you for meeting me today."

Ignoring the agent's outstretched hand Bob said, "Whatever. You need to skip the weak shit and get right to the business because the next time we speak my attorney will be speaking for me."

The agent laughed and said, "I doubt that, but okay, tough guy, I'll get right to it then. Six years ago there were seven people murdered in Brooklyn, New York, at an Urban Style clothing store. I have proof that you and your crew were the people who murdered those seven people. But I'm here to offer you a chance to miss those seven murder charges that will definitely give you a life sentence, and save yourself."

Bob started laughing though inside he was scared to death, petrified actually. *Fuck!* "First off, me and my crew as you called my friends don't do murders so I don't know what the fuck you are talking about. Second, I've never been up top to New York in my life."

"If you say so. Then my key witness against you, Athony McGhee, must be lying when he told us that he helped you get well by providing medical attention for you when you were shot in the shootout in Brooklyn six years ago. Athony seemed to recall very detailed information about that day. He also gave me some serious information about a man named William Hunter."

"Who?"

"Oh, excuse me, you most likely knew him as Won."
*Shit!*

"I can tell by your shocked expression that you now have a very good idea where I'm headed with this. Let me continue so the picture can be crystal clear for you, Bob. Athony McGee, aka Magoo, worked for Won for several years doing different things for him. Everything from running heroin to cocaine to murder on the East Coast with his Bronx Bloods connections. Won was rumored to be a high-ranking official of a criminal organization called the Network. Though the Network is in fact real, people in law enforcement never were able to get any real proof that this criminal organization really existed. That is until Athony McGhee or as you know him, Magoo, was captured for four murders in Yonkers six months ago. Since then he has given us some valuable information about this somewhat mythical criminal entity.

"After doing my homework I found out that Won was found murdered in his home six years ago. When I brought this to Magoo's attention he told me an interesting story about how Won was beefing internally with the Network's leaders and was involved in an intricate plan to take over leadership of the Network. But he was murdered before that could happen. What makes this Mario Puzo–like is that Won made sure that if something happened to him before he could take over the Network that his protégé would take the helm of the criminal organization. And that protégé of his is your main man Taz. Since we've been watching you guys we've had time to check Taz out as well as each member of your crew. Tari Winston, a drop-dead gorgeous Amazon-like white woman. Billy Joe Trent, aka Wild Bill, a short man known to be very violent yet he's never been arrested for any crimes. Robert Burns, aka Red, a calm and cool-mannered big man known as serious muscle for Taz and your crew. And of course you, Bob, the somewhat wild man of the crew who has calmed greatly since being shot and the birth of your children, Bob Jr. and Gwendolyn, named after your lovely wife six years ago.

"A lot sure happened six years ago in you guys' lives I'll tell you that. And we also know of the two members of your crew who were murdered in you guys' beef with the Hoover Crips of Oklahoma City. Quite a bloody war that one was I might say. Now see I have the facts but what I don't have is the proof of the Network's real existence, or what they're currently into. The rumors float from drugs, murder, extortion, all types of things. What I want is proof, proof of what they are into so that can lead to proof of their existence. And you, Bob, my friend, are going to get me all the proof I need."

Bob started laughing nervously and asked, "Really? And how are you going to make me get you this proof of all of this fairytale gangsta story this Magoo guy has given you?"

"I figured you would try this tactic and normally it would work but you see, Bob, I do have some proof. I have proof that you were at that clothing store in Brooklyn. See if what Magoo said was true about you being shot in that shootout in the clothing store that means your DNA was left on the scene of those seven murders. So all I have to do is have your DNA taken and see if it matches any of the DNA found on that particular crime scene. Once I get a match that places you in New York, the state you said you've never been, that along with Magoo's testimony and I can pretty much promise you it would be over for you, Bob. Circumstantial, yes; but still enough to get a conviction and a life sentence for you."

Bob stared at the little FBI agent and wanted to reach across the small table and wring his fucking neck. *Fuck! All because I didn't wear that fucking vest. No, all because of that rat-ass fucking Magoo. Fuck!* Bob said to himself.

Sensing that he had definitely reached Bob the agent smiled and said, "You can give me the proof I want about the Network and assist me in bringing down this infamous criminal organization and be able to keep your freedom and all of your riches. You're quite wealthy, Bob. I'm sure you don't want to lose all of that for being loyal to people who I'm sure if were in your shoes would give you up in a heartbeat. So, what is it going to be?"

"Don't call me, I'll call you. I need time to think about this shit. My wife already thinks I'm having a fucking affair with your fucking calls so stop."

"Done. Just don't have me waiting too long. If you do you won't be called; we'll be coming to get you. And if you're thinking about warning your leader Taz then know I will go all out to get you that life sentence for those seven murders in New York. Don't fuck with me, Bob. Help yourself or it's over for you, pal." With that said the agent stood and left the McDonald's with that confident smile still in place.

All of this shit that was going on in their lives and now this had to be added, too. *Shit. Beefing with Danny Orumutto in California. Beefing with Saint Tramon on that council business. Sacha's and Taz's drama as far as their relationship and the murder of Keno. Mama-Mama dying and now having to bury her in a few days and now on top of all of that shit the Feds are all over me wanting me to turn fucking snitch to bring down the Network. What the fuck am I going to do? This is truly a nightmare turned reality,* Bob said to himself as he got up and went to the counter and ordered a Big Mac combo. He thought better whenever he was eating and right about now he knew he needed to think very seriously about this situation. Because crossing Taz and the crew meant instant death. *Fuck!*

# Author's Note

I never intended to do a part three for the *Gangsta Twist* stories but thanks to my devoted fans here it is. I hope you enjoyed this installment of *Gangsta Twist*. Don't worry you all got me started so there will be one more final *Gangsta Twist* book. *Gangsta Twist 4: The End of a Nightmare*. I figured I might as well put together one last mean gangsta twist so stay ready. I give you my promise that I will not disappoint. Everything will be addressed. All questions will be answered and the finale of this series should leave you, my fans, satisfied. What will happen with Bob? Will Taz and Sacha still remain married? How will the beef end with Saint Tramon? How will the war end with Danny Orumutto? All of this and some more surprising twists and turns along the way is expected in *Gangsta Twist 4*. So be patient I'm in the lab right now! Take care and may God bless you and yours always. Thank you for your continued support.

**SPUD**